# THE S

❧

# TO OUTWIT GOD

# THE SUBTENANT

❦

# TO OUTWIT GOD

Hanna Krall

NORTHWESTERN UNIVERSITY PRESS

*Evanston, Illinois*

Northwestern University Press
Evanston, Illinois 60201

Translation of *The Subtenant* was funded with the assistance of the
National Endowment for the Arts.

Printed in the United States of America

Library of Congress Cataloging-in-Publication Data
Krall, Hanna.
    [Sublokatorka. English]
    The subtenant ; and, To outwit God / Hanna Krall.
        p.  cm.
    "The subtenant originally published in Polish under the title
Sublokatorka . . . To outwit God originally published in Polish under
the title Zdążyć przed Panem Bogiem . . . English translation
originally published 1986 under the title Shielding the flame . . . by
Henry Holt and Company"—T.p. verso.
    ISBN 0-8101-1050-4 (alk. paper). — ISBN 0-8101-1075-X (pbk. :
alk. paper)
    1. Jews—Poland—Warsaw—Persecutions.  2. Warsaw (Poland)—
History—Uprising of 1943.  3. Holocaust, Jewish (1939–1945)—
Poland—Warsaw.  4. Edelman, Marek, 1921–  .  5. Warsaw (Poland)—
Ethnic relations.  I. Krall, Hanna. Zdążyć przed Panem Bogiem.
English. 1992.  II. Title.  III. Title: To outwit God.
PG7170.R28S813  1992
940.53′18—dc20                                                    92-15923
                                                                        CIP

The paper used in this publication meets the minimum requirements of
American National Standard for Information Sciences—Permanence of
Paper for Printed Library Materials, ANSI Z39.48–1984.

# CONTENTS

The Subtenant
1

To Outwit God
129

# THE SUBTENANT

*Translated by Jarosław Anders*

# I

Dear Sir,

(again that intonation of your favorite actor, Zbigniew S. It was supposed to be a matter-of-factly "sir" with a short crisp *r* at the end—not this shifty, endlessly rolling consonant. Such an *r* may be fine in a semidocumentary film, in which your favorite actor pretends to be a real-life storekeeper, but "dear sir" in my letter was to be neutral, though polite).

dear sir,

I have been lying on my Yogi mattress all day thinking about the last night spent in your company on the subject of grandfathers.

First, there was *The Dream of the Innocent*, and then the grandfathers of the actors. The actors stepped down from the stage to tell us about their ancestors—it was probably about historical continuity or making history more accessible, in any case, they all came to us to say something like that: my grandfather, a legionnaire, here you can see him (they would show us a photograph) right next to Marshal Piłsudski, organized a rally in defense of Polishness, and the rally was to be attended by Stefan Żeromski, here he is again, the third from the right, waiting for the arrival of the great writer. . . . And my two grandfathers (they showed two photographs, each grandfather in a different uniform) were fighting against each

*3*

other—one on the Russian, the other on the Austrian side—
and one day, during the battle of Stajenka village, they suddenly faced each other, literally brother against brother, bayonets in hand, Stajenka is a living legend in my family and
the bayonet of the Austrian grandfather started our collection
of side arms, what concerns the Russian grandfather, he later
became a bosom friend of a certain Lieutenant Schmidt, the
leader of the mutiny on the ironclad Potemkin, we also have
the original of Lieutenant Schmidt's letter, but please ladies
and gentlemen, don't forget to give it back—and the actors
would pass around photographs and letters of their grandfathers, how many grandfathers there were, and how well
documented, even later, in the "alcohol-free" room in the
Terminal restaurant, I barely had time to recover when I was
hit with yet another grandfather, this time belonging to your
favorite actor, Zbigniew S.

His name was Oscar Staemmler, still with "ae" before they
changed it to Sztamler, which only once appeared to sound a
bit awkward and even created an unpleasant confusion, and
he was, like everybody in his family, for many generations, a
German and a lawyer, to be more specific he was a legal
counsel to Jagiellonian University.

It was a beautiful story: Grandpa Oscar, summoned by the
Gestapo, accompanied a group of professors to the university—to Room No. 55; the professors, together with Grandpa, were sent to Buchenwald; the Staemmler family raised
havoc, the unfortunate mistake was discovered, sincere apologies were offered to Grandfather Oscar, who nevertheless
said—please pay attention!—"I thank you very much, gentlemen, but there must have been some misunderstanding,
I am a Pole, and I wish to remain with the others." And
Grandpa Oscar, whose family spoke only German, remained
in Buchenwald out of his own free will, ended up in Auschwitz, and returned after the war as a Pole, Sztamler (which

4

name, as I've already mentioned, became the source of a certain unpleasant situation, but that was much later—twenty-three years after Auschwitz) and that's how Polishness got started in my family, concluded the actor Zbigniew S. his story in the Terminal restaurant.

It was probably quite natural that we all fell silent at the table, moved by the story as much as Zbigniew S. was moved—even you kept tactful silence behind your glasses until our solemn meditation was interrupted by Zbigniew S., who looked at you inquiringly and asked with a measure of effort, though in a composed and kind manner: and you? how about your grandfather? Your answer was quick and decisive: "My grandfather built outhouses."

Right on the mark. There was consternation, even panic at the table, because, in all honesty, your builder of outhouses did not sound too good after Grandpa Oscar, who chose Polishness in Buchenwald. With great presence of mind Zbigniew S. came to your rescue: you mean he was a carpenter? a woodworker? (An artisan that is, a good workman. The Staemmlers, though lawyers, always respected honest labor.) Alas, you evidently could bear the brotherly, democratic kindness of your friend no more. You let us wonder for a moment and then you said: a carpenter? why carpenter? He was a prime minister. His name was Sławoj-Składkowski.

I am bothered by the tone of my account of Zbigniew S.'s grandfather. "Solemn meditation . . .", "composed and kind . . ."

How could this little irony, that quite inappropriate smirk, seep into this exquisite story?

(Beautiful, not exquisite. "Into this beautiful story . . ." and so on).

You know how?

Me too. I only pretend to ponder the question, when in fact I knew the answer from the very beginning. At first I did not recognize that feeling and it really caused me some problems—it was when I received a letter from a man who served under Major Krall (let's assume that I, the narrator, bear the name of the author of this book), and who was eager to tell me about the major's death, because the major died right in his arms and spoke his last words to him—but now I am perfectly sure that feeling is envy. It is envy for the words: "I thank you very much, gentlemen," which Grandpa Oscar was able to say in Buchenwald, and envy for Major Krall, who died in the arms of his faithful soldier.

*I cordially invite you to visit with us*—wrote Major Krall's soldier in his letter—*our house is small, but we always, with greatest pleasure . . .*

Dear Sir.

I felt an immense urge to go there, to sit at a table in the small house. . . . Until this day I feel the shadow of a tree I would see behind the window—it is hot but the trees fill the house with cool dusk, the lady of the house takes teacups out of a large cupboard and says, this year my apricots did not come out quite right, and I sit there with tears in my eyes, tears my host pretends not to see, and hear about the death of Major Krall, my father.

From that time on I started to invent many various lives for my father. Just like the hero in the story by Stanisław Benski, the director of the nursing home in Warsaw. The institution has fifty Jewish residents, which makes it the largest Jewish community in Poland, and it is a real treasury of subjects for Mr. Benski's stories. The hero of one of them has a very inadequate life because he spent the whole war in New York. On Easter 1944 he was eating kosher frankfurters with matzo and somehow missed the ghetto, the "Aryan side," and Treblinka. For that reason he is ashamed to show his face in public. Surrounded by reliable sources he composes a new, more appropriate life in which everything is just as it should be: he did not go to America, he is in Warsaw under the bombs and planning to sneak to the "Aryan side" to see the Wieczorek family. So far so good, but around 1941 his wife, Róża, has a nervous breakdown. She spent the war in Samarkand, therefore she should also do some homework, but she does not wish to be in the ghetto. "I hate the sight of blood, I used to run away when the butcher was killing a chicken, so how could I stand all that? No, Gabriel, you are asking too much. Let us say I died of a heart attack, I am already dead." "My dear wife," says her husband, Gabriel Lewin, "if all Jews were like you, the ghetto would die out in no time at all and the Nazis would have nothing to do, they would have nothing to be proud of in front of their führer. As for me, I have joined the Jewish resistance, and I am already fighting in the forests. . . ."

The same with me.

I sit and compose new lives for my father.

For example: my father is in a POW camp (I basically stick to the soldier's letter) and my mother and I are waiting for him. My mother, sad but unbroken, takes odd jobs like selling cigarettes or baking cakes, and never loses her estimable dignity, she is also very careful about appearances, every evening she washes her only white blouse and irons it in the morning, and she forbids me to laugh. "Maria," she says, because in matters of importance she uses my given name, "it is improper to laugh when your father and your fatherland are in slavery." She would admonish me one day in June 1940—I was happily and noisily riding my bicycle—crying: "Maria, how can you? France has fallen!"—which I would not understand and I would pedal into the garden, obviously into a garden, it would all happen in a garden, yet I would preserve the memory of that moment as part of our family tradition. We would decorate our Christmas trees only with white and red tissue, and after the war there would be gatherings of veterans and parades of the Major Krall Scouting Troop from his native town. I would always receive invitations to these events, pamphlets with my father's small photo in a four-cornered cap nicely printed by one of his soldiers, now an owner of a photographic studio.

I have one more little episode in store: a slap in the face. I do not know how to reconcile all the details—the death in the soldier's arms, the POW camp, and now a slap in the face in his wife's presence, but it doesn't matter, after all I was too small in 1940 to ride a bicycle, let us not be fastidious; what matters is that a German officer slapped my father in the face right in front of my proud mother, and that incident has to remain the gloomiest wartime experience of my family. Until today I tell the story with a lump in my throat, as the most painful thing, "and then he comes up to my father, and he. . . ." emotion drowns my words, but the woman to whom I try to tell about this great humiliation looks at me without comprehending and waits for some sort of conclusion, ready to express her compassion as soon as she learns what was the great tragedy. "He hit him, and then what?" As it turns out there was nothing more. That was the whole thing: the father, an officer, slapped in the face. And that woman, that idiot, burst out laughing: "And that's it!" It is difficult to calm her down. "And nobody smashed his skull with a rifle butt because he did not walk fast enough? And when he was on the ground nobody kicked him with heavy boots (your daddy cried a lot—said the janitor who was there—and then they hit him again and again . . . )." "No," I say as if I wasn't sure what that other one means. "There was nothing more," and finally the other woman smiles apologetically: "Yes, that must have been terrible. An officer slapped in the face," she says in a calm voice, just like any normal woman talking with another normal woman about the horrors of war.

What we have so far is: an officer slapped in the face, gatherings of veterans, and "Maria, France has fallen," and I think all that could make quite a pretty life, at least something to ruminate about with the author of the letter in the early evening on a hot June day—but unfortunately I was unable to go. My father could not have entrusted his last words to my host because he entrusted them to the ceiling of a barrack that stands on the right side behind the gate . . . a small barrack with No. 41 on it. Its walls are stained and bluish gray and there are little grooves on the ceiling. At first I thought that plaster was peeling off, but I learned later that those grooves were made by human fingers. The guide explained that when the gas was poured in and people started to suffocate, they would scratch the ceiling with their nails trying to get out— hence the traces in the plaster. It is quite possible that some of those grooves are traces of my father's hand. Why shouldn't they be, after all.

**II**

She put on a knitted woolen cap: a Norwegian pattern, elk and snowflakes with two woolen braids on both sides, a cheerful, funny cap, there is no doubt that only an absolutely and thoroughly bright person would allow herself to wear something like that. One girl, the partner of Zbigniew S., literally snatched that cap from her during each break in-between shooting to count the stitches: how many for the elk, how many for the snowflake, and when the two of them were bowing their heads over the Norwegian pattern they were absolutely and thoroughly bright.

And now a question: what does it really mean to be bright?

It is hard to explain exactly but we can use the examples of, let's say, Krystyna Krahelska* and Rywka Urman.

It is August. Krystyna has tied up her long hair in a bun, has written "Boys, ready your bayonets," has helped a wounded partisan, and is running in the sun. She is running among sunflowers, but she is so tall she cannot hide, even when she bends, and the bullet hits her in the back. She is lying on her back, still among the sunflowers, still looking into the sun. And brightness is when you die so beautifully

---

*Krystyna Krahelska, a poet, soldier in the Home Army, and heroine of the Warsaw Uprising. Famous for her beauty and uncommon courage.

and brightly. (Nothing reveals darkness and confirms brightness better than death.) And the incident with Rywka's child happened in the Warsaw ghetto at 18 Krochmalna Street. Rywka was standing in the yard, her hair disheveled, her eyes mad, with the body of Berek Urman, her son, lying in front of her. Berek had died the previous day, but we shall put some dots here, because we are trying to tell what the hungry Rywka was trying to do with the body of her son . . .
. . . . . . . . . . . . . . .
and we shall pick up the thread a bit later, when they are already surrounded by the crowd. The crowd is silent. It stands still and stares at Rywka without a word. Finally someone calls the police, a report is written, and a cart from the funeral society Eternity takes Berek Urman away.

Despite the dots one can still have doubts about whether we have used the right example. There are certain limits of good taste that no one should cross, and the whole distinction between brightness and darkness is rather questionable, why not something from literature or history, Cain and Abel, for instance—pretentious yet better than Rywka. Martha and Maria? that's it. The gospel and Velázquez, the original in Vienna, a copy in the National Gallery, two sisters are visited by Jesus, so Martha immediately starts to busy herself with supper, while Maria "sat at the Lord's feet listening to His word."

The painting shows Martha in the foreground—a tired, sad, and homely woman cleaning a fish, further on her sister, bright, spiritual, and definitely slimmer, sits at Jesus's feet. (Someone told me I could use the word *ailée*. Winged. This is from the French *aile*, a wing). "My Lord," says Martha turning away from the fish and interrupting their conversation, "My Lord," she says in a voice that is meant to be polite but sounds like the nagging of a fat grumpy woman, "my sister has abandoned me to serve you alone, please tell her to help me." To which Jesus—certainly annoyed by the voice from the kitchen—replies: "You worry a lot, but your sister has chosen a better part, which will not be taken from her," and they return to their conversation, while Martha, rejected by them, and thus rejected by everybody, returns to her fish.

Yes, these are clear and educated examples, and we would like to stop right here, but Tadeusz D. wants to defend Krysia Krahelska. That's what he calls her—Krysia. It seems that by contrasting her with Rywka someone tried to blame her for her death, therefore he tells at length about the wonderful person she was, and also about her father and her fiancé, whom he knew personally and remembers well. The father, a district administrator and social worker, was a noble as well as tall and handsome man, said Tadeusz D., he had a spreading white beard that reached down to his waist, the fiancé was an airman and participated in the Battle of Britain. "I understand," she told Tadeusz D., and she really understood right away. Who else would Krahelska's father be if not a tall, handsome man with a spreading white beard, and who else would her fiancé be if not a heroic airman defending England? "Tadzio, can you imagine," she said, "Rywka from Krochmalna Street with a heroic airman?"

She would have a father with a long beard, that's more likely, a father with a Hasidic beard, side curls, and a yarmulke, a father who would come every day to the synagogue even when the war started, and the ghetto, and all that business with the Jews, he would come day after day until it dawned on him that with a beard like his he would never be able to go to the "Aryan side." He would never be able to go there with the beard or without, who on earth would take in a man with such an expression in his eyes, with the eyes of a Hasid who shaved his beard for the first time in his life!—but he still does not know that and he is still thinking—what if I go out and they see my beard? Yet he comes to the synagogue like before, as if nothing had happened, he comes every day with other bearded Jews and puts on his tallith and tefillin, until one day he notices the absence of one Hasid. He did not die, he was not deported, so what happened? It turns out he had shaved his beard, just in case there was some opportunity, and now he cannot show his face in the synagogue. On the next day another Jew does not show up. And then another. From that time on there are fewer and fewer bearded Hasidim in the synagogue and the prayer grows more and more feeble, until there are just three or four of them left and the prayer becomes almost inaudible. Someone who told that story to Father B. claimed that all those prayers were useless anyway, because there was no God on their side at the wall. When Father B. insisted that God was everywhere that person repeated that perhaps He was but He stopped right at the wall on the Aryan side.

He could have been the God of Marcion, the founder of one of the first Christian sects. Marcion believed there were two gods: a kindly and tolerant god, and an evil, perfidious one. Unfortunately, they divided their duties and the perfidious god deals with people while the kindly one tends to the rest of the universe. It sounds plausible, although one cannot exclude another division: both of them deal with people, but the kindly god takes care of the bright, and the perfidious god of the dark ones. The bright God of Father B. simply had to stop at the wall.

She explained everything—what is darkness and what is brightness (with examples from literature: Hemingway—bright, Kafka—dark, Singer—bright, Dostoyevsky—dark, and so on), and then the bespectacled guy comes up and with a quick move of his hand tears the cap off her head, the cap with elk and snowflakes, the cap that only truly bright people can wear, and says: stop it.

Dear sir, that was rather rude. Is anybody bothering you

when you, the grandnephew of the prime minister who furnished Poland with public sanitation, pretend quite unconvincingly to be dark and try to hide your bright offshoots? On the contrary. One looks the other way, what darkness, one says with compassion and indicates that we, the bright ones, can understand the dark pretty well.

III

Time for genealogy.

The daughter of Major Krall must be from somewhere—everybody must be from somewhere and especially a major's daughter. My genealogy, that of a major's daughter, should read as follows:

Jan Kalasanty Krall, the oldest recorded member of the family, was knighted in 1678 in the presence of King Jan Sobieski, and he figures in three armorials. I should be able to find more details about Jan Kalasanty's merits that earned him his knighthood in the archives, after which I should set out to look for his traces throughout the country. I shall visit several parishes, browse in the parish records, look into an attic or two, and having gathered enough documents I shall start a family chronicle with our genealogical tree and information about the ancestors.

During my expeditions with a sleeping bag and a tape recorder I shall meet other people traveling with backpacks and engaged in similar pursuits, and those will be most pleasant meetings with intelligent, well-bred people.

This is how "The Book of the Kralls" will come into existence. Thus far we are still not sure who will be its heroes, but at least one of them will participate in the uprising of 1863, and he will be my great-great-grandfather, Adam

Joachim Krall. After his return from exile in Siberia he purchased a small estate with the money of his not-so-young wife. Shortly afterward he bought more land and had to hire more hands, over whom he held a tight rein, just like over his own family, although he certainly wasn't a tyrant, far from it, and the relations within his household were quite cordial. My great-grandfather could be an artisan. That's right. The Kralls, though figuring in three armorials, never shunned manual labor, and my great-grandfather was a simple piano tuner, though also a man of perfect pitch and a great lover of music. Before the Independence he organized the first Polish militia in his hometown, worshipped Marshal Piłsudski, and brought up his boys in an exquisite manner.

My grandfather, Wincenty Krall. An autodidact. He constantly worked on himself and managed to climb from the rank of a telegraph operator in the Celestynów railway station to a deputy station manager in the Wilno district, with a salary of four hundred prewar zlotys (when a dollar was five zlotys). Before his death he donated a manuscript of *Mr. Balcer in Brazil* to the National Library*—no one knows how the manuscript came into his possession, but it was probably through his friend who printed this book, I found a beautiful thank-you note from the library among the family papers— and throughout his life he displayed a truly democratic sensitivity to human suffering. He gave his own shirt to a shivering tinker, he helped the daughter of a local peddler with her homework, and he saved a child from fire with total disregard for his brand-new suit.

Thus we come to Grandfather's sons. The younger one is a famous inventor—even the Japanese are going to purchase

---

*Mr. Balcer in Brazil* (1910), an epic poem by the Polish positivist writer Maria Konopnicka that deals with the sad fate of the Polish peasant abroad.

one of his patents—and the older one, Major Jan Ludwik Krall, is my father, who died in the arms of his soldier, or was taken prisoner of war, or—which is a totally new hypothesis—was arrested by the Soviet security troops in the Lublin district in 1944 and sent to Siberia.

Now that we have established our genealogy we shall have to mention—no use putting it off any longer—the apartment. It is a generations-old residence of the Kralls that was finally destroyed during the Warsaw Uprising, a place where my mother, the major's wife, waited for the return of her husband, decorated Christmas trees with white and red tissue, and instructed her daughter: "You should not laugh, the Fatherland is in slavery."

There is really no way to avoid this apartment and the meeting between me, the major's daughter, and the other one, the sooner we put this tasteless scene behind us the better.

It is—I don't know if I've mentioned it already—a spacious, a bit dark apartment on the third floor in the center of the city. It has a kitchen door, a front door, five or six rooms, and maid's quarters.

She crouches under the windowsill in one of the rooms.

The other one.

She crouches and listens.

Someone is coming, one can clearly hear the footsteps.

Someone is whistling. "Golden chrysanthemums in a crystal vase . . . " I don't know why he never finishes that tune only whistles a couple of bars and stops.

"I shall take an advance to buy her a bouquet . . . " the final bars come from a distance and there is silence.

Silence in the courtyard and in the whole dark, empty apartment.

She is still crouching there, perhaps waiting for more footsteps. But nobody comes.

How does it feel—such silence in a huge, empty apartment?

I told her not long ago: "You know, my mother said that the most shocking thing was your awareness. You were five years old and apparently you understood everything. Is that true?"

She did not remember.

"But of course," I said, "my mother told me you never ever coughed behind that stove when strangers were in the house, you never cried and you never looked out of the window although you were so lonely. And in the afternoons you never wanted to pee between three-thirty and four."

"Really?" she asked. "I never came up to the window? That's interesting."

Not only did you never come up to the window during the day, but you never complained at night when we turned off the lights so that you could look at the street. You never complained it was dark and you could see nothing.

We took you for a walk several times.

We pulled your scarf deep over your forehead and pulled up your collar but that was not enough. Your eyes were still there, and the eyes were the worst. My mother had a wonderful idea: a stone. While walking down a street you would push a stone with your foot, like in the game of hopscotch, so that you could keep your eyes down and avoid suspicion. What could be more natural than a girl absorbed in a game of hopscotch, incapable of lifting her eyes from a stone? So we went—I, a well-behaved daughter, my mother, and you with your stone. Knock—you pushed it with your foot and hit a flagstone. I would watch it unwittingly. It is amazing how clearly one can see flagstones. Knock—a smooth flagstone, no cracks, knock—a flagstone with a black fracture in the middle—knock, blades of grass in the joints . . .

From time to time we would play a little scene for the ladies who were passing by. "Please leave it alone, you'll ruin your shoes," my mother would say, but you wouldn't pay any attention as if you were deaf—a naughty girl who does not listen to her aunt, and I, an indignant daughter, a good one unlike you, a little girl who takes care of her shoes. And above our heads my mother would smile and exchange understanding glances with other aunts of normal girls.

What are you laughing at?

I don't know why I remember that stone so well.

You had your moments of weakness, admit it, and you tried to lift your eyes. Not much, just a little bit, at least to the level of other children, and only for a moment when you thought that nobody would notice. Wasn't that so? But my mother reacted with relentless vigilance: "Keep your eyes down!" (I remember that sharp, muffled whisper well, but I don't feel like describing it in more detail.) So you quickly lowered your eyes and jumped on another flagstone.

You don't seem to be laughing anymore.

My Favorite Director of semidocumentary films told me yesterday about a monk whom he saw years ago in some railway station. The director was standing inside a car and the monk dressed in a brown robe was running down the platform short of breath. The door had closed a moment before he reached the train. The train was still standing so they had a couple of seconds to look at each other, and My Director saw the pale face of the monk, who was helplessly touching the door. That's all. Nothing important has happened. Some monk was late for his train, but the Director felt such a terrible pain growing inside him that years later he would recall it in order to describe a similar sensation—of grief, pity, who knows what to call it.

I told the Director that I understood him well, because as he was telling me the story I saw, or rather physically felt—somewhere between my collarbone and my heart, but closer to my breastbone, it's hard to explain exactly—the motion with which you, admonished and guilty, quickly returned to your stone.

I wonder whether anybody ever noticed you raising your eyes and whether he or she had enough time to observe them.

Do you know why I am asking that? Because your lowered eyes remind me of Catoblepas from one of Pliny's tales as told by Borges. Catoblepas was a wild beast—medium size, with a great head of sad and unpleasant appearance, swollen eyelids, and lazy gait. Its head was so heavy that he had to wind his long thin neck around his body. It was a lucky coincidence that the creature could not lift its head because its eyes had a terrible property: whoever looked into them died. "If I only opened my swollen eyelids—Catoblepas told St. Anthony—you would already be dead. . . . "

Do you see the striking analogy? The eyes of Catoblepas killed others, yours could kill you.

Why are you staring like an idiot?

I told you an interesting story, full of foreign names and intriguing words. I feel that occasionally we can embellish our tale with a literary reference. It presents both of us in a rather favorable light, there is nothing funny about it, and don't behave like a savage.

Listen . . .

Have you ever tried to figure out when you started to understand?

Do you listen?

I asked you a question.

I asked you: Have you ever tried . . .

"No," she said. "I have not."

"And hasn't it occurred to you that perhaps you always understood?"

"Do you think so? That would be interesting."

"But how does it feel—that silence? Do you happen to know how to describe silence?"

"Try to do it," she said, "through whistling. Silence is when the whistling in the yard has stopped and you are left with only the curtained window which you do not approach."

"You know, we felt pity for you."

As I was sitting at school—of course, like all girls my age I went to school—I often wondered what you were doing in that empty apartment. On my way home I would stop at a store and buy you cutouts, you know, those paper dolls with dresses, which we later played with in your maid's quarters.

You could go everywhere in the apartment until three-thirty, but after three-thirty you had to stay in your room. My grandfather returned from work before four. He had had a stroke and was quitting smoking, which made him very irritable, and in order to save his nerves we concealed your presence from him. Grandfather would never go alone into the maid's quarters, so the arrangement did not pose any problems except one. Between three-thirty and four you were not allowed to pee. Grandfather had a very regular stomach and he used the toilet soon after his return.

Did I say we felt pity for you?

The large dark apartment of the Kralls was one of many in the life of our subtenant. Each one was as large and dark as ours. She told me that all of them looked surprisingly similar. The same study of the absent man of the house whom you knew only from photographs—tall, slender, with a mustache and a four-cornered cap. Further on, the room of the boy who never slept at home, the piano in the sitting room, the grandfather who spent hours filling cigarette tubes, and a prewar faithful maid.

It is interesting that the women in those apartments were also similar to each other. No makeup, hair smoothly combed into a bun—the usual type of a strong, resourceful lady.

I asked if she remembers them.

She said she certainly does. She still visits them to try their apple pie, or brings some of her own. In the summer she meets them in the mountains: they take walks with their sweaters tied around their hips and order tea in mountain lodges, but skip the cake because their pensions do not keep pace with the cost of living. When they die she buys obituaries signed "with gratitude." After each funeral she thinks that someone has departed again from her only true world. Then she plants arborvitae and instructs the caretaker to clean dead leaves from the grave.

I asked her if she remembers how lonely she was in each of these large and dark apartments.

She thought for a moment and said she did not remember that.

I asked if she had any idea how to describe loneliness.

She told me to try it through a plant. A tall plant with a velvety stem and a small yellow blossom. Perhaps it was a mullein. One day she saw it near the wall of the Albertine convent, and some other time on a sandy railroad bank near a road barrier, and then again at a wire fence, and thus she learned to recognize it.

"Through a flower?" I was surprised.

"Because this is the only thing you recognize. You are going to new, strange people, the wall is new and strange, and the fence, and even the sky, because the clouds you tried to remember when you were leaving have long since disappeared (you are trying to push your sweaty hand into the hand of the man who walks beside you, but the man is so tense from having to be with you in the street in broad daylight that he cannot possibly notice your hand) and only the light yellow flower is always the same, intimately yours.

And that is loneliness. When you notice the flower, you immediately calm down. You know that everything can be new and strange, but at least the earth is the same, beyond doubt."

# IV

There appeared, as previously mentioned, a new version of the death, or rather disappearance, of my father, Major Krall. It seems that in the summer of 1944 his Second Reserve Communications Regiment with forty-four Polish officers mostly from the Home Army was surrounded on the Bug River by Soviet security troops and all the officers were arrested.* I have learned the story of the Second Communications Regiment from its political officer, Bernard Rajnicz, and I immediately figured out how useful it may prove for my new version. In any case, the life of Bernard Rajnicz should intersect several times with the life of my father. It would be quite logical: the fate of people like Bernard inevitably crosses over with the fate of Major Kralls, just like my life and the life of our Subtenant.

I wish to state it finally in plain and unambiguous terms: I, the daughter of Major Krall, am the bright version of the fate of our Subtenant. (Or perhaps the other way around. The Subtenant is the dark version of my life.) Similarly Major Krall could be the bright version of Bernard Rajnicz.

*The underground Home Army was supported by the London-based Polish government in exile.

Here is the genealogy of Bernard Rajnicz, who from now on has to become one of the heroes of our tale.

First of all—the name. Rajnicz is not his real name. His real name is Rainisch. Nice, isn't it?

Bernard found it in an encyclopedia under *RAINISCH Marianna, 1838–1936*, and learned that she was a leader of a women's movement in Austria. He also found it in Vienna right across the street from his hotel. It was a large, beautiful piano store. BERNARD RAINISCH AND SON. During the day the name stood out in dark letters against a lighter background, and at night it glared with a blue neon light. Bernard felt an urge to walk inside, ask for the owner, and say: "My name is Bernard Rainisch. Pleased to meet you." Unfortunately he was unable to do it, because he was no longer a worthy Austrian Rainisch but merely Rajnicz.

He received the name together with his commission upon graduating from a Soviet military college. When he saw it on his ID he immediately reported the error: "No error, comrade," explained the commander. "It's just better this way." Perhaps it was better, but later on it was worse, much worse, because Bernard R. (that's how we are going to call him for the sake of the truth) hated Rajnicz more and more.

Back to the genealogy. Unfortunately we cannot give him, despite his wish, a grandmother who was the author of several noble and progressive books on women's rights in Austria, or a paternal grand-uncle Bernard the piano maker, because such antenati would never bring him to communism. But a grandfather who was an innkeeper, and who was killed with a corkscrew by a drunk in the Carpathian Mountains, and a daddy completely ruined by his two lifelong litigations—such progenitors will bring him to communism the shortest possible way.

Bernard R. had to become a Communist, it was inevitable.

"Have I already reached my communism?" asks Bernard R., who has just finished the story about his father's litigation against a certain Mr. Gasthalter, with whom he endeavored to produce wine but the wine turned into vinegar, and against the prewar Polish government, which refused to recognize his service in the Austrian army for his retirement benefits.

"No, not yet."

Therefore Bernard R. tells about his sister, Rosa Cecilia, who was very beautiful and studied German literature, but who could not find a husband or a real job and had to support the whole family by giving private lessons, and about his high school, which provided him with a free uniform, free lunch, and free tuition.

"I was the only student in the school who, thanks to his certificate of poverty and his mathematical skills, received a free uniform, free lunch, and free tuition. Have I already reached my communism? Because I think I am quite close."

Perhaps he was really close in this free uniform of his. Especially when at age fifteen he read a pamphlet summarizing Marx, and everything wonderfully and mathematically came together: profit, surplus value, and class struggle. At age sixteen he took this pamphlet to the Lvov slums and told his friends, a hunchbacked seamstress and an unemployed baker who had nothing to eat and barely spoke Polish, that they were related to a certain wonderful idea that would soon triumph everywhere. They did not have to know the details about Marx's polemic with Bakunin, because Bernard, who had leafed through the pamphlet, assured them that only Marx was right. They were quite satisfied to know that from now on they did not have to catch up with the world, which neither needed nor wanted them. It was the world that would soon join them, and they would become its elite: the hunchbacked seamstress, Bernard in his free uniform, and his father, who was still producing vinegar through the clear and exclusive fault of his partner, Mr. Gasthalter.

Now that we know where Bernard R. got his communism, we can return to our main subject, that is, the circumstances of Major Krall's disappearance.

The time is the end of July 1944, the place—the western banks of the Bug River. The Second Communications Regiment has just been formed, and Rainisch has just become Rajnicz and received the rank of political officer. The regiment's commander, Colonel Malarenko, has called the officers for their first briefing.

It is a hot summer day. It is Poland again. The officers are standing in front of a porch and waiting for their commander. Bernard is passing a cigarette to a young lieutenant with a blond mustache. They smoke together leaning against the same warm pine tree and the sleeves of their uniforms stick to brown, soft resin. The lieutenant picks a lump of raisin and lifts it to his mouth. Bernard looks at him and thinks that it would be good to win him over for communism. That may not be easy, he thinks. These are no longer unemployed bakers but prewar officers who spent the war in the Home Army or partisan units. Their faces are calm and masculine, their uniforms properly buttoned up. It occurs to Bernard that their parents must have paid their high school tuition. It is a trivial reflection, but Bernard does not mean the money. It is rather a touch of regret that fate gave him a worse part, an unjust share of humiliation. The fate of the dark ones—as he would think if he knew that primitive distinction. Yet he restrains himself and even thinks with satisfaction that now it does not matter anymore. Here they are—sitting together in the same uniforms, on the same bench—they, Polish officers, and he, a

Polish officer, one of them after all, at last one of the bright and calm ones.

The commander approaches, the officers salute. The commander says that he *privietstvuyet* (he is greeting you, translates Bernard), and that the first thing he has to say is the following: *Vy pomnite, tovarishtschi, vot chto. Kazhdyi oficer dolzhen byt chekist.*

Silence.

Bernard starts to explain. He translates for Major Krall, who sits right opposite to him (it could have happened, after all, that Major Krall, whose grandfather was in the uprisings and whose father worshipped Marshal Piłsudski, sat face-to-face with Bernard R.): "Remember comrades, each officer should be a chekist."* And Bernard sees in despair a chasm opening between his communism and these people. Bernard has to redeem his communism in the eyes of the major, so he interrupts the commander and says: "Gentlemen, I am quite aware that in our society the word *chekist* does not evoke the best possible connotations, but do not take it too literally. The commander simply wants to underscore the need for vigilance, because we have expensive weapons and . . ."

The officers still look in silence at Bernard R. and Bernard makes his last effort: "Listen. Land will belong to the peasants, factories to the workers. It will be good in Poland, you'll see."

The officers remain silent, and Colonel Malarenko interrupts his briefing, gets into his car, and drives away—probably to file a report against Bernard. In the evening two commissions arrive—each acting on a different report. At night the security troops surround the regiment. By morning

*Cheka: secret police, predecessor of the NKVD, GPU, and KGB.

it is clear that all the bright ones are gone. Yet Bernard remains . . . after all.

Now Bernard R. gets into his car and drives away. "Listen, Tolek," he says, "they took my officers." "First of all calm down, Beniu," says Tolek, the chief of personnel. Now Bernard starts to shout: "They took all my officers! Do you understand?" And Tolek Fejgin, the future director of the Fifth Department in the Ministry of Security, replies: "You are a nervous wreck, Beniu." And he transfers him to the Fourth Regiment of Heavy Tanks, with which Bernard R. will end the victorious war.

Bernard R. told me the story of Major Krall's disappearance and fell silent. To be honest he should be able to summon some comforting words, express some regret, but the major is the last thing Bernard R. has on his mind right now.

He seems to have succumbed to some kind of self-pity. For himself, the one who remained.

Colonel Malarenko was a real disaster: he appeared only to deprive Bernard R. of the opportunity of being with the bright ones.

"A real disaster . . . " Again that sarcastic tone of the narrator from the first chapter, when she was telling about Grandpa Staemmler choosing Polishness in Buchenwald. Back then it was envy for the man who had the chance to utter the words: "I am staying with the others." And now? Isn't it because Bernard has failed to say exactly the same words? Yes, that would be the right line for that night, but we should remember that the only alternative was the Fourth Regiment of Heavy Tanks.

What is the matter, then?

Of course I know what the matter is. I only pretend to ponder the question.

"Dear Bernard R., do you have to call him 'Tolek?'"

Bernard R. is evidently surprised.

"Anatol Fejgin, the director of the Fifth Department."

"We were calling each other by our first names after all. Everybody was for me 'Tolek,' or something else. And I was Beniek from Lvov."

Do you remember (continues Bernard R.) the scene from the movie *Man of Marble*, when the hero arrives in Warsaw to seek justice? He climbs the stairs at Party headquarters and is met by a man with gray hair. When I saw him I almost leaned toward the screen to see if it was someone I knew. If it were me climbing those stairs I would certainly know him— someone with whom I wrote pamphlets, or worked in a party cell, and he would know me, too. "Hi, Benio," he would say.

"I don't deny it. I was one of them."

So much about the new variant of Major Krall's death, and the irritation caused by the name "Tolek."

Soon after the major and his colleagues were taken away the Fourth Regiment of Heavy Tanks entered Lublin. The next day Bernard R. visited Majdanek.

He entered a gas chamber.

He touched an oven in the crematorium. It was still warm.

Ashes in the oven were still warm.

When leaving the compound Bernard R. was thinking differently about many things that had happened in his life.

He knew, for example, that the disappearance of forty innocent men was a terrible thing, but he also knew that in this camp four hundred thousand innocent people were killed. What is forty against four hundred thousand . . . It is the war—thought Bernard R.—These are still the costs of this terrible war.

And the forty men whom he had no time to convert to communism blended inside him with the ashes he touched with his own hand.

**V**

As for us, we visit Majdanek every 5th of May.

That's how it looks: She buys flowers on the 4th in the afternoon, and calls me in the evening all upset to say she bought the wrong kind. "Tulips. Is that all right?" "It is." "No, too modest. Carnations would be better, wouldn't they?" "We had carnations last year." "You see!"

In the morning on the 5th of May we put three bunches of flowers on the back seat of our car and set out on our journey. As we go she says all sorts of things. For example: "Look, Ryki. There is a church on the right." And there is a church. "There is a road right behind that church." There certainly is a road. "We were driving that road in a horse cart, my mother and I, and my mother's brother was running behind us and shouting: Don't leave me here, please! He was falling behind and clinging to the cart with his hands: Please, take me with you! Mother turned away and was looking straight ahead, but I saw him until the very end. You won't see him anymore, I finally said, you can look now. And my mother turned around and looked."

"You have told me all that already," I say. "Really? I don't remember." "Last year in the same place, when we were passing the church." "Well, perhaps." "Two years ago you

*30*

told it, too," I say absentmindedly because someone tried to pass us crossing the solid center line. "When will those people learn to drive?" She starts paying keen attention to the road and expresses her indignation at a cyclist who did not signal his turn early enough. Then she tells me about Naples: "They drive like maniacs there and yet you hardly ever see an accident. Unbelievable. Have you ever been to Naples?" she asks with curiosity. In short, we engage in a normal conversation between a driver and a polite passenger.

We reach our destination before noon.

We pass MAJDANEK cafeteria, we park in front of the gate and take our three bunches from the car.

Our barrack No. 41, "Bad und Desinfektion II" [Bath and Disinfection II], is on the right side directly behind the gate. We enter only when it is empty. If there is a guided tour inside, we wait quietly until the voices subside.

We pass through the first room. We walk on our tiptoes— not in order to be quiet, but because our pumps get stuck in the planks of the floor. In this room the prisoners were undressed and shaved, says a sign, but we don't read it. The hair was sold to a German company P. Reimann, fifty pfennigs per kilogram, the total amount of seven hundred and thirty kilograms was sent to the Reich, but we've also known that for a long time.

One year we overheard a guide explaining that all sorts of things were made from the hair, for example socks for submarine crews.

We were quite puzzled by that, and we talked about socks on our way back. First of all: how do you spin human hair? Needless to say it has to be spun into a thread. On a spindle? On a spinning wheel? Or maybe on some sort of industrial machine? Probably on a machine. After all it was three quarters of a ton.

And why socks, of all things?

Probably they were warm, and it must be chilly on a submarine.

Perhaps they are exceptionally light? On a U-boat every gram counts, just like on a spaceship.

Maybe they are delicate and do not chafe your heels?

Or perhaps they help with rheumatism. Service on a submarine must be rather unhealthy, especially if you have rheumatism, and socks from human hair may have some special medical effect.

One year she said: "And if a U-boat sinks together with its crew, and the crew is wearing the socks, the hair will die for the second time, is that right?"

One year she said: "Judging by the photographs he had short hair. How much could it weigh—tell me?"

We proceed through the second room—the washing room with taps in the walls—and after a dark, narrow corridor we reach a compartment with a small barred window. One can look outside, because it is the window through which they poured gas and checked to see that everything in the chamber was in order. We do not look. We walk matter-of-factly without glancing around, it is evident we are no tourists, we are here on some sort of business. On the right side there is an open door with a wooden barrier. We've reached our destination.

Each of us knows exactly what to do: she unwraps the flowers and I fold up the paper, I stand behind the barrier and say: "All clear." She climbs over the barrier, jumps to the other side, and enters the chamber. I step back to watch the entrance, because some time ago a guide started hollering and threatened to press charges. She lays the flowers in the middle of the floor and carefully arranges the ribbons. She looks around. A bulb is glaring on the ceiling. The walls are bluish gray with darker stains, and you can see shallow grooves on the ceiling. When the gas was poured in and people started to suffocate, they scratched with their fingers . . . and so on.

She touches the ceiling and the walls with her hands as if expecting to recognize his marks.

When a guided tour approaches I say: "They're coming." She jumps over the barrier and takes another bunch. We know it was here, but we do not know which of the three chambers was HIS, so she puts flowers and touches the ceiling and walls in each of them. After we are done with the third bunch we turn back, we pass the compartment, which is now on our left side, we walk through the washing room and the room in which they were shaved, and we exit the same way we came in (the door is heavy, it has an iron staff, and it is often closed, so one has to push hard to get out).

Each year we make the return trip, and she never forgets to be surprised: "Look," she says, "I'm out. I was lucky again."

There are two slabs of concrete behind our barrack. Several steps from there behind a wire fence the town begins. A meadow, single-family houses, gardens, a warm breeze blows from the gardens—it is usually quite warm on the 5th of May. We sit on the slabs and look at the calmness, grass, houses behind the fence, the tourists—luckily nobody comes behind the barrack, everybody follows the designated trail.

She asks: "Are you hungry? I brought some sandwiches."

Once I tried to refuse, but she replied: "I am at home, I want to eat so I eat." And she opens her bag.

Later she says: "I have no issues with him anymore. On my way here I try to remember everything that has to be resolved, but now there is nothing. No requests, no problems, perhaps only a plea for the trip back—from the barrier to the door. There is the sky, the grass and warm breeze behind the door, Father, everything is fine, really."

On our way back to Warsaw:

"It must be somewhere here. Yes, this road. They were

herding them along that road, and Grandpa was carrying . . . well, guess what . . ."

(Of course I know what.)

"He was carrying a samovar, can you imagine?"

(You told me.)

"It must have looked funny."

(At least the Director, to whom I told the story, was laughing at this large, elaborate piece of junk—to use his words.)

The crowd in the road—terror, shouting, everybody grabbed something in a hurry, and now they are carrying all that stuff—furs, suitcases, linen, perhaps a sewing machine—all the sensible things that one takes for a journey when one is driven away from home. And he is clutching a samovar.

They are bumping into him, nobody pays much attention, and yet it is a sort of curiosity: among the madding crowd—a tall old man with a long, gray beard and a samovar in his hands.

At that moment Mr. Zygmunt, Grandpa's Polish prewar partner, appears. He offers to take something for storage until the end of the war, but what? Not the grandpa with his beard, with his eyes—out of the question. But it never occurred to Grandfather to ask for himself. Why don't you take this—he says and hands Mr. Zygmunt the samovar. The partner is surprised, he offers to run to the house and salvage something else—silver, perhaps?—but Grandfather is adamant: "No, Zygmunt. This will do."

The question of the date emerged only as we were passing Puławy. It is fairly easy to establish the year, but please note that we know the exact day. The 5th of May. This is a slightly delicate matter, and I am always curious how she is going to wiggle out of it. 5–5–1942. Two fives. The 5th of May. She learned the date directly from him, in Moscow, and on top of that, in the apartment of the daughter of Pushkin's great-grandson. I cannot help it, it was at the daughter's of the poet's great-grandson, in Moscow, on Smolenskaya-Naberezhnyaya Street. She was in Moscow for the exhibition of achievements of the Polish People's Republic. The exhibition included furniture and interior design. The walls of one of the model interiors were decorated with paintings by contemporary Polish artists, and her painting *Portrait of a Sad Girl* (*Portryet grustnoy devchonky*) was among them. She hung it herself—with a measure of disbelief—over a white living room set, after which she went to Smolenskaya-Naberezhnaya to have tea with the daughters of the poet's great-grandson. Katia was retired, Natasha was a philologist, and her husband was a physicist in the Dubna Institute. The poet's self-portrait in profile— the original sketch—was hanging over an escritoire from Tsarskoye Syolo. The younger of the two sisters turned out to be a perfect medium. The physicist from Dubna asked: "Dukh, ty kto i komu ty pryshol?" [Who are you, spirit, and to whom did you come?] And when she already knew everything she wanted to know, the physicist explained that an electromagnetic impulse sent by the human brain can take material form. "Vy nye vyeryte, konyechno?" [Of course, you don't believe?] asked the physicist.

"Nyet, pochemu. Konyechno vyeru." [No, why. I do believe.]

The shouting continued throughout the night, but in the morning it was already quiet. The streets were empty. The day before, her mother had brought them some money, and later she regretted it: if she had brought them food they could at least have taken it for the road. They did not have far to walk. It is a five-hour walk, six at the most, from Kalinow to Majdanek.

If I had brought them bread, they could at least have eaten it as they walked.

She told her cousins about the grandfather and his samovar during a huge family reunion in London. They were very interested in her story and asked whether it was a silver samovar. No, it was brass. And how is that possible? The tray was certainly silver. Before the war someone visited Grandfather in Poland and clearly remembered the silver tray, on which the butler brought the mail into the sitting room. "In white gloves," added someone in English, because the whole conversation was in English. Everybody agreed. The butler in white gloves brought the tray into the sitting room. That's quite possible, she consented, but they were still somehow disappointed. "Listen," somebody said in a conciliatory tone, "the fact that the samovar was made of brass does not mean that the tray could not be silver." It was evident that the silver tray and the butler did make a difference.

There were thirteen cousins, about thirty people including the wives and children, and everybody looked at her kindly, almost tenderly. They were delighted that she spoke English, that she came to London on a British Council scholarship, and that she was wearing a silk dress. Only that unfortunate detail about the tray! After the soup the atmosphere improved, and someone asked her: "And how about Granny?" meaning Grandmother Hanna, the wife of the grandfather with the butler and the samovar. She panicked, because her grandmother was a very religious old lady, but before her death of starvation she asked for a "kotlet." "It doesn't have to be kosher," she said. "Let it be a pork kotlet." And now one had to tell it in a relaxed manner, without hysteria, and with the proper sequence of tenses. "*It was during the Uprising,*" she started uneasily because she still didn't know how to handle the grandmother's wish (she could imagine the shame of a pious Jewish woman asking for pork!), but she realized it was all to be told in English, so Granny would not ask for a kotlet but for a *pork chop.* Could a woman asking for a *pork chop* still be her grandmother?! And everything went rather smoothly, as it always does during a polite English dinner, and she thought that the worst part was definitely behind her, when they suddenly remembered the photographs. God have mercy, they have photographs? They rushed out, rushed in, cleaned the table, and she saw a young girl with a white veil who looked just like her mother. Beside her sat a man with large, dark eyes, so she guessed it was her father. "This is my father," she said aloud. On the reverse side father sends his regards from Warsaw to London, the 20th of May, 1935 (*s* in the word "sends" and in the word "Warsaw" had an elaborate hook). "*He will scratch the ceiling,*" she easily found the proper English words, "*in the barrack on the right side.*" Then a middle-aged man with bright eyes looked at her. "This is Uncle Szymon," she explained. "He will be running behind the cart. Mother went back there after several days but everybody was gone. Since that time she often dreams about him as he runs and shouts. 'You know,' she says, 'I dreamt about him again. He was running and shouting something, but I could not hear the words, only his lips were moving.' After each dream Mother goes to the cemetery, and if Mr. Fenicer is sober she asks him to pray on the grave of Grandma Hanna, the mother of Uncle Szymon." "And here? I'll be damned—this is Aunt Rosa. What good looks she had! She would not have to hide at all were it not for her habit of suddenly looking back in the street, in 1968 she started doing that thing again, and she had to be locked up in an institution." She could not logically explain why she was telling all that. "You acted like a hooligan," I said. "Worse than that. You acted like the hero in one of Sławomir Mrożek's plays, the guy who undresses during a reception in order to show his war scars. Can you explain why on earth you were telling them all that stuff." "So that they would know," she said but this answer convinced nobody, and quite rightly so.

The one good thing resulting from her trip to London was

that after she had returned she finally took a good look at the samovar.

She found a crumpled newspaper at the bottom.

She straightened it out.

She saw a roll of paper.

She unrolled it and saw a narrow metal plate with two holes in it, as if for nails, and also a small roll of parchment . . .

The parchment was covered with Hebrew script.

She learned that it was a mezuzah, or "doorpost." One used to nail mezuzahs to the post of the main door in the houses of religious Jews, and they contained two verses from the Books of Moses. The first one starts with: "Hear, O Israel: The Lord our God, the Lord is one . . . ," and the other ends with " . . . that your days be multiplied, and the days of your children, in the land which the Lord sware unto your fathers to give them, as the days of heaven upon the earth."

# VI

The officer in the properly buttoned uniform who sat opposite Bernard R. during the July 1944 briefing in the Lublin district could not possibly be Major Krall. I know that the major returned from the September 1939 campaign, was arrested at home, and spent the rest of the war in some officers' POW camp. How could he be in the Lublin district in 1944 if he returned home right after the war? It is more likely he was among those sitting in the district government building in Bydgoszcz and listening to Bernard R., chief of the Military Political Council in Western Pomerania, explain the current international situation.

Yes, I am more and more convinced that he was there: one year and one month after that July night he was sitting in a large amphitheater among his friends, who, like himself, have just returned from the camps and were curious about their new fatherland and about the young captain whose task it was to explain the background of the electoral defeat of the British Conservatives. At least that was the subject of Bernard's first lecture.

Bernard R., his hand still in bandages because a couple of days earlier he was sneaked out of a hospital by his friend from Tarnopol, Wilus Sz., first gave a general overview of the situation in Europe, and then advanced the idea that by throwing out Churchill, that reactionary puppet, the English nation had clearly chosen democracy and progress.

Bernard R. was wounded while inside a heavy JS tank. Those tanks had terrible ventilation and after three consecutive rounds from the cannon the crew would start to suffocate. Germans knew about that property of the JS, which stood for "Joseph Stalin," and waited for the third round, when the suffocating crew would open the hatch to get some air. Bernard R. was wounded while taking air after three consecutive rounds, and was sent to a hospital, from which four months later he was sneaked out with the help of Wilus Sz., one of the brothers Sz. from Tarnopol. Wilus Sz. was known for two things: for conducting political debates with his brothers while quartering meat and brandishing his cleaver (they had the largest butcher shop in the whole of Tarnopol) and for his passionate speech to the officers during the victory roll call in May 1945: "We've finished with Hitler—shouted Wilus with fire—and now we are saying to our internal enemy DAVKE NO!" "Excuse me, captain," whispered an officer who was sitting next to Bernard, "but what does it mean, *davke*?" Could Bernard say that Wilus Sz., who finished four grades in Tarnopol, had problems distinguishing Yiddish from Polish? No, Bernard R. could not possibly say such a thing, so he answered: "This is an old Party expression of ours, even from before the war." "Aha," agreed the officer. "That's very interesting." And Wilus Sz., who now runs a very successful dry cleaning business in Malmö, sneaked Bernard R. out of the hospital—his hand still in bandages, because the wound turned out to be a really nasty one—and made him chief of the Military Political Council in Western Pomerania, so now Bernard had to explain to Major Krall and his colleagues the reasons for Churchill's downfall and the Tory defeat.

He had just given a general overview and was expressing,

in strongest possible terms, his opinion of the reactionary puppet, when suddenly one of the officers rose from his seat and exclaimed in outrage: "Winston Churchill was one of the greatest statesmen and war heroes, and calling him a puppet seems highly inappropriate."

Bernard R. was dumbfounded.

Not that he denied the officer the right to speak out, far from it. Bernard R. was simply amazed that someone could call Churchill a great statesman and a hero. In the world from which Bernard R. emerged in his heavy tank Churchill did not exist, and Joseph Stalin was a great statesman. In the amphitheater of the district government Bernard understood for the first time that another world was possible—a world in which J.S. did not exist yet Churchill did. It was such an enormous discovery that Bernard R. remembers it to the present day.

I do not claim that the man who spoke out was Major Krall. I do not think, either, that he was the man who got up during the next talk and volunteered the opinion that the Polish political orientation was being dictated by geography. Bernard R., who wanted to be loved for his communism and not for geopolitics, was very upset by the incident yet unhappy to learn that the officer was later expelled from the army. He even asked around whether the punishment wasn't too severe. He was reassured, however, that the demotion would spare the officer much more unpleasant consequences. In 1947, when the officers from the POW camps were being arrested, Bernard R. realized that the expulsion was probably a lucky coincidence, and rid himself of any remaining qualms of conscience.

Major Krall was not the officer who volunteered his opinion on Churchill, nor was he the one who talked about geopolitics, but I think, in fact I am positively sure, that he was among those arrested in 1947 for conspiracy against the Communist government.

Major Krall was taken from his home in the morning.

It was on the 24th of September—someone knocked on the door and some officers walked in. They told him to get dressed, and when he was ready one of the officers ripped the insignia from his uniform. They told him to walk in front of them.

Where was I at that time? I had to be somewhere in our apartment. I must have been asleep and I heard nothing.

No. I was asleep but I heard some voices and footsteps and I saw my father leaning over my bed (later I was never sure whether it was reality or a dream).

No. I heard the noise, I sat up in my bed and after a while I sneaked into the dining room where my mother found me and quickly led me away.

No. I was asleep after all. I woke up at the usual hour before school, I walked into the kitchen, hot milk was on the table as usual, I was surprised that my father had left so early, and only then my mother came up to me crying, and told me what had happened. "We are alone again," she said. At the gate she was already calm and it was the same stern calmness with which she used to admonish me not to laugh too loud. (Do not forget that your father and your fatherland are in slavery.)

I still remember my way to school and the misty cool air. I always remember the temperature and the color of the air. That morning the air was pale gray with a tint of purple. I felt coolness on my knees above the socks. I don't think I was sad. To be honest, I do not remember the feeling of sadness from my childhood. I suspect that it is a certain peculiarity of my organism: it produces antibodies at the first sign of sadness. And this is all that remained of the day when my father was arrested: mother crying yet calm, hot milk on the table, and chilly, pale gray air.

I could reconstruct the further events concerning Major Krall from two sources: from documents and from the testimony of Bernard R. The documents contain information about the trial of fifteen officers from the Pomerania military district accused of conspiracy, notes from death row written by one of them, letters from prison, and several other materials. The testimony of Bernard R. concerns only the trial, in which he appeared as a witness for the prosecution.

The proceedings were held in the basement of the Military Information Office in Warsaw. Present were judges, prosecutors, and investigating officers. The defense was not admitted owing to the confidential nature of the trial.

The major would have sat on one of four benches in the dock. (From the documents: "We were seated in four rows at some distance from one another. The room was guarded by armed soldiers.") The judges were seated on the major's left side. ". . . above their heads was a huge banner saying: WHO IS NOT WITH US IS AGAINST US. WHO IS AGAINST US IS THE ENEMY. THE ENEMY MUST BE DESTROYED."

One of the first to testify was Colonel Tadeusz Jan Z. (From the documents: " . . . born 1894, height 177 cm, companion of the Virtuti Militari and four Crosses of the Brave in the Polish-Bolshevik war of 1920, the son of a landowner . . . ") Probably one of the major's fellow prisoners in the camps. The court asked his family name. "Z.," answered the colonel. The court asked his Christian name: "When I was born a certain rich and influential aunt was visiting our estate," started the colonel, taking the court by surprise. The court repeated the question. "This is very significant for my case," insisted the defendant, "because when I was born, a certain aunt was visiting us . . . " After the third attempt

Colonel Z. managed to finish his statement, which I quote from the records: "When I was born a certain rich and influential aunt was visiting our estate. That aunt, known for her great veneration of the Polish kings, wanted me to have the name of Jan. My father, however, an ardent democrat and a great admirer of Tadeusz Kościuszko, insisted on Tadeusz. A family council was convened and after three days of deliberations I was given the names of Jan Tadeusz in order to satisfy both sides. Of course as a democrat I use the name Tadeusz, especially since my father was so attached to the memory of Kościuszko that he distributed half of his estate—about 450 hectares of cropland—among his peasants. As my father before me I was always a true democrat and since the age of sixteen I spent most of my time in the servants' quarters." Then Colonel Z. touched upon more-contemporary events, providing ample details about an organization that never existed, quoting conversations that never took place, and thus becoming the main witness for the prosecution. No one knows why Colonel Z. so testified. His behavior remained a mystery until the very end. His testimony did little to ameliorate his own situation: he was sentenced to death together with the major and four other officers.

They were locked up in the same cell.

Thanks to the documents I can reconstruct the major's life on death row.

"After the morning toilet and breakfast the prisoners would tell each other their dreams. If someone dreamt about potatoes, it meant a visit from the prosecutor, new interrogations, and torture. If one dreamt a forest or a road lined with trees, the case would be sent to the president's office and the decision would be negative. Crosses signified a speedy execution. Climbing a mountain or a priest saying mass meant a successful appeal. Birds in flight augured the prosecutor's consent to a family visit . . . That was our occupation until lunch. After lunch the cell became more agitated and the prisoners grew more tense. Anxiety increased until 5 P.M. when the condemned were called for execution. At 5 P.M. a warden called the names through the bars. The one whose name was called would say good-bye to the inmates and leave the cell. The cell remained frozen in gloom. In total silence the inmates would spread their straw mattresses on the concrete floor and wait until 9 P.M. At that hour one could hear a shot, or several shots, from a high-powered handgun. The shots brought some relief. The prisoners would pray: 'Rest in peace,' and fall asleep in full light, because the lights on death row were on from dusk till dawn. There were many days like that during my six months in the cell. . . ."

One day five officers sentenced to death were taken to the office of the prison supervisor and informed that the president of the Polish People's Republic had commuted their sentences to life imprisonment (the act of mercy was preserved in the documents of the case). They were moved to ordinary prison cells, started ordinary prison life, and could write letters to their families. The documents in my possession contain twenty-four such letters, all written by the same man to his wife, Dela. Each letter starts with "Dear Dela," displays the prisoner's name and "b. 13 Dec. 1896" in the top left corner, accompanied by a date and prison name—Rawicz, or Potulice, or Wronki—in the top right. In the middle of each page the word CENSORED was stamped in red ink.

If Major Krall was sentenced to death and then pardoned, if Major Krall really existed, he could certainly have written those letters to his wife, Dela. Dela—short for Delfina. Isn't it a magnificent name for a major's wife and my mother?

"Dear Dela," he would write with an elaborate ornamentation preceding each *D*. The major would have beautiful, calligraphic handwriting, and each capital letter would seem chiseled, especially the *D*'s and *W*'s, as in "Wronki,"

"Ward," "Death," and "Dear." Each of his *W*'s is a real masterpiece of calligraphy: a thin horizontal line at the top followed by a strong, decisive stroke of the first vertical, a gentle arch in the middle, another bold vertical, and a delicate loop over the second horizontal line: *W*.

Dear Dela! Rawicz, 3 September 1953.

I am glad to hear that you are feeling better, but I am really worried about Aunt Hela's health. Please give her my most sincere regards and kiss her hands for me. Also give my kisses to Granny . . .

Dear Dela! Potulice, 5 January 1954.

. . . Janka brought me clothes. I left them in deposit because I don't need them right now. I have the feeling that I shall not be using them for some time. . . . I doubt if all that would do me much good because all that is lasting too long, and I am not getting any younger, or stronger. . . . Please write to Aniela to say that I thank her for her letters. I thank Hela in advance for her promised letter. Tell her to write about Syla—whether she has recovered, and how is Stach's health. I kiss the hands of our Granny.

Dear Dela! Wronki, 20 September 1954.

The prison is quite close to the station. . . . If you visit Frank and his family give them my regards, and kiss Helena's hands. . . .

Dear Dela!

. . . thanks a lot for sending me 15 injections of extra-strength vitamin B-1 . . .

Dear Dela!

Aniela wrote me that Maryśka suffers from eczema on one hand . . .

Dear Dela!

. . . you have to explain to our son that a gentleman must apologize for such misbehavior directly to the person he offended, even if in his opinion he didn't do anything wrong.

He is growing up in a house full of women, and he has to understand that a man who offends a woman cannot consider himself a real man. Please make him understand that.

Such were the letters. No weakness, no suffering, not a moment of doubt—only once, and even then immediately back to pleasantries: thank Aniela, and kiss the hands of our Granny . . . Escape into gallantry, relatives (how many relatives they had, how many . . . ), a gentleman's honor, and calligraphy, because no other world imposed by external forces should be as much as acknowledged.

Only a calm, bright man in a properly buttoned uniform can write such letters.

And the final document in the file: a copy of a deposition by one of the officers.

"I, the undersigned, confirm that retired Colonel Bernard Rajnicz, whom I knew in the army from August 1945 to September 1947, while called upon as a witness by the District Military Court in Warsaw in February-March 1949 to testify against me and my companions accused of alleged membership in an illegal military organization . . . , testified in my case, as in the cases of some of my codefendants, in a factual, objective and truthful manner. . . . In several particular instances his testimony was clearly in favor of the defendants.

"Both I and my codefendants appreciated the objectivity of Col. Rajnicz.

"I am also aware that his objective testimony has exposed Col. Rajnicz to serious personal and professional complications. My internal passport number is . . . . Col. Jan Kryska."

# VII

Bernard R. came to our last meeting with an even more incredulous smile and more astonished eyes than ever. The reason for his incredulity and laughter are all these stories he is
telling me. For example he is telling me about himself, with
the Marxist pamphlet in hand, calling on the hunchbacked
seamstresses in a Lvov slum, and before I have time to write it
down, he is choking with laughter: "Can you picture it? I
promised her that the whole world would soon join with her!
Ghhhhh," because he laughs with a strange aspiration as if
trying to cough out a fish bone stuck in his throat. "So how do
you like it, eh? Ghhhhh," and he waits for me to join him in his
amusement at the fifteen-year-old boy with a pamphlet in his
hand. But I take no part in this enjoyment, on the contrary, all
right Bernard, I say. You were right. After all who else could
make the hunchbacked seamstress from a Jewish slum a member of the world elite? And Bernard stops laughing and looks
at me intently—"do you really think so?" But he knows perfectly well that he was more than right, because were it not for
communism he would never have escaped with his comrades
to the East and would be dead in the sands behind Lvov. Were
it not for communism he would not exist at all. Once, during a
New Year celebration—the first one after 1956—he struck up
a conversation about Stalin with a *Pravda* correspondent.

"Comrade, of all people you shouldn't talk like that about him. You owe him your life!" his interlocutor replied. The correspondent was certainly right and Bernard R. became so embittered that he almost burst out crying: So that's how it was, so he couldn't even be a revisionist like the rest of them, he couldn't hate Stalin like the rest of them, because he still had to love him a little? . . .

As I said, Bernard came to see me even more astonished than usual, because a day earlier he learned in the Nymph café that he was a swine. He has lived for thirty-five years with the conviction that he was not a swine! Yes, he visited seamstresses with his pamphlets, he gave talks on Churchill, he even won elections, but he never had blood on his hands. An now he suddenly meets his victim in the Nymph café.

He was paying his bill when he sensed someone's presence behind his back. He lifted his eyes and he saw the General. "It's been thirty years," smiled the General, so Bernard invited him to his table, and they started a conversation on the relations between philosophy and mathematics. Still smiling, the General said: "That was some talk you gave back then, Colonel. You practically finished me off, but you were a great speaker. . . . "

It took Bernard some effort to recall the event the General was referring to.

It was in 1948—the time of Gomulka's "rightist deviation." They were sitting at a briefing—the General with the presidium and Bernard R. in the first row, dressed in a new uniform with a lieutenant colonel's insignia and basking in the glory of a successful electoral campaign in Western Pomerania. There were two districts in which the Communists actually won the elections in 1947: Western Pomerania and Gdansk. Both chiefs of Security and Propaganda groups in those regions, that is Bernard R. and Jurek Krupiński, who recently visited our country to attend an anti-alcoholism congress, since he has made his career treating alcoholics in Australia, received the Order of Polonia Restituta. There was a small celebration with President Bierut and all the S & P chiefs, Bernard R. and Jurek Krupiński accepted their orders, and in the intermission Bernard asked an old veteran from the Spanish Civil War known by the name of Kubuś: "So how did we do in the elections?" To which the said Kubuś replied: "What does it matter, Benio? The ballots have already been destroyed." "How come?" asked Bernard R. "I did my best to win and now it doesn't matter?" And he was growing more and more bitter, and unfortunately also more and more loud, so Kubuś had to smack him in the mug and lead him out of the room, and the celebration continued without the hero.

As we see, Bernard R. had a good reason to feel great in the first row during the briefing, and as soon as he heard the General distancing himself from Gomulka, he asked for recognition. Why did he choose to speak against the General? Bernard does not remember. Perhaps it was for that one sentence that just came to his mind, that one should beat his own chest, not that of Gomulka—at that time it was a new expression, and who knows whether Bernard wasn't actually its author—and his speech was really very impressive. "Good job," said Kubuś, the veteran from Spain, during an intermission. That was all. And thirty-two years later this man tells him in the Nymph café that after that briefing he expected to be arrested any time. He would wake up early in the morning and listen whether they were coming to take him away, and it never occurred to him that a twenty-eight-year-old lieutenant colonel from the first row delivered his speech on his own, out of the pure joy of living because everything around him was so wonderful.

Bernard R. was transferred to Warsaw.

He won the elections, received his medal, condemned the

rightist deviation—everything was great—and one day Tolek Fejgin, now a powerful director in the Ministry of Security, calls to tell him about the trial of fifteen officers from Bydgoszcz. "Just drop by, Benio, we need you as a witness, I'll explain everything right away," says Fejgin but Bernard R. responds that no explanations are needed, he remembers the men well and knows what to tell the court.

On the twelfth of February 1949 Bernard R. entered the basement of Military Information Headquarters.

He saw the bench and a banner: WHO IS NOT WITH US IS AGAINST US. WHO IS AGAINST US IS OUR ENEMY. THE ENEMY MUST BE DESTROYED.

From the moment of Bernard's entry into the room I should reconstruct the court scene in utmost detail. First of all Bernard glances at the defendants. Then the court asks a question—probably about the activities of the accused, or whether the witness recognizes them. Bernard looks at them with more attention and notices the major. It is quite possible that for a fleeting moment their eyes meet. A moment of hesitation: he locates that face in his memory, sees the warm pine trunk, the officers on the porch and the major sitting right opposite him, listening with curiosity, yet without irony, to his awkward explanations. . . . No, Bernard excuses himself, those men no longer exist (besides, as we have already established, the major was never in the Lublin district, so how could Bernard recognize him in the courtroom, but that is not important), from that moment on, however, the strange feeling never leaves him. Once again he is facing the other ones. Now he is calm, he is bright—he is facing them again.

The court repeats the question.

Now one should describe Bernard's state of mind in minute detail. This is really important because Bernard, having seen that pine tree, knows perfectly well what will happen next. As in a dream we dreamt only once but remember forever. There will be the porch, only this time without the young lieutenant with a blond mustache, who a moment ago put a lump of resin into his mouth, and without the major tilting his head ever so slightly while listening, without hostility or offense but with keen curiosity, to his explanations. There will be nobody on the porch except himself, totally alone. While standing on the porch, in the basement of Military Information Headquarters, Bernard decides that this time he will not surrender his men.

The court asks for the third time whether the witness recognizes the defendants, and Bernard feels pressure in his throat. Not really in his throat but somewhere lower, right above his stomach—pressure, or perhaps a spasm. No, not a spasm, just pressure. It is interesting: Bernard has already experienced the same sensation twice in his life. It happened for the first time in Lvov when he had read the Marxist pamphlet and a certain acquaintance of his said: "I can put you in touch with some people?" "The Communists?" Bernard guessed immediately and the man nodded. Bernard felt the pressure and heard himself say: "Yes, of course." When he recalled the scene much later he realized that the pressure occurred even before he uttered the word "yes" but after he had made his decision. It was like a signal that the decision had been made and Bernard was already on the other side.

It happened again eight years later in the Fourth Regiment of Heavy Tanks. He had summoned all his men and told them that the political officers should be with their soldiers, inside the tanks. He added that it was not an order but a request. They agreed. "All right then," Bernard R. smiled to his political officers and felt the pressure in his throat, because there was really no need for them to die in the tanks. "Why should we die, if we can live," thought Bernard R., but his spasm told him the decision had been made and he no longer had anything to do with it. (A military historian once asked Bernard R. why so many political officers from other regiments survived while nearly all of his men died. "Because only we were riding inside the tanks," explained Bernard, and the historian admitted that he had never thought of such a simple explanation.)

For the fourth time—let us skip chronology for a moment—Bernard recognized the sensation in March 1981, how many years later? My God, forty-five years after the meeting with the Communists in Lvov.

The pressure preceded his reply by only one second:

"Yes, of course," he smiled with gratitude at a young bearded Solidarity man with the image of the Black Madonna pinned to his sweater. "Of course," he repeated realizing how much they were forgiving him, and how much trust they were showing by giving him the job, the last chance in the last round.

"What is this moment before a decision?" I asked Bernard R. "What is this spasm? Is it already a sign of brightness because one has made his choice, or is it still darkness because one is afraid of his choice?"

"It is the fear of darkness," said Bernard R. and, what's interesting, he said it without thinking, almost automatically.

For the third time he felt the pressure while standing on the empty porch, in the basement of Military Information Headquarters. At least he should feel it, because that would be much better.

Without suggesting which version is true the author feels obliged to present yet another possibility, this time without the pine tree and the porch but only with the bench and the banner WHO IS NOT WITH US IS AGAINST US. . . . THE ENEMY MUST BE DESTROYED.

According to this version Bernard R. would like very much to help the court vanquish the enemy (there is no doubt these men are the enemy, innocent people are not put on trial). But because he did not care to see Fejgin, he has no idea what these officers are accused of, he does not know what would speak for or against them, so he decides to tell the truth. What could be more useful to the court in destroying the enemy?

After just a few sentences the accused officers realize what is happening and start showering him with questions, to which he dutifully replies for several hours. When he decides he has told everything he knows, he clicks his heels and leaves the room.

The next morning Bernard R. is called to the meeting of the powerful Party Supervisory Commission. "What the hell was that about?" they ask. "What did you tell them?" "What do you mean?" Bernard R. is surprised. "I told the truth." "What kind of truth?" "Plain, objective truth," replies Bernard R. relaxed, because according to this version everybody is tense—the defendants, the court, and the commission— and only Bernard R. is relaxed. Why should he be afraid, after all, if it all belongs to him—his court, his enemy, his truth. "Objective truth," insists Bernard R. with his childish ease and has to be reminded that for a Communist there is no such thing as "objective truth." The truth is what serves the revolution, and "objective truth" is the domain of the petit bourgeois, that is, of capitalists. Such are the grounds for the official reprimand to be put into his personal file: bourgeois objectivism.

And the rest is the same in both versions: death sentences— act of mercy—and a letter starting with: *I, the undersigned, confirm that Colonel Bernard Rajnicz summoned as a witness . . .* and ending with his internal passport number, signature, and date. This letter was placed on Bernard's desk by a silent man, whose face Bernard did not remember. When he studied the letter—without too much attention although with a measure of curiosity—the man added: "If you ever have any problems, Colonel, and if we could help in any way . . ."

The letter was dated 6 April 1968.

The help from the officers proved unnecessary. Bernard R. was a genuinely talented mathematician even in his Lvov high school, thanks to which he was granted a free uniform and a free lunch, and later in Soviet-occupied Lvov at the university. There, parenthetically, he also received a reprimand because he volunteered the opinion that until Polish professors learned Ukrainian, as required by the Soviet authorities, they should be allowed to lecture in Polish. The reprimand was for "Polish nationalism"—the first of his Party reprimands, which preceded by nine years the reprimand for "bourgeois objectivism." He was a gifted mathematician, so he quickly filled some gaps in his education and in 1968 started writing a long, laborious dissertation on the theory of cybernetics. The theory should be able to explain a lot, like, for instance, the role of accident and necessity in the historical process (hardly an issue of primary importance), as well as the rather painful fact that Bernard failed to couple the hunchbacked seamstress with a certain idea soon expected to triumph in the world.

# VIII

Our Subtenant found me after the war.

I lost sight of her during the 1944 Warsaw Uprising, most likely in its second week, but I remember well our last period together, especially the day we went out into the yard.

We went out in the afternoon. It was still warm, the shooting had subsided, and a lot of people were standing around waiting for the announcement. Suddenly I noticed something strange happening to the Subtenant. She wasn't listening to the voice from the loudspeaker but cocked her head and looked at the gathering with the most satisfied expression on her face. I remembered that expression years later while watching the film *La Strada*. Masina stands in the crowd admiring the acrobatic feats of her lover. "And how about that?" her silly smile addresses the onlookers. There was something of that smile in our Subtenant. She was wriggling her body, watching the people's reactions, absorbing them, exchanging smiles—in short she was taking an active part in the gathering. Then she decided to go for a walk. "They are shooting again," I tried to stop her. "Uh-huh," confirmed the Subtenant, and I noticed undisguised pleasure in her face. "They are shooting. Let's go." She grabbed my hand and dragged me to the next yard. "They are shooting," she repeated. "Shooting at everyone. . . . " I turned back and she followed reluctantly, still looking around, waving her hands, jumping up and down. She was unusually lively, in a mood for celebration. There was really something strange about her, and I started wondering what it might be.

"How warm," she said, "look." She stopped and outstretched her hand toward the sun with a gesture of someone checking for rain.

I realized at the time how strange our being in the street was. Here we were, walking for the first time in broad daylight, without her constantly adjusting her scarf, without kicking a stone, without thinking about her eyes—for the first time since we had our Subtenant. "It's warm, isn't it?" she repeated, talking constantly. "And scary."

"Everybody is scared, aren't they," she assured herself with joy.

They are shooting at everyone.

We returned home and sat down at the table facing the window and we started to draw. There must have been a fire nearby because we saw an orange reflection on the wall. The Subtenant looked at it, then reached for red and yellow crayons. "Here you are," she handed them to me with a polite smile.

She found me all by herself shortly after the war. One day we noticed a scrap of paper attached to our door: "They told me at No. 48 that you are here. I am at . . . " followed by an address with the letters "C.H.," which we did not understand.

Sometime later I went to a small town near Warsaw. I saw a garden and a large house with a porch. It was really nice. The hall was bustling with children, who would also have looked nice if not for their shaven heads. One of the girls ran out to bring our Subtenant. She was dressed in an oversized sweater from UNRRA and had black fluff on her head. Her hair was starting to grow back.

"It's nice here," I said. "Uh-huh," agreed our Subtenant, who, needless to say, should have a name by now but no name was coming to my mind. "Do you want to see the Home?" she asked. She took me to the dormitory. I found three girls there. One of them had a white scarf wrapped around her head. She noticed me, got up from her chair, extended her hand, and curtsied: "My name is Anusia." I observed something unnatural about her face but I couldn't figure out what it was. The second girl, a tiny one, looked just like the bright, chubby child staring at a jug in one of Wyspiański's paintings. Her hair was unkempt, she was called Sabinka, and she also curtsied to me. The third one, Ruta, asked me if I had ever seen a fresh honeycomb. Since I had not, she reached into her bedside table and produced a piece of wax dripping with thick, dark honey.

Later I was introduced to the headmistress and we made a tour of the whole house. I saw a concert piano. "Just like the one in your apartment," commented the Subtenant, "do you want to hear me play?" And the common room. "Here we take our ballet lessons and language lessons." I understood that Our Former was under the guidance of civilized ladies in a house of polite, well-bred children.

From that time on I visited her every so often. Her friends came to know me well, and upon seeing me one of them would call: . . . and here, unfortunately, we have to find some name, because they could not possibly call: OUR FORMER!

Let's say they called: "Marta! (if she wasn't in the dormitory at the moment). Maryśka has come to see you."

I think it works fine, although I am a bit annoyed by that diminutive form. I much prefer Maria, and I would put Marta in the vocative but I understand that "Marta! Maria came to see you!" would sound too artificial coming from Sabinka.

Sometimes I had to wait for Marta. I would sit in front of the house and hear Czerny's études or Bach's "small preludes" through the window, or the ballet teacher's voice: and full *battement*, please, and with more grace . . . I had the impression that the headmistress spared no effort to make visitors realize what careful education her pupils were receiving. At least each time she saw me waiting she informed me that Marta was dancing or playing some instrument, just like any young girl from a good family would after returning from school. Finally the young ladies arrived, breathless, and we could go behind the railroad tracks and into the forest saturated with thick pine fragrance, which was supposed to be good for our lungs.

But first we walked along the tracks.

Do you remember how we walked along the tracks? I, on a narrow path along the rise, and you on a rail, showing the toe steps learned during your ballet lessons. As you walked, you were telling me news.

The new medicine from Switzerland was helping Anusia.

Yes, one day it became clear that the medicine was helping Anusia, because we found one hair on her head. A thin and delicate one, like on a baby, but a real one, no doubt about that. Her brows and eyelashes hadn't started growing yet but that was just a matter of time. Only then did I realize why Anusia's face seemed unnatural to me: it was a face without eyebrows and eyelashes, totally hairless, with a scarf tight around the skull. From that time on you looked for a new hair on Anusia's head every evening, and after a week you found two more, also on the right side. Finally a whole spot of fluff appeared at the top. "Is it there? For sure?" asked Anusia delighted, and you decided it was time to take up a collection for a comb.

In the distance one could see a road crossing the tracks. On the left side, on a slope, grew light yellow flowers with velvet stems.

Sabinka's mother was found. Sabinka was the bright one, from Wyspiański's painting.

I had to stop, because you had just demonstrated full *batte-ment* with your leg at the hip level and with perfectly positioned feet (your teacher was a very meticulous woman and demanded daily practice), "and one—two—listen, it's really interesting," you said, "her mother was found, but she told them to leave her alone because she wasn't coming anyway. The headmistress may look for that German who made Sabinka. They say he made her by force. Do you know," you paused on the rail, "that it is sometimes done by force?" (Yes, we both found it very interesting.) "And if the headmistress wants, she may call that German to visit Sabinka, but never bother her, said the mother."

Don't look at me with such disgust. The information about Sabinka combined with the ballet practice perhaps isn't in the best of taste, but you can't deny, can you, that you went on to demonstrate a jump from third position to fifth, when the jump must be both light and powerful.

"And now nobody calls Sabinka other than Kraut. Nobody in the whole Home. Haven't you heard it yet? Sure, she is a Kraut. And you liked her so much, you see. That Kraut. That-kraut, that-kraut, and-as-high-as-you-can-go-and-as-high-as-"

At the road crossing we would turn into the forest. It was aromatic from heather and resin—and quiet. At last no children, no voices—silence . . . That was the best thing about the forest, wasn't it?

Strange: In our large, empty apartment you waited for hours for the sound of footsteps and whistling to interrupt the silence. Here you waited the whole week for the forest that would free you from the presence of people. On Sundays you waited for me at the gate early in the morning and you were even ready to skip the fabulous Sunday breakfast of cake and hot chocolate in order to run, as soon as possible, to the tracks, beyond the crossing, and into the forest.

*60*

You didn't like me to come into the house. On those occasions I would talk to other girls, and you would keep an eye on me indicating that I was there only for a moment, I just dropped by and I would soon leave, of course with you, because I came to see you, and only you could claim me.

Then we would walk along the railroad and turn into the forest, and we talked about everything I was not supposed to learn from your friends.

You talked about the school.

In the mornings you marched in pairs, a long column of shaven heads, through the whole town (every day you wondered whether some casual onlooker could distinguish your faces. You came to the conclusion that it was impossible because all your faces looked alike. That gave you comfort. Why should you bother about the onlookers who stopped in the street if they could not recognize your face. Besides, the townspeople soon got used to you and weren't looking anymore), but you could return all alone, not muffled by anybody's presence, so you tried to walk slowly, as slowly as possible. . . .

You told me about the new girl.

Her name was Olga. She made everybody laugh because she wasn't sure the war had ended. The forest ranger who gave her shelter did not tell her, so she kept working for him and running to the cellar each time she heard strange footsteps. When the voices subsided the ranger would give her a sign to come out again. One day she found a scrap of newspaper and read a sentence that made her ponder. I don't know what it was—maybe something important, like Potsdam, or maybe a small ad: someone had returned from the camps, someone was looking for somebody. In any case, after reading that sentence Olga sneaked out of the house and went to the nearby village. She was very cautious but nobody paid any attention to her—and also she didn't see any Germans. She went to the town: no Germans either. Then she walked up to some gentleman and asked very politely: "Excuse me sir, is the war still going on?" The gentleman looked at Olga's eyes and hair. "Don't be afraid," he said, "the war has ended, don't be afraid. . . . "

Thus Olga was brought to the Home. She was still very cautious and suspicious, which made you all laugh. You teased her even more than Jakubek, who didn't know he was a boy, and the tutors had to threaten to stop serving you powdered scrambled eggs in order to make you cut it out.

You told me about Ruta's attic. . . .

No, not yet, that was after the medical examination. You told me about the painter who taught you drawing. He was old and gray, he talked in the soft voice of a sensitive artist, and painted your portraits with large breasts, much larger than real. One day he pointed to some rubbish on the ground and told you in his quiet, gentle voice: "I would gladly pick it up myself, but it would be easier for you. You are closer to the earth." You looked at his wrinkles and said: "Who knows who is closer to the earth, sir." You told that to the painter? Not to Mrs. Helena Boguszewska, a writer who paid you a visit? Never mind, they were all gentle people who reacted with genuine horror to your arrogance and one had to calm them down and apologize in front of everyone, right in the middle of the room. But unlike Ruta, the painter did not capture our attention. Ruta was the hero of our many walks and all possible aspects of her case, both technical and moral, were thoroughly discussed.

Right after the medical examination the headmistress called her in and started asking about something Ruta could not understand. Whether somebody, sometime . . . perhaps in that attic (because Ruta spent the whole war in a village attic). "Aha, that thing," Ruta finally guessed. "And how did it happen, my dear?" the headmistress inquired. "But you must not tell the other girls, God forbid, because nice girls do not talk about such things." Ruta returned to her room and told you all about the conversation and the attic. The girls did not understand, so she had to throw in more details. "Did it hurt?" "Sometimes." "When did it hurt?" they kept asking soberly until she told them. "And when it was smaller, did it hurt?" "Almost nothing." She explained patiently again and again, until all of them understood, even the Kraut, who was the youngest and in principle understood very little. It was impossible to explain to her, for example, why she was a Kraut. "Were they good to you?" asked the Kraut. "Sure they were," Ruta was surprised. "Why shouldn't they be?" "Did they give you food?" "Sure they did. They even gave me toys. . . ."

"They were good to her," you said on Sunday on our way to the forest. They gave her shelter, they brought her food, they packed all the cracks in the walls with moss so she would be warm, and they carved wooden toys for her, and when they had to leave they told her not to cry because they were around and they wouldn't allow anything bad to happen to her. "Our whole room," you said, "decided they were good to her, and the headmistress wants her to remember their names, because they deserve severe punishment." We were puzzled. Punishment? We stopped at one of the toppled columns, the usual destination of our walk. We often wondered what they were—no ruins, only two white columns in the middle of the forest. But punishment for what? Just in case, you told Ruta to keep her mouth shut if the headmistress asked her again about those names.

Soon it turned out that the Swiss medicine did not work after all. Anusia lost her hair and she was bald again. Bald on the head, under the armpits, brows, everywhere.

On our way back we would walk together from the forest to the tracks. Right in front of the barrier I would turn toward the station and Marta would pass the crossing. She would steer right, to the cluster of tall yellow flowers, pick one of them, and go straight toward the Home without looking back at me. That's how it was every time. She turned to the flowers, picked one, and walked on.

At first hardly anybody knew about the Home. Sometimes a priest would bring his trophy—German chocolate. He would stand quietly in the doorway to the dining room, untie his sack, and hand everybody a bar, and when the sack was empty he would pull the strings together, smile politely, and leave without a word. . . . A certain lady started an apiary, and was running around the garden with a net over her face and a smoking pot to scare the bees away. . . . And I kept visiting the Home, "the daughter of our Marta's guardian." That is how the headmistress introduced me, thus providing me with an ideal status: everybody in the Home understood what a "guardian" meant. Guardians were those resourceful women without makeup and with their hair smoothly combed into a bun who lived in spacious dark apartments— therefore I was greeted with amiable, almost melting smiles from the teaching staff.

As the news about the Home spread, the number of visitors increased.

First to appear were members of the Commission for the Investigation of Nazi Crimes and one had to tell them a lot of stories.

Rafałek told them about the coal box with a double bottom in which he spent the war. Anusia told about a tomb, which the cemetery caretaker allowed her to leave only at night, and when she finally left it in the daytime she no longer had any hair. Bronka, who had blue eyes and therefore did not have to sit in any strange place, told about her brother Szlamek, whom she hid in a brick kiln, and how his frozen toes broke off in winter. One had to tell all that politely and in full sentences, and also to demonstrate Anusia's head and Szlamek's feet because the headmistress said it would help to bring the malefactors to justice.

Next there came representatives of charity organizations and American philanthropists—they also wanted to hear, in full sentences, about Rafałek and Anusia, but there was more sense to it because it was not about bringing anybody to justice, but about parcels with clothes, egg powder, fountain pens, and halva.

The humanists also came—historians, painters, writers, poets, who liked most of all the story of Jakubek surviving the war dressed as a girl, because he was circumcised. His name was Zosia, he wore dresses and giggled like a girl. What is more, he did not know he was not a girl, he learned it only in the Home. The humanists were quite taken by the story, just like Achilles, they said, and told us of Thetis, who, upon learning about the Trojan War, dressed her son as a girl. Jakubek was very flattered by this comparison. Unfortunately, he did not reach for the sword produced by Odysseus but still preferred dolls and giggling. Everybody was very amused by that, and only the arrival of Olga, who did not know that the war had ended, turned our attention away from him. Of course Jakubek eagerly participated in our pranks with Olga until the guardians threatened us with breakfast without powdered eggs, and the whole fun ended.

One had to talk to the humanists in full sentences because, as the headmistress explained, they wanted to save it all for posterity.

Our Former Subtenant was not on display because a story of someone hiding in a spacious, empty apartment could not be of any particular interest. She had all her hair and all her toes—should she perhaps tell about the interrupted whistling outside the window? No, our Subtenant was of little use to the judges and philanthropists and was slightly embarrassed by the fact. Sometimes she as much as indicated that it was my fault that she had nothing interesting to tell and therefore did not get halva and fountain pens, but, to be fair, Anusia and Ruta shared with us their surplus, and none of us ever remained penless. Hardly a Sunday passed without a visitor leaning against the door in the dining room and telling us about the horrors of war and the brotherhood of man, and reassuring us, or explaining something. Perhaps no one should be surprised by that, because there was hardly a place in the whole of Poland, and perhaps in the whole world, more suited for self-scrutiny, expiations, resolutions, and other humanitarian emotions.

Only three persons said nothing and asked no questions: the priest with chocolate, the beekeeper, and the poet Julian Tuwim. Yes, Tuwim did not repeat Mrs. Boguszewska's mistake, and was not deceived by those little cynics in the bodies of seven and ten year olds. He glanced at them only once, asked one question, and, it seems, got frightened by something, because he left immediately without as much as looking back. When he visited later on Sundays the children tried all kinds of tricks—they played hopscotch or "merry-go-round," they laughed cheerfully like children—but nothing worked. Tuwim would pass them quickly without looking and run to the newborns, to whom he would read his poems for hours.

One day a tall woman in a dress with a floral pattern appeared in the doorway. Women rarely came to the dining room—judges and philanthropists were all men, so when one of them appeared at the side of our headmistress, the children saw it as a warning and had enough time to scatter around. Internally, of course—tumbling into themselves like into a bomb shelter—because on the outside they remained solemn and attentive through the entire new brotherhood of mankind. This time there was a woman, which took them by surprise, they had no time to screen themselves against words, and they were assaulted by the high-pitched, earnest voice of the headmistress greeting the famous author Zofia Nałkowska.

The writer leaned on the door frame.

Her diary says it was on the 12th of November, so why did she wear a floral dress, could it have been so warm in November that year? If it happened today, the Subtenant would hardly deny herself the pleasure of scrutinizing this elegant lady, especially her neck, because shortly before her visit the writer confided in her diary that she had had a careful look at her neck in the mirror and was quite pleased with what she saw: the neck turned out all right, "as if washed in milk"—these were her words. Back in their bedroom, before an evening conversation with Ruta on the obvious subject, but after counting Anusia's hair, they would deliberate on the writer's décolletage, and one of them would certainly say: is it possible to observe one's aging body in the mirror and to limit oneself to the neck? Why didn't she look at herself in profile and watch with concern her breasts and her belly? Of course you would say that, because I would accept the writer's sagacity with understanding. "This is a valuable suggestion for all of us," I would stress each word, "truth is truth, but there are certain limits of good taste that no one should cross, especially in literature." "And in the case of an aging woman this limit runs somewhere along the neck line?" you would want to be sure. "Of course, if SHE believes so."

The author leaned against the frame of the door. *I speak from my heart, although I feel somehow awkward . . .* she would say in her diary. Well, only two people spoke in the Home without feeling awkward. One of them was the priest, who delivered his speeches in cardinal numerals and only in his mind: One—two—three—ten—thirty—fifty—one hundred and twenty . . . The sole indication that he was delivering a speech was the gesture of his index finger. At the end he would nod his head, meaning that there was enough, that the number of seated children corresponded to the number of chocolate bars. At this moment the tension at the tables subsided. The other person was Julian Tuwim, who spoke without awkwardness but only among the newborns on the second floor. He would begin with the words of his poem: "Hallo, lo, lo, lo, this is the birds' radio, dio, dio, dio, from the birch wood . . . " Apart from these two, all speakers were awkward, therefore the writer blamed herself needlessly.

As we can learn from her diary Nałkowska visited the Home in the time between her preparations for a meeting with the French essayist Parrot and the meeting itself: *In the morning I was kidnapped in a car and delivered to O. by a strange woman who loved flowers and bees . . .* followed by the description of the speech and *lunch with some of the tutors. One of them was a widow of a man who died fighting in the ghetto uprising, one was a gray-haired, distinguished lady, whom I met long ago in Belmont, and whose name I cannot recall. . . .* Followed by an observation: *When I stepped among the children, I thought for a moment that there was some misunderstanding—all of them had Aryan features, almost no dark eyes or curly hair. What does it mean? But that's exactly why they were there! That's why they survived the camps, basements, holes in the rubble. A peculiar kind of selection.*

We read the still-unpublished fragments of Nałkowska's diary thanks to the book's editor, Hanna Kirchner. A strange woman who loved flowers and bees, the distinguished acquaintance from the prewar salon . . . We could hardly believe it was about our Home, but we were pleased nevertheless: despite the final sad observation the sentences exuded normalcy and good taste. "Perhaps everything that passes through her system turns into elegance and style," pondered Our Subtenant. "It turns into brightness," I explained. "Elegance and style are only form." "I wonder if you can train yourself for brightness," wondered Our Subtenant, whom I prefer to call just that, although I don't know why. "Try it," I said, "at least try."

Let us say, therefore, that Our Former is now a painter, and that one day she decides to paint the Home. Her life could turn out that way, after all: she is a middle-aged painter and she decides to return to the world of her childhood. Apparently that's what sometimes happens to artists. . . . So she paints the Home.

She paints a little girl—a small, sad girl with disproportionately large eyes.

Then she paints several small girls, their heads next to each other, their eyes too large and separated from their faces, growing on little stems like the eyes of tadpoles.

Then she paints a crowd of sad girls, and this time one can see neither earth nor sky behind them, the whole painting is filled with heads that disappear in the perspective like cobblestones, or like gravestones in a Jewish cemetery.

We (her daughter and I) look at these paintings with embarrassment. "And this is what you learned from Mrs. Nałkowska?" I ask. "And this is what you call your training?"

# IX

Dear Sir,

Our Subtenant started to train herself for brightness.

She came to like her hair smoothly combed into a bun, straightforward glances, white shirts, and shoes with flat heels. Later she would complement her appearance with some casual, funny motif like, for example, a cap with elk. Indeed, she was ready to begin.

The day when she started her training . . .

Wasn't it on a warm, slightly hazy morning . . .

It was Thursday, June 1956: sunny since early morning but not too hot—just pleasant, calm warmth.

We were standing in the middle of a crowd on a crossroad in the center of Poznan.

Nothing was happening yet, people were just standing along the sidewalks on a clean, wide street waiting for something. Nobody knew what it was, but it was in the air, it was coming from everywhere, and it was probably going to happen in the street, which was still empty. Everybody was trying to be as close as possible, the crowd thickened, luckily some tall guy pushed his way to the front, so we followed him and got a good view of the empty street.

We did not wait long, shouts were heard in the distance, and something started to approach us.

It was a demonstration.

It was coming from far away, from the depths of the street. It looked like all mass demonstrations organized on the First of May, only this time the people walked differently, slower, and they were wearing their gray working clothes. It was the first time that I saw such clothes during a demonstration. Sometimes during those official marches people were also wearing working clothes, but they were clean and fresh—evidently a costume—while those we saw were authentic.

The workers in front of the column were looking straight ahead, their faces concentrated and motionless. (Today I think they must have been overwhelmed by the solemnity of the moment and their own role, and they were trying to prove worthy of the occasion.)

People from the sidewalks started to shout to the people in the street. "At last!" shouted someone and people began to applaud. Of course I also started to applaud. We raised our hands high above our heads so that the others would notice us, and shouted "bravo" and "at last."

The Subtenant looked around and saw more and more people—practically everybody—clapping their hands. They were clapping and shouting. ("They were greeting them with such joy," she would say a couple of days later to a man named Werner in a park near the Citadel, "with such relief.")

I guess she must have been surprised by that universal joy.

Later she realized she was probably the only person on the sidewalk who felt no joy.

Later she noticed that the tall boy who had helped us get to the front was looking at her. She felt that glance even before she lifted her eyes: he was watching her attentively in the middle of the strange crowd, in which only she was different from the others—not overjoyed and not clapping. Obviously she did not think what was the right thing to do. She had no time to think, because when she understood what she was doing, she was already standing with her eyes down and looking at the cracks between the flagstones with blades of grass growing between them. (Kicking a stone was out of the question. Too little room.) *Bread and freedom*—the boy read one of the slogans carried by the people in the street. I wanted to whisper to her that she could lift her eyes, but people started chanting together with the demonstrators: free-dom-free-dom and drowned out my whisper. I saw the boy speaking to her: she lifted her eyes from the ground and understood her mistake. She gave him a flirtatious smile and raised her hands over her head, like the rest of us.

"In my opinion," I told her recently, "that's when your training began. When you lifted your hands."

Now you should shout. "At last." If possible, with much relief. And you did shout, didn't you?

But of course, you were clapping and shouting with the rest of us.

It was a very nice feeling to be with us, filled with joy on the sidewalk, wasn't it?

("You were shouting 'at last'?" asked the man named Werner. "Yes," you said. "Of course. I also shouted 'bravo' and 'freedom.'"

—"But why?" asked Werner. "In order to be with them," you were surprised by his lack of comprehension, and quite rightly so, because what is brightness if not the ability to be with the others?)

It is high time to explain who Werner is. Who he was, because he has been dead for the last eighteen years. He used to have a different, beautiful, and poetic name, but I had to change it because the woman we called is still alive, and so is her husband, who always answered the phone, and their children.

I told that story to My Favorite Movie Director, and now the man who used to be known by his real, beautiful, poetic

72

name lives a new and strange life as Werner on film tape. Unfortunately the story in the movie takes place in contemporary times and Werner is still alive but older by eighteen years—old, short, and gray-haired. The real Werner was neither gray nor short, but that is of little importance because the tape is shelved in several metal boxes and nobody can see it. Sometimes the Director will rearrange the boxes in a perfect pile, or some gentlemen will organize a private screening, after which they invariably proclaim: No, this film will never be distributed. Perhaps it is better that way, because why should some moviegoers watch old, gray Werner?

(Recently the Subtenant raised the issue of the film with my former husband, Jakub. He greeted her very warmly and proceeded to explain patiently why the film will never be distributed. They were talking in Jakub's spacious office—not at his desk but at a table in the corner. That was because an old friend from the Home treated her to a private dinner. The Subtenant told me all about the dinner, about the spacious office, and about Jakub's strange new way of walking, as if each of his feet wanted to go its own way, but I interrupted her: "Were you waited on?" "We were . . . " "In tails?" "No . . . " the Subtenant was surprised. "But the waiter was wearing a black suit? And had a napkin over his arm? And was bustling around?"

"My God," I said. "The waiter in black . . ."

My God . . . )

Their conversation did little good for the film of My Favorite Director, but that is not important, there is no good reason why moviegoers should see old, gray Werner, who in reality has never had time to grow old and gray. The real Werner was tall, slender, distracted, and smiling a bit senselessly as if he were constantly amazed, or apologizing for something, and this amazement increased with age. He had problems with walking and he put his feet inside while bending his knees. He mentioned once, without interrupting his laughter, that being beaten on the soles of the feet is not an entirely pleasant experience. He died, as I said, a long time ago, but since he lives in the movie, he is sitting now at a table and speaking about hands. "She had ugly hands. . . . " he says. "White and chubby, so plump she couldn't even take off her wedding ring when her husband went to prison. When I was living with her she would hide her hands from me, because they were ugly and there was this wedding ring from a spy. . . . Since they locked him up, he had to be a spy. . . . That's what I kept telling her for a whole year until she believed me . . . and I moved in with her. . . . "

I met Werner through the Subtenant and her calls to the woman with ugly hands. Her husband always answered the phone, so Werner dialed the number and the Subtenant asked to speak with Anna. "May I speak with Anna?" she would say in a nice, polite voice, and when Anna came to the phone she would hand the receiver to Werner and discreetly leave the room, or the telephone booth. On several occasions they called from a booth near the Atheneum Theater because Werner loved Kafka's *The Trial,* and he used to call after each performance. His favorite scene was when Joseph K. does not receive a summons to the court, yet reports for interrogation of his own free will. He is innocent, but since he was charged there must be a reason, a higher imperative that he still tries to understand. He is innocent, but he reports for interrogation of his own free will. The moment when Joseph K. becomes certain that there must be some higher imperative never failed to put Werner in a good mood. "Yes, yes," he would repeat several times looking around until the audience started to shush him, "that's how it was," he chuckled even louder and slapped the Subtenant on her knee, there was no way to quiet him down, and finally they had to leave the theater so that Werner could laugh at will. When he finished

74

laughing, they would go to the telephone booth on the corner. Werner would dial the number and the Subtenant would say: "May I speak with Anna?" Then she handed the receiver to Werner and waited in the street. Werner would leave the booth after a couple of minutes, less cheerful than during *The Trial*, and the two of them would go for a walk toward the Vistula.

These calls became the Subtenant's everyday routine, and when Werner was less sober than usual she sometimes had to call several times during a day. "May I speak with Anna?" she would say when the male voice answered, and she left Werner whispering shyly into the receiver.

We wondered why Anna never answered the phone. Did the man expect Werner's calls and prefer to be around? And if so, didn't he suspect the trick? Once, after the usual "may I speak with . . . " he asked who was calling. "Marta," she said truthfully. He did not ask anything else and called his wife to the phone as usual. From that time on, after hearing her voice he would say—with a smile, as it seemed to her—"Good afternoon, Marta."

[Twenty-five years after "may I speak with Anna" I met a nice elderly lady—tall and slender, wearing a pearl gray dress and pearl earrings. As I saw her I thought that at her age I would certainly be neither pearl gray nor slender, but an acquaintance of mine told me I shouldn't worry because I shall not live to be her age—no one of us will. Over coffee and homemade cookies that beautiful, tall lady called Anna would once tell the author of this book the following story:

I met my husband during the last prewar vacation in Lvov at the house of my aunt, who rented him a room. Jarek was handsome, he painted beautifully and wrote poems. My aunt whispered that he was rumored to be a Communist. I had heard a thing or two about communism, I understood it was supposed to be something bad, yet I knew next to nothing about the whole idea. Jarek's father was a Greek Catholic priest, and Jarek would probably never have come across communism were it not for his high school friend, a certain Bernard R. Late at night I heard them through the wall discussing unemployment—I knew that unemployment was a terrible tragedy, but I had never met anybody who was unemployed. Neither had Jarek, but he read about them in his books and heard about them from Bernard.

After the vacation I returned to my school in Warsaw, and Jarek went off to study architecture in Liège.

We were married after the war and after Jarek's return, but because he stuck with his communism I couldn't show him to my aunt from Lvov for a good couple of years. At that time Bernard was replaced as his best friend by Werner. I have no idea where he came from. He appeared one day when Jarek was not at home, he asked if he could wait, and sat on the windowsill. From that time on he visited us often. They would sit at the kitchen table and talk about politics, or Werner would tell some stories—during the war he met some people who now became prominent, most of all he liked to tell about Nowotko ("the Old Man" as he called him), and I would serve them tea and apricot jam.* We felt good together. When Jarek was away Werner sat on the windowsill, watched me bustle around the kitchen, and waited. He kept silent, smiled as if he were constantly astonished by something, and looked at me. It is strange that I always win the affection of those activists—I, a quiet person, removed from all politics, a graduate of a convent school, with the picture of St. Theresa over my bed—Saint Terenia, we

*Marceli Nowotko, first secretary of the Polish Workers party, the Communist party established in Poland under German occupation during World War II. Later murdered by a member of the Polish Workers party on the orders of the KGB.

would say, because she was in fashion at that time, only after Jarek's arrest I got angry and took her off the wall, and hung our marriage portrait in her place. And I think it was because I was a calm, healthy, totally normal person, and each activist needs some normalcy in his hectic life.

My husband was arrested in 1949.

They came in the morning, ransacked the house, and told him to get into the car. I ran to Werner. He calmed me down and promised to straighten everything out with his friends, whom we knew only from speeches and photographs. After a few days he came, terribly depressed: it looked more serious than we thought. Jarek was accused of espionage. Werner was so broken that this time I had to comfort him. "He'll get out," I said, "after all he is innocent." But Werner was surprised. "Innocent? After they've arrested him and presented evidence? Unfortunately," he repeated with sadness, "we do not understand everything yet. WE DO NOT UNDERSTAND." He was saying it as if he wanted to share with me that terrible thing, that shame.

He did not change.

He would come, sit on the sill, and wait as before.

We both waited.

Sometimes he would bring me coal from the basement or would nurse my daughter when she was sick.

I asked him whether he was not disturbed by the fact that he was taking care of a spy's wife, but he explained I wasn't guilty of anything.

After a year he moved in.

Soon afterward they came again, early in the morning and told him to get into the car.

When I managed to obtain a visit I asked him whether he still believe Jarek was a spy.

During the interrogations he confessed he had killed No-wotko.

I think he confessed not under torture but for me, because he had made me believe Jarek was a spy.

I waited on, this time alone. Odd jobs and chores of a single mother absorbed me more that the question who was I really waiting for.

I did not have to decide because they released the "spies" first, and the "deviationists" sometime later. My husband was the first to come home. I don't know when Werner was released, we were in Finland at that time and Jarek was beginning to build his first church. I came to like that church. Behind the altar there was a huge glass wall and behind the wall stood a tall wooden cross. The altar seemed without limits and was always changing because the cross was sometimes bathed in sunlight, sometimes covered with snow, or with dead leaves. Thanks to this church my husband won international recognition and new contracts abroad, but I would come there often, and try to read in the semidarkness, under the cross that was sometimes wet from rain and sometimes warm from the sun. I would read letters received from Poland.

After our return from abroad Jarek was offered a chair in architecture and I started to use my knowledge of Scandinavian languages as a translator.

The telephone usually rang in the afternoon when we were back from work. The telephone was in Jarek's study. He would come to the kitchen, or to the children's bedroom, and hand the receiver to me with a smile: "Marta is calling."

I usually said there was really nothing new, or complained about the grades of my older son, or asked him whether Woszczerowicz was really so great as Joseph K., and that I finally must go and see *The Trial*.]

After leaving the telephone booth they would walk toward the river—Our Subtenant in an American skirt, a keepsake, many times remodeled, from the humanitarians visiting the Home, and Werner placing his feet inside. They were in no hurry—neither of them was. When they were hungry they would stop for some rice porridge—one zloty and a half—and they would walk on while Werner explained the world to Our Subtenant.

I don't really know why she had to understand the world and be assured that it can be justly arranged. Perhaps it was because she was from nowhere? The window in our apartment she never approached, the Home where we visited her, and the pale yellow flowers at the railway crossing did not compose themselves into any particular world, therefore she entered eagerly, almost gratefully, the one promised her by Werner. It was a good world ruled neither by the bright nor by the dark people, but only by class war and surplus value. Ten years earlier my friend Stefan M. was told by the chairman of the county Young Communist League: "I care nothing about your nose, colleague. All I care about is to hang this bastard Mikołajczyk by his balls."* "I knew nothing about Mikołajczyk," says Stefan M., "and I knew little about what balls are for, but I knew quite a bit about my nose, so I joined the League when I was twelve years old." People need the brave new world for different reasons, and what concerns Our Subtenant, she received its coherent version during the first year at the university. The vision was in the shape of a cardboard box full of letter-size brochures. One of them was entitled *Pay—Price—Income,* and another *The Origins of Family, Private Property, and the State.* To be sure, the Subtenant did not find too many facts in the box, but she found plenty of conclusions that cleansed life of all mystery. Right now she was a bit worried about the simplicity of these conclusions and

*Stanisław Mikołajczyk, leader of the anti-Communist movement in postwar Poland.

the eagerness with which they were accepted, but Werner was able to explain that as well: it is difficult to live with too much mystery therefore we are susceptible to simple answers.

It is quite possible that all these serious thoughts nested in her head quite accidentally, and—as Simone Weil said—having noticed their error they tried to break out by all possible means. ("I do not know where they come from and what they are worth, but just in case, I think I must not interfere with the process. . . . ") All that is not important. The fact remains that I, the major's daughter, did not need anybody's worlds, while the Subtenant, who was from nowhere, did need them, so she took walks with Werner, and the longer their walks, the closer was the light in the labyrinth of history, which was the favorite metaphor of our friend. "In the labyrinths of history," he would say, usually in the vicinity of the Old Town embankment, because they were walking along the Vistula toward the Citadel, "each generation needs its own light, its own assurance that the world can be just. At the beginning of our life this light is at arm's length. As the twilight approaches it moves farther and farther away, but without this hope, and without the bitterness, life would be miserable."

("Listen," she said one day. "Shouldn't one be looking for a way in this labyrinth in a totally different area?"

"Which area, for example?"

"God."

"Not really. In God we are looking not for justice but for meaning. You open up to Him when you want to know what justice is *for*.")

At that time the light was closer than ever before, because the little misadventure that ruined Werner's feet did not dim it at all, and our Former Subtenant could take a trip to the Poznan Trade Fair with a clear conscience.

She went on Wednesday, June 27th 1956.

The next day was Thursday—sunny since early morning but not too hot, no, just pleasant, quiet warmth.

A demonstration was approaching from the depths of the street and the people on the sidewalks were shouting with relief: "At last!"

Our Subtenant was being deprived of yet another world.

Dear Sir, it was time to start our training without further delay.

# X

My profession.

I think I am a painter, and not a bad one.

I wear loose sweaters and shoes from the Hoff collection, I have my own method of mixing the ground, I buy canvases and paints only of the best quality.

I started with "small" realism. My style was rather obtrusive because I limited myself only to several objects that I rendered with a near-photographic accuracy: a plate, a herring, or, even better, a cleaned skeleton of a herring. Most of all I liked to paint exquisite little skeletons complete with a head and fins, invariably accompanied by an empty bottle of vodka. . . . Sometimes I painted houses. They all had identical windows and in each window there was a person—brushing his or her hair, making love, washing clothes, grinding meat, or driving a nail into the wall. Some critics wrote that I ridiculed those people, but in reality I sympathized with them.

The windows and plates were not bad. I even found imitators among my colleagues of the younger generation, the journal *Kultura* published a rather big article about them, and the Pegasus TV show devoted at least five minutes to my work representing a plate with turquoise flowers and an empty bottle of "Zytnia" vodka, but nothing caught on like my strange girls.

I started painting them for art galleries: such portraits were fashionable at that time, and they sold for ten to twelve thousand zlotys. I thought I knew a bit about little girls, so why shouldn't I try?

The first paintings did not come out too well. One of them depicted a figure with terrible, huge eyes on stems, and another one a crowd of heads that filled all the space and disappeared in the perspective like cobblestones, or gravestones in a Jewish cemetery. Marta looked at the paintings with embarrassment. "So that's what we've learned from Mrs. Nałkowska?"

If I had known the words of Tadeusz Kantor—about the place of birth one leaves behind and art that must be a form of return—I would have tried to defend myself, but I heard Kantor much later, on the twelfth of December, when all the portraits, as well as the door frames and the roof, were ready. My answer was rather vague and nonsensical, but I never repeated my mistake. My girls stopped being afraid, they were calm, good-natured, and they brought me fifteen thousand a piece, because the public is not particularly crazy about brazen sadness, and quite rightly so.

The girls were usually standing in a green landscape. With a pretty sky, pretty light, as if hesitating where to go, as if, to be honest, they had nowhere to go, although it was so pretty around. (At first the backgrounds were neutral and flat, but now they are meaningful, as important as the main figure.) Sometimes the girls were walking across a meadow. I liked them when they walked against the background of a bright, optimistic cloud, with the horizon neatly balanced between the cloud and the earth. I liked them when they held some plant in their hands. One day it turned out it was a yellow, very long flower that reaches beyond the frame of the painting and must have got entangled with the cloud.

I noticed—this is quite interesting—I noticed that my girls

never looked at us, except the one with a ribbon in her hair. She was looking with only one eye because the other did not exist, but her ribbon was huge and pink. A certain man from Zurich bought it for his gallery, and the poet Barbara Sadowska wrote a poem:

*childhood—this doll*
*with an eye crushed into her*
*skull a Doll from a pile of dolls*
*in an organdy dress*
*with a ribbon of fear in her smoldering*
*hair*

*this feeling of bare feet*
*against a mist of stone*
*the obvious darkness of steps*
*whiteness approaching*

Thanks to the gentleman from Zurich I opened a dollar account and went for a trip to Italy.

I started sending my girls to important exhibitions; the catalogs were written by experts. I won one of several awards during the exhibition "The Fate of an Artist—the Fate of Man," Andrzej Wajda spoke at the opening, and the wife of my professor started calling me "our Marysia."

After my return from the Biennale I said in an interview that the best way to attain brightness is to articulate darkness. The only sensible thing to do with darkness is to turn it into art, like Charlie Chaplin, Woody Allen, or Bruno Schulz.

I was asked what I actually meant by brightness and darkness. I said I could only give some examples: Maria and Marta, or Rembrandt and van Gogh. Yes, van Gogh was bright, his ear notwithstanding. Michelangelo's Pietàs are bright, except for the unfinished one in Milan. (Perhaps he was removing darkness from the stone as he sculpted?)

I give interviews rather often, therefore I keep a certain amount of useful thoughts at hand, though only those I have first tried out in the salon of my professor's wife.

The distinction between the bright and the dark ones was not received too well, it required too much explaining and was a bit embarrassing. First, the guests argued that such a distinction did not exist because darkness and brightness coexist in each person and at every given moment, then they wanted to know whether I saw them as dark or as bright ones. The answer "I think you are a dark person" is tactless, even if it puts one in the company of Dostoyevsky, and finally I had to give up my ruminations on brightness altogether. I like, however, to make another statement: "Some people live, some people depict." It was intended to mean that some people live real lives—they build, they destroy, they rule—and some other people depict their real lives in books, films, and paintings, or whatever they have at hand. I indicated that only "real life" really matters, but my statement contained a measure of hypocrisy: I know perfectly well that the real world exists only so that we can depict it.

Thus, thanks to my strange girls I entered the world of exhibitions and salons. I felt quite good in the company of my girls, especially in the more unreal moments of the last year, like when everybody was anxiously waiting for a general strike. I did not feel any anxiety. When my daughter was leaving for the university—with a sleeping bag and a camping mattress—I told her she had to survive and gave her some good advice on the subject, but later I returned to my girl in a wreath, or rather to the thistle in the foreground, which needed some more faded blue. The sense of unreality disappeared immediately because the only real world was in the meadow with the thistle.

Recently I started to paint a dream. It was a real dream that repeated itself many times. I dreamt a girl on the roof of a very tall and old building. She probably thought she had hidden herself well, but she was perfectly visible from the street. Down below there were people waiting for something. The girl knows what it is: a very tall ladder.

Nothing else is happening in the picture. Nobody walks, there is no wind—perfect silence. This total immobility of people and of the air is terrifying. And this is what I have to paint.

My painting is not ready yet, although I already know quite a bit about it.

I know, for example, that everything is very distant and very clear. Stones in the road, cigarette butts, people—their hair, rings, shoelaces. . . . I will even mark warts on the face of a certain lady, I'll do it with a good brush, a zero, or a worn four, though four would probably be better. Only the window frames are unreal—pink, fluorescent—pure pigment directly from the tube.

Can you paint fear?

("Do you happen to know how to paint fear?"

"I asked you a question, Marta."

"Do you happen to know . . . ")

I also tried to paint other people's dreams—Marta's dream about a bird, or Jacek's dream about betrayal. Marta dreamt that someone had left for vacation and entrusted her with a black bird. She placed it in a white empty room, she put out some water and crumbs, but the bird did not want to eat and Marta was very sad. What is more, the bird did not fly, it only flapped for a moment in the air and dropped to the ground. I think it must have looked like a Malczewski painting:* a girl walking across a meadow and a dark bird circling over the grass in front of her. I think that if birds could dream, the inability to fly would be their worst nightmare.

The dream about betrayal that my friend Jacek Kuroń

*Jacek Malczewski (1854–1929), a Polish postromantic, symbolist painter.

started to dream in March 1968 recurred always in the same, unchanged form.* It is incomparably more difficult and I am not sure whether I will be able to paint it. I don't even know whether it should be in color or black and white, dynamic or static. Certainly the first part has to be in black and white—the part when Jacek is still standing in a strange building without walls among a group of boys whom he calls "children," and he suddenly notices guards approaching them from the street. He realizes that both he and the boys have just escaped from prison and the guards are coming to arrest them. If he says anything, everybody will jump and they won't have the slightest chance, so Jacek—and this is the beginning of the part in color, in sharp, chemical color as in test tubes or neon lights—Jacek turns away and leaves alone. Later he sees this strange house again, this time from a distance—the boys and the guards who are coming to take them away—and feels such dreadful shame, unbearable even in his dream. He wakes up, realizes that this time he has betrayed nobody, and looks around his prison cell with great relief. . . .

I cannot paint the dream about betrayal. It's too bad, because I had a terrific idea: I wanted to place Jacek's portrait in the house without walls. He posed for me a couple of days, drinking whisky, roaring with laughter, coughing, grabbing my hand and telling me stories.

"My life reached its apogee when I was four years old. It was during a performance of *The Two Who Stole the Moon*. When the Bad Wizard was pushing the boys into his sack I charged onto the stage with a terrifying scream in order to save them. Everything I did later in my life was just a repetition of that experience: terrible fear drowned in a scream, and my charge onto the stage to save the boys."

*Jacek Kuroń, one of the most prominent leaders of the anti-Communist opposition, cofounder of Solidarity.

He also told me about goodness—that he is pathologically good, he cannot suffer the death of any creature, even a cockroach. When the boys in prison organized cockroach concentration camps—with roll calls, barracks, and a crematorium—he would bribe them with cigarettes. They released one inmate for a cigarette, and would even close the camp for a whole pack.

Or about fear, to which I shall return later.

Or about the revelation of Hirsz N. In return for his survival in the ghetto Hirsz N.—the largest supplier of wine must in Poland—decided to believe in Jesus Christ. But he couldn't make himself do it, so he was asking for a sign. "You are one of us," he prayed to Jesus, "so give me a sign. Try to understand that I cannot believe in You just like that, without any sign." And Jesus gave Hirsz a sign. He appeared to him in a dream in a Mokotów prison cell. Hirsz covered a stool with a towel, placed a picture of the Virgin Mary on the stool, and started to rock back and forth in front of the picture for hours. Sometimes Jacek would say: "Do something, Hirsz, because I really have to go. . . ." Hirsz would interrupt his prayers and say: "Just a moment, let me cover our Lady's eyes." He would cover the eyes of the picture, and Jacek could finally piss into the bucket.

The story of Hirsz N. was an answer to my question why Jacek started doing what he was doing, was it perhaps an order from God, because such things do happen from time to time. Well, God appeared to Hirsz, not to Jacek.

There were no more stories, or whisky, or roars of laughter. It was December 1981 and martial law and my friend Jacek could no longer pose for his portrait. Yet I already knew that I would never be able to paint his world, and I was even a bit angry with him for that: "Your life is too difficult," I told him. "Couldn't you live a bit easier, so that I could paint it all?"

# XI

I am still a painter, although I am no longer sure it is such a good idea. What if I were a photojournalist? So many advantages: contact with real life (and probably social awareness), everyday observations, a couple of generalities—as in early Fromm—about "elevating the mundane to the level of art," and also a number of inexplicable phenomena that, so I am told, sometimes do happen in photography. For example, during the development process one suddenly glimpses a meadow in bloom in the background although the object was photographed in the studio, or a shadow of a person that was certainly not there. Such a meadow could have happened to me, why not. . . . No, that doesn't make any sense, I am staying with painting.

It is January 1982, I am a painter, and the roof as well as the pink window frames are ready.

I also think I've found just the right kind of light for the girl on the roof. I have known for a while that the light should be very pale, but I imagined a friendly kind of light, like in early afternoons in the beginning of summer.

On the 14th of December I tried to paint the light of the previous morning—bright and indifferent (I remember well where I saw it: near the Saxon Garden, when we were walking toward St. Anne's Church), and I left it like that.

That's not much. . . . Will I be able to finish the painting?

"Will I be able to finish the painting?" I asked a seemingly well-informed person, a Solidarity activist Janusz O. one month before the Sunday morning. "How big is it going to be?" asked Janusz, probably because he is a mathematician. "Ninety by seventy-five, but all I've got so far is the roof and window frames." "November, December," he started to count. "Will you be done by the end of December?" "So soon?" I tried to bargain for time. "Yes," said Janusz O., "I think you have time . . . we have time until the end of December."

And look, it is the end of January and I still have time.

Of the more important things what remains now is only a certain meeting. I am trying to play for time, and that's why I am providing so many details about my working methods, but one cannot avoid the subject forever, just as one could not avoid the window in our Subtenant's room.

Well, then. The meeting.

It would be best if I got up and shouted something in a shrill, unfortunately hysterical voice in our Subtenant's defense, or at least I should do it in the case of Bernard R. It would provide us with perfect symmetry: Bernard defended my father during the trial, and now I am defending him. Perhaps that would be a bit too symmetrical, but nothing doing, I finally have to rise from my seat and ask for recognition . . .

*I do not remember who informed me about the existence of Jews,* someone wrote in a Catholic weekly. As for me, I remember it quite well. I do not mean the information itself, because I was informed about the existence of Jews in whispers during the war. It was in connection with our Subtenant, the window and the curtain. What I remember is the word "Jew" spoken aloud for the first time after the war. It wasn't even "Jew" but "Jewish," or, to be more precise, "once-Jewish."

*90*

"This is once-Jewish property," a nice elderly man encouraged my mother. He was a social worker who distributed powdered milk and clothes for children. "You can see for yourself what good quality it is," he said and showed us a soft beige overcoat—too big for me, evidently made for a boy a couple of years older. I winced. "Take it, it's pure camel hair," insisted the man. I tried it on reluctantly and I put my hands inside the pockets. I felt some crumbs under my fingers. I pulled my hand out and saw flecks of tobacco. "How old was he," I asked the gentleman. "Fifteen, but don't worry, you'll grow into it." "Little rascal," I thought. "He made cigarettes for himself, of course he made them on the sly, in the street, what an insolent brat." "Don't cry," said my mother, "the gentleman will find you a smaller one." I shook my head, turned around and walked away in my new coat, with tobacco in my clenched fingers. But why am I telling all that . . . Yeah, because someone did not remember who informed him about the existence of Jews.

(I was growing very slowly and I was wearing the camel-hair coat until the last year of high school. At first the tobacco was sitting at the bottom of the pocket, later there was less and less of it because I had the habit of pinching it in my fingers, and finally I had to pick it out of the seams, but it lasted until the very end.)

. . . I rise from my seat and ask for recognition.

I have to do it because I am the bright one and because a terrible injustice is being done in my presence.

I do not mean to say that I behaved in such an exemplary fashion in the case of every injustice. Not at all. During the long years of my dealings with the regime I worked out for myself a fairly well-functioning technique of nonbeing. It all boils down to the ability of being outside the reach of hands, and eyes, of humiliated people. Let us say it is late evening, and someone is kicking a woman in a deserted street. There is nothing I can do. What technique do I apply? Cry? Thrust myself into an uneven, absurd battle? The only perfect technique is to be on the other side of the street. Not to *cross* to the other side, because a decent person would never do something like that. The trick is to *be* on the other side from the very beginning just in case something terrible is going to happen. It has worked perfectly throughout my life: I was not present when they arrested the kulaks or the Home Army fighters. Unfortunately I had to be present when they sentenced the officers because *they* had crossed to my side. But all the rest belonged to the world that was not mine.

All right then, I get up from my seat and raise my hand. That man is sitting next to me and almost certainly he is not Bernard R. The previous day, the 19th of March 1968, they showed a mob howling anti-Semitic slogans on TV, and today the man is evidently scared. He is scared in the corridor and in the conference room, and someone better give him a tranquilizer because his eyes are blinking, evasive, these are the eyes of people who had to hide behind somebody's wardrobe during the war. If he were not sitting next to me, if he were sitting somewhere else, at a different meeting, on somebody else's street—nothing would happen, that's for sure.

I would not get up.

My hands would not shake, and I would not say, in my somehow, alas, screeching voice . . .

The phone rang as every evening. Our Former Subtenant was calling from a city situated one thousand two hundred and sixty-three kilometers to the East. "Are you there?" "I am," I said. She kept silent for a while. "That's good." "I am here," I said. "Go to bed."

At first she called in the morning. She was receiving Polish newspapers with a day's delay and when she asked: "Have you read it?" I knew she was thinking about the new wave of anti-Semitism. "Don't worry," I told her, "it has no significance." "No significance?" she repeated with uncertainty. "And how about that . . . ?" "Some moron," I was making light of it. "Do you know," she was asking, "if everybody in Poland thinks that way?"

Later she called during the day. "Are you there?" she asked. And then in the night. "Listen," I tried to speak some reason to her, "go to bed. Is your family asleep?" "They are." "So why aren't you?"

I also did not sleep. I was lying wide awake waiting for the phone to ring. I guessed that she was trying to behave normally in the presence of her husband and daughter, and only when they went to bed did she begin her vigil. "What are you really waiting for," I asked her when the phone rang. "Absolutely nothing can happen to you." "I know, I am just sitting here, that's all."

Strange thing: on that particular night in March 1968, nineteen years after my father's arrest, I started to imagine his vigil. That is how it must have been—my mother was asleep, I was asleep, and he was listening. The vigil must be concentrated and lonely, undisturbed by anybody's presence.

Later, who knows why, I have imagined the Subtenant's grandfather: he has already cleaned his samovar, hidden the little scroll of prayers inside, and he is waiting. Then—I imagined her father: still on his bunk, still before the trip to the barrack on the right side (I hope that the thought of his daughter's safety brought him some comfort). Then I imagined Oscar S., who had chosen Polishness, and the next morning they were going to transfer him to Auschwitz. Then the General—after Bernard R. has criticized him during the briefing. Then Werner—awake at the side of a woman whose husband, imprisoned one year earlier, still considered him his friend. And I also imagined the waking hours of the boy whose coat with tobacco in the pockets I was wearing until not long ago. He had to know that sooner or later they were going to come to take him away. It was summer, so he did not take his coat, but he had to take something important, a stamp collection for example, like Henryk Z., my colleague from the office. What else could a boy take on the road to Treblinka if not his stamp collection? He was young, so perhaps he managed to jump from the car on a bend of the tracks? Maybe, like Henryk Z. he scrambled to his feet only to see the others, those who had jumped before him, already naked and digging their own grave? Perhaps the boy undressed too, but an officer of the SS noticed the album and asked what it was? He leafed through it and told the boy to get dressed. Stamp collectors take care of each other.

I am not making much sense. If all that happened to my colleague from the office, it could not have happened to the boy. God produces such stories without duplicates.

Then there was the boy from the Polish-Bolshevik war of 1920 who was to be executed for desertion at the Warsaw Citadel in the morning. The story was told to me by a soldier from the execution squad, that is, by Jacek's father. "Hey, boys," the boy called to the soldiers as they were training their rifles at him, "wait a minute. Anybody from Żyrardów?" And when the squad remained silent, he added imploringly, "Because if anybody is from Żyrardów, tell them there that I am dead, and no longer living." So let us add the fear of this boy.

It is surprising how many of them there were. . . . The whole night was populated by those waiting men lying wide awake.

I can guess they were afraid, but I cannot imagine their kind of fear.

Did they feel it physically? If they did, where did they feel it? In their throats, on the skin of their hands, above their wrists?

Perhaps they were sweating?

Were they afraid of something particular—like pain? Their own betrayal? My father must have been afraid that he would betray somebody during the interrogations if they were going to beat him.

"You have to conquer your fear," Jacek instructed me as he was posing for his portrait. "Tell yourself: here I am, and here is my fear. Not I, the person who is afraid, but I *and* my fear—something intimate, something personal, my fear, my very own fear. And then you have a chance to conquer it. Each fear calls for a different technique because each fear is different. My fear—continued Jacek—has to see everything until the very end, therefore I try to see it. When I was in prison, I told myself that I'd get fifteen years, so when I finally got out I'd be fifty. From that time on I spent my days meticulously preparing myself for old age. Now I am practicing everything they can do to me when Solidarity comes to an end. Will they take me away, or will they shoot me right on the spot? OK, they'll shoot me, but where? In front of the building, or in the yard? I would prefer the front because there are more trees there, and more people. I still haven't conquered that fear because I would really like to end my life with dignity and I still have not invented the proper way."

Did my father conquer his fear?

Did he invent everything till the very end?

Death row? The warden who calls the names through the bars? Did he invent his own name called from behind the bars? and 9 P.M.? and the shot?

Did he hear that shot from a distance, as if it were meant for somebody else, or right next to his head? Does one really hear HIS shot?

It was difficult for the Subtenant's father to conquer his fear because he could not invent the barrack with bluish gray plaster, the one on the right side, behind the gate.

"Have you conquered your fear?" I could ask her one night, but I couldn't really do it because I haven't met Jacek yet. Besides, even Jacek did not know because at that time (exactly at that time) he was beginning his prison career, his shameful dreams about betrayal, and his old age.

The comparison between her anxiety in the city situated one thousand two hundred and sixty-three kilometers to the east with the nights of the grandfather, father, the boy, and the Communist Werner appeared to be rather inappropriate. "What can possibly happen to you," I was asking angrily, although it was me who was thinking about their vigils. "What can possibly happen?"

"Nothing," she agreed. "Perhaps only that I will be afraid. And that it will be the fear from your apartment. Fear is the only thing I am afraid of."

The phone rang as every evening. Before she managed to utter her "Are you there?" I said: "I've done it." "What?" "I did what a decent person does under such circumstances." "And what does a decent person do . . . ?"

She rises from her seat.

She asks to be recognized.

Hoping that nobody notices her trembling hands, she speaks:

THIS IS NOT THE MARXIST WAY.

Ah yes!

A person who has had twenty years of solid education in *their* world does not explode with anger, does not exclaim "THIS IS DISGUSTING," or "SHAME!"

Her anger is articulated in their jargon. Her shrill, not to say hysterical, voice tries to explain to those present that anti-Semitism is at odds with "our ideology" . . .

The room is silent.

The chairman whispers something to the director. My friend, a former prisoner from Ravensbrück, tries to come to my rescue and mumbles something about the ethnic factor, or something like that.

I knew that the chairman was looking at me. I was wearing a white blouse with a shirt collar and a dove gray V-neck sweater—an example of modest elegance of a person from a good, patriotic family.

"You, a daughter of a war hero, from a patriotic Polish family, should be able to understand . . . "—that was my last chance, offered in a soft, kind voice.

We learned about the Order of Virtuti Militari awarded to my father for his part in the September 1939 campaign by a pure accident and from a book published abroad. We received the book half a year after his death and it was too late to tell him about the honor.

I was going to tell them to keep my father out of it, but I was not sure whether I would not shout out about that book, too, if I rose from my seat one more time.

I was finally shushed down and our director took the initiative, assuring the listeners that he had many Jewish friends before the war, but considering the foreign policy of Israel . . . Upon which a quiet man next to me suddenly woke up from a slumber and mentioned an interesting article on the Middle East which he had read in *Le Monde* and was more than ready to summarize for us.

The chairman gave a sign and people started to leave their seats. I had the impression they were leaving the room with a bit of distaste, as if they had involuntarily witnessed some obscene spectacle, in any case they were walking rather quickly, and even my friend was steering straight for the door without waiting for me, but she had been in Ravensbrück, had diabetes, and therefore much must be forgiven her. Only the man next to me was still going on about the article from *Le Monde* and was ready to go on, but nobody was listening to him.

It was snowing and raining outside.

The man was still standing nearby, he was probably still afraid, and he must have thought I would hide him somewhere.

I opened my umbrella and walked right to him.

"You stupid Jew," I said. "Now you feel it, don't you? When they came to take my father, you did not feel a thing. When they came for the peasants and for the Home Army, that was historical necessity, right? But now they finally got to your ass, and you suddenly noticed! . . ."

. . . I was speaking to the man under my umbrella quietly, without raising my voice, until I finally turned around and walked away taking my umbrella, my friendly profile with my hair combed into a bun, and my honest, sincere eyes.

# XII

Painting doesn't make sense, I am definitely changing my profession. I must have a solid job—a psychologist? lawyer? if a psychologist, then I was always a practitioner (contact with life helped me to maintain a measure of common sense even during my fascination with Pavlov), although I have also harbored some broader intellectual ambitions vented in a number of articles in professional journals, as well as in a doctoral dissertation in progress.

I am writing a dissertation on victimology. I have read in some book that this interdisciplinary area of knowledge analyzes the world in terms of harm, suffering, and humiliation, and I came to the conclusion that such an ambitious and noble discipline should not overlook the problem of darkness. I turned for help to a great authority in the field, the author of many publications, Dr. Lech Falandysz from the Institute of Criminal Law at Warsaw University, and asked him to be a director of my dissertation.

"What is the problem that you are trying to solve?" he asked me at the beginning of our conversation.

"Whether a human being is condemned to darkness."

"That is a good question," he praised me without showing much surprise. "But did you define the notion of darkness?"

"Well, not exactly."

"That doesn't matter. Some basic notions such as 'human being,' 'universe,' 'happiness,' or 'God' have never been clearly defined yet they function rather well in philosophical discourse. Therefore you will not define darkness, although you'll try to come close to some kind of a definition as you proceed with your thesis, yes? Does darkness possess any symptoms?"

"Denigration, humiliation, anguish, murkiness . . . but that does not bring us any closer . . ."

"Can we deduce darkness from something else?"

"From the Bible. Darkness of the Bible, brightness of the Odyssey. Darkness is vertical, brightness is horizontal. Sometimes it affects whole countries. The Vilno district breeds brightness, but the Carpathian region produces darkness. Do you think it may have something to do with the land?"

"So you'll also introduce the notion of brightness, which will represent everything that is not darkness. Or is it the other way around? But we cannot put Man in such an awkward position. If we separate darkness and all the rest is brightness then we stand a good chance of being bright, which should be a source of some encouragement.

"Is it possible to transcend the borders?

"Is it possible to switch roles?

"How about the hereditary element?

"Are there people especially susceptible to darkness? Ellenberger and Mendelsohn, the fathers of victimology, believe that some people have a natural tendency toward being victims. Do we observe something similar here?

"Is blackness a subjective state connected with consciousness? We can take two different positions: only the self-perception of darkness is the source of suffering, or darkness is an objective state perceivable by others. I am sure you will argue for the latter position?"

"Self-perception of darkness is connected with pride. The sense of being marked, you know . . ."

"In science we call it 'labeling.' Man becomes someone else when he is 'labeled' by institutions—the press, the welfare system, psychiatry, the courts. Here, however, we are dealing with a special case: self-labeling. A form of consent to blackness, a choice."

"The choice is between good and evil, not between brightness and darkness. Man consents when he no longer has any choice. (Perhaps the essence of darkness is, after all, an internal consent to darkness . . . ?)"

"But this is called 'internalization'—acceptance of a role imposed by others. But let's proceed. Is it possible to fake darkness? Or brightness? We are onto something interesting here. You have just discovered there can be false brightness, Madam, but not false darkness.

"Let's go on. How can one help the dark ones? Clinical treatment, perhaps? Mendelsohn proposed something like that for people susceptible to victimization.

"Well then, institutions for the dark, is that right? Little use for drugs, rather psychotherapy.

"Should we opt for compulsory or voluntary treatment?

"Perhaps one should punish darkness?

"Training? Well, what do you think, Madam?"


Thus I slowly sketched the outline of my doctoral dissertation and defined my subject. The title should be rather factual: *The Psychological Aspect of Victimology and Victimization and Some Methods of Prevention: A Case Study*. The bibliography should include several works in foreign languages: *Schwarz-Weiss Theorie; Théorie de la bicouleur; Iz voprosov kontrastnovo, dvutsvietnovo ponimanya litchnosti*, as well as some others.

The day we outlined the subject there was a street demonstration of bus and garbage truck drivers. For the second day in a row buses and garbage trucks were blocking the central intersection and the drivers wanted to turn left, toward the government buildings, in defiance of an explicit order from the authorities. Janusz O., the Solidarity activist who told me we had time until the end of December, was trying to persuade them to go straight ahead.

I asked Doctor F. whether in his opinion we would survive all that, because people have started asking that sort of question again, but he did not know: he has come to no conclusion on this particular subject. "Man has to make a decision about his own survival. I haven't made that decision yet, therefore I don't know whether I'll survive."

He was right, of course. When on the eve of the general strike I ordered my daughter to survive, I started with the same statement: First of all you have to decide that you will survive.

The next day the drivers, decorated with wreaths of flowers, drove straight ahead, and again we did not have to make the decision for ourselves, and Janusz O., a mathematician and a climber, the conqueror of Gasherbrum III (7,952 m, the tallest unconquered summit), and Gasherbrum II (8,036 m, the first climb on the north-western wall) told me how he spent the night with the drivers trying to persuade them not to turn left. "They wanted to fight till victory, and for them victory meant turning left. What is more, they were surrounded by a crowd that wanted them to turn left, and the drivers claimed they could not disappoint the crowd. The strike was coming to an end and it was time to make a decision—explained Janusz O.—I took the microphone and said: 'At noon we are driving straight ahead.' If I had to compare the two events in my life that required the most courage: the climb on Gasherbrum in the Himalayas and the sentence 'We are driving straight ahead,' the Himalayas would appear incomparably easier."

Janusz O. scored his new victory, drivers decorated with flowers drove straight ahead, and I was able to return quietly to the outline of my dissertation.

First, the introduction. One should start with the basic concepts of victimology and a brief history of the discipline: it was founded by two Israeli lawyers, Drabkin and Mendelsohn. . . . My director suggested that I elaborate on the connection between the fate of the Jewish nation pushed by history into darkness and the birth of victimology (the Jews were too bright for the world, so the world shoved them away, but their whole history is a climb toward brightness. Perhaps the notion of the chosen people was an attempt to deal with that issue?), yet I interrupted these rather interesting speculations. "I am not interested in darkness on a macro scale, Professor. I want to analyze one particular case."

So that much for the introduction. The first and the most important chapter will be my presentation of the case under study and of the level of victimity displayed by the analyzed person (it would be good to quote some numbers—for example, the quantity of darkness contained in the organism—which always makes a dissertation sound so much more objective). I would also describe the process of "sinking into darkness" until the moment when Our Subject decides she is inferior to every other person. That would be the conclusion of the process of "secondary victimization," or acceptance of one's own inferiority, explained Professor F. It is believed that some people occasionally manage to break out of it.

And the practical conclusions: methods of therapy.

Therefore:

I finally gave up painting, I stick with victimology, I am working toward my Ph.D., and I have some good suggestions concerning the treatment of dark individuals. The therapy will be simple: in order to practice brightness, one should experience darkness thoroughly and up till the very end.

In Holland the "camp sickness" is treated with LSD-25. The drug activates certain brain centers that hide suppressed memories. The patients ramble, cry, and talk about the camps. This therapy is reported to give very good results.

I would rather avoid such drastic methods, it is enough to experience everything once again and without avoiding sadness.

The technique of survival depended on the rejection of suffering and compassion. *From the fiery ovens . . . we were saved by our cunning and knowledge . . .* —that was our shrewdness. Sadness distracted while survival required the highest possible degree of concentration; sadness weakened while survival required immense strength. "And now you are going to survive without rejecting sadness," I told the person on whom it is my duty to test my method like a doctor testing the new drug on himself. "Please sit down," I say, because I am going to write about her in the second, or even in the third person. I am analyzing a case, and scientific research requires proper distance from the object of study. "It is nice that you agreed to be my subject. Sit down, my dear, and try to survive once again."

I would start with the mullein. I looked through the notes I collected on you and the mullein made me wonder. Recently one reads a lot about the importance of touching, experiments were conducted with a small orphaned chimpanzee that was given various objects to handle—a coil of wire, a wet sponge, a teddy bear, a stone—and it was established that the chimpanzee likes to play with things that are light, warm, and dry. The mullein is mossy and warm, is it not?

"It is rough." She took off her rings and started to arrange them on the daybed. "Its stem is hairy, and you can hardly break it off. It splinters and hurts your fingers, and oozes bitter juice, it certainly wouldn't appeal to the young orphaned chimpanzee."

"Why did you try to break it off? One has to go to the mullein, not tear it out and take it. It should exist in its own place: tall, neat, strong—like your friends from the spacious apartments."

Quite unexpectedly we found ourselves back in the familiar apartments, that is good, now we should gently encourage the object of therapy to say something more about these apartments.

"One of them had a tile stove," I prompted her. "Do you remember the stove? You know, a week ago I saw a similar one in the apartment of a certain gentleman. A huge, white stove?"

"With a festoon at the top?"

"With stucco work—a rocaille, which in French means an ornament in the form of pebbles and sea-shells. That gentleman told me about it. The style goes back to the time of Louis XIV. It was definitely a bright stove, because objects can also contain darkness or brightness. I think we can use the apartment with the stove in order to demonstrate a certain method."

"There were dried roses in a silver bowl standing on the ledge, and the door had chiseled bars."

"The echo of a fireplace. In the country estate they had a real fireplace. This one was only a surrogate. . . . "

"When everybody left, the apartment was silent and empty, one could open the stove door and watch the red embers. They arranged themselves into sprawling, strangely bright cities. Sometimes I would populate them with people and invent their names and life stories, but the stories had to be short and tragic, because the embers quickly died out and the cities disappeared."

105

" . . . Do you know at what hour they would sit down at the table in the country? Guess? At noon. In the summer they would sit on the porch. It wasn't stuffy inside, no, the windows were wide open. One could hear the buzzing of bees and see the flickering of warm air.

"He says that this world ends with him, as does the memory of the cool porch on a hot day. There was a wardrobe by the stove."

"It was very practical," (she rearranged the rings, this time starting with the thin ones and gradually moving on to the large and heavy ones she bought in a bazaar in Samarkand. She bought them from a stall next to a tearoom in which bearded old men were holding saucers of tea on wooden trays. "Where are you from," asked one of them. He did not hear the answer. "Where from? Where is it?" "In Europe, between Germany and Russia." He pondered for a moment and shook his head. "Impossible. There's no room there." "That's right," she agreed. "And that's where I am from"). "A very practical wardrobe . . . a part of the backboard was removed and one could squeeze between the garments to the other side."

"You are talking too fast.

"There was a wardrobe by the stove.

"When your hosts had visitors, you would crawl into the wardrobe, feel the gap in the backboard, and sneak behind the stove. It was possible to sit there, and some light came from above, so you could take some crayons or a book with you. When the visitors left you could come out and the daughter of your hosts would examine your finished drawing. I would prefer if you told it in the first person. . . . "

"Most of all I liked drawing little girls. They all had a certain common feature: they were bearing themselves with elegance, and their sleeves were always in two different colors. That detail irritated the daughter of my guardian. 'Look carefully,' she said, 'do you or I have sleeves in two different colors?' 'No, we don't.' 'Then correct it.' 'No.' 'Correct it,' she would push the right crayon into my hand. I knew that if I didn't correct the color, she would leave me, annoyed by my stupidity and stubbornness, and I would be alone again, so I would follow her order. I am telling this because I recalled these drawings not long ago in a church during the funeral of the daughter of one of my guardians. I brought red carnations decorated with a purple ribbon because that was the only color the florist had in stock, and during the whole ceremony I apologized to her for that. Then I remembered the sleeves of my little girls and apologized again. Later, as always, I thought with envy about her religion, and I prayed."

"It is good that you prayed for her. The angel who appeared to the children of Fatima told them to pray for the dead. 'Many souls are doomed forever because there is nobody to pray for them,' said the angel."

"I always pray for the same thing. That He be. What can one pray for? Just be there, I tell Him. Look: I never bother You with anything, I have no requests or favors to ask You apart from that one thing, and if You would like to do something for me, that is all I ask for. Just be. Will You?"

"One day you were sitting home alone and somebody entered. Don't try to put it off anymore. We had the stove with the rocaille, and the stove's owner, and Samarkand, really, one cannot put it off any longer.

"You were sitting home alone and—you don't know how it could have happened, is it possible that your host forgot to lock the door? never mind, you were sitting on the floor near the window and a man walked in."

"He was surprised.

"He stood in the doorway, his hand on the knob, and looked at me. 'Good morning,' he smiled as one smiles at a child. 'Good morning,' I said."

"What did you say?"

"Good morning. I might even have curtsied."

"No, you did not curtsy.

"What did you say to the gentleman who entered so unexpectedly?"


Why should she tell about the girl?

Why should I write about The Case?

Why on earth should she tell people about the girl . . . ?

She would have to tell it if—let's say—she couldn't bear the torment caused by her obtrusive presence, but she can bear it. She would have to tell it, also, if she started the process of self-therapy, because such reactions do occur from time to time. Apparently it happens under one and only one condition—when someone has lived for a while a different life and does not want to return to the old one.

Let us say: One day Our Case has learned that she could be a bright one.

When should it happen?

Not during the Pope's visit, not yet. Not before the strike, certainly not, the instructions about the art of survival given to her daughter and her return to the painting with the thistle in the foreground suggest a safe distance, but it could have happened on Sunday, the 14th of December 1981, the first day of martial law, when she was walking through the eerily bright snow toward St. Anne's Church. (A poet, Ryszard Krynicki, was walking with her: a day earlier, during the Congress of Independent Culture, he gave her his book with the following poem:

*Yes, I have survived*
*Now I must cope with an equally*
*difficult task: to get on*
*a streetcar*
*and reach my home.*

As she was walking she felt the blinding, cold sun and she did not think about any painting she could use it for—only the next day did she realize it was the light surrounding the girl on the roof.)

Without asking anybody she knew where to go. She knew everything from the very beginning—from the morning of that day: she should put on several pairs of pantyhose and shoes with flat heels (until that day she could never decide which shoes to wear with which skirt), and she would reach the snow-covered steps in front of the door to which someone's hand has attached a note about the dissolution of the congress, and then she would go to St. Anne's because churches were the only safe place and because someone had to send some warm clothes to those detained in the internment camp. Everywhere she went she would meet people who came to the same place because they, too, knew exactly where to go, and the strange feeling of belonging with everybody else would not leave her until the end of that day.

The next day the feeling faded away, but she already knew that she could belong. I told her: You can have it till the end of your life. It's enough to undergo therapy . . . it's enough to live the darkness up till the very end.

"Good morning," says the strange man and smiles as one smiles at a child.

You are sitting by the window . . . you're not standing, no, you're sitting because someone could see you from the street. And what are you saying to him?

I am talking to you—you, sitting by the window. What are you saying to the strange gentleman?

You are saying nothing, nothing, you are quickly getting up and walking toward the wardrobe. . . . For goodness sake! what got into you? You are opening the wardrobe right in front of the man who is watching you?!

You, who never ever came up to the window when you

were alone. You never coughed behind the stove when strangers were in the house. You never wanted to pee between three-thirty and four. You, of whom the daughter of your guardian would say (she was sitting on her snow white starched bed) forty years after the drawings of little girls and several months before the mass with red carnations: "The most shocking thing was your awareness, you were five years old and you understood everything." ("Really?" you would ask her with a polite, incredulous smile.)

Sometimes your mother comes. She always wears a black dress, she sits on the edge of a chair and holds your hand. "They took daddy away, and I gave him money. If only I had given him food, he could have taken it for the road, and now . . . If I had brought him bread, at least he could have eaten it on the way . . . " She tries to cry very quietly, afraid to disturb this huge, strange apartment, and you, silent and calm, stand at her side. "Well, what's done is done," you say at last. "At least I am alive." You withdraw your hand from her hands, and you quickly walk away, afraid that her sadness may still catch up with you. (It is frightfully difficult to crawl out of sadness, therefore one has to be always on guard, and one must never allow oneself to get entangled in it. "Well, what's done is done," one has to say calmly, then withdraw one's hand, and walk away leaving her alone on the edge of the chair. . . . )

So you, who never coughed and never wanted to pee, now open the wardrobe and walk inside in the presence of a strange man? You hastily push the clothes aside and with outstretched hands seek the passage behind the stove.

Listen? Why are you telling all this?

When a certain Dutchman suffering from the camp disease was treated with LSD-25 he started to mumble something about wooden clogs and sand. Later it was revealed that while in the camp he fell into a ditch and felt something soft under his feet, there were corpses covered with sand, and the sand was getting into his clogs. But what is so horrible about the wardrobe you are just opening?

This is not horror, this is just shame: you are hiding, and somebody is watching you. Nobody should ever see you hide in the wardrobe because this is so shameful.

What is more, you understand you are acting like an idiot: it is not enough that someone found you in the apartment, you are trying to hide, and what is he going to think about you? He may think you are some idiot!

You are starting to cry. Not out of fear, as the man wrongly assumes, but out of shame and anger. Your crying can be heard from inside, from between the coats, because you cannot find the passage. "Calm down," says the man, trying to disentangle you from the coats. "Calm down, little girl," says the man.

This is going to be your therapy. In our clinic we are going to get you a beautiful bright stove. Strange memories of things forgotten will open up inside you and you'll tell, for the first time in your life, the story about the man, the clothes, and the wardrobe. "If I had brought him bread, he could have eaten a little on the way . . . " your mother will say to you, and you'll stand at her side and listen to how the street looked on the next day when father, and people with suitcases full of linen, and grandfather with his ridiculous samovar were gone, and only stains of blood remained on the pavement, and feathers from yesterday's pillows were drifting in the air. You will experience everything you did not want to experience because sadness was distracting you and depleting the strength you needed to survive.

You will talk it out, cry it out, or shake it out, laugh it out, even yawn it out—because it is not enough to live through all that, one also has to act it out, and there are six basic ways of acting out blackness.

And when you finally and absolutely get everything out, we shall banish that little girl once and for all. My dear, we will have to tell her one day, I gave you a lot, didn't I? Paintings and salons, family, and white wine on a beach in Epidaurus . . . sure, I didn't give you a happy childhood, but the wine was well chilled and—what you shouldn't forget— accompanied by a dish of squid, quality stuff after all, and now we shall say goodbye like civilized people, and not a day longer shall we stay together, do you understand what I am saying?

If she still does not want to leave and tries to push her sweaty little paw into your hand, one should pause for a moment and say—now piss off, and right away, do I make myself clear?

Then she will stop and probably wish to say something in response to your farewell.

She could say something like this: "I shall go, but do you realize what I'll be taking with me?

"I shall take away your joy of looking at the Narew River from the tall embankment (from the place where you can see the older part of the forest and sandbanks with a shoal on the other side), and the joy that the river exists, and that warm rain is falling, and that wine is well chilled, and also the knowledge that the river, the rain, and the beach in Epidaurus were all undeserved gifts because you deserved nothing except barrack 41, the first one on the right side behind the gate.

"I shall go (she might say) but then you may come to the conclusion you actually deserved all that.

"To believe that you deserve everything is a terrible sin.

"I shall go, she will say, because you want to be bright, calm, and strong like Delfina, Major Krall's wife, like the daughter of your guardian, like the ladies from the apartments. You'll meet them at the mass in St. Anne's at eleven o'clock. You will not ask Him: 'Be there.' You'll know that He is, and you'll ask Him for a short sentence for the striking workers. The man kneeling next to you, who has come here for the first time in thirty-seven years, will read aloud a litany handed him by the priest (you'll be surprised but you'll understand that he, too, wants to be with the others). After the mass you'll linger for a moment with your friends, you'll talk with them and express your outrage at the fact that a famous actor wears a suit from Dior, and you'll quickly calculate how many food parcels for the imprisoned one could buy for the price of just one suit. And when you'll be making your rounds with a money box the gentleman who lives in the apartment with the stove will smile at you and give you a donation.

"Now and then certain cracks may appear in your new persona. One day it may turn out that you never make any preserves for the winter. This is a mistake, by all means you should make preserves, the other ladies already have at least forty jars of jam, not to mention fruit jelly or mousse? Embarrassed, you will quickly correct the blunder, but it would be much more difficult in the fall when it will become evident you have nowhere to go. On All Souls' Day you have nowhere to go, you know well what I'm talking about. The others will go to visit graves—how many graves they have, dear sir, how many—some of them will need more than two days to visit all the cemeteries, and you don't have a single grave! Well, you don't, do you. ('You don't have any graves?!' asked the surprised gentleman from the apartment with the stove with the rocaille, whom you would have met—if you had any graves— holding a money box at the cemetery gate, and you would have smiled at him, and given a donation for the renovation of the cemetery.) But don't worry. The therapy I am prescribing is your best chance. Yet there is one thing I have to warn you about before I go (the little girl could say, but she will say nothing, she will just withdraw her sweaty hand and leave without a word): you may recover from blackness, but brightness is incurable."

# XIII

This book should end on Sunday, December 13, 1981, a couple of minutes after ten, when I saw Our Subtenant for the last time.

It was freezing cold.

We were standing on the steps of the theater since early morning, we were standing in front of the door with a note about the disbanding of the congress.

We were standing and making lists of the detained. The wind was blowing. The day before, Tadeusz Kantor was talking about art, which has to be a return to the world of childhood, and now we were making lists of the detained. I felt lumps of frozen snow under my shoes and I was thinking that obviously it wasn't really happening, it was a dream, most probably a dream dreamt by the Subtenant. At the very beginning, at six o'clock in the morning when I heard the vigorous, masculine voice on the radio announcing the introduction of martial law, I decided that it was not really happening and I refused to accept it. I reached for my knitting needles and started to knit ski socks with a Norwegian pattern for my daughter. At eight-thirty, when they were reading the ordinance, I was just finishing the heel and when they played the anthem for the third time I was finishing the first sock. After an hour I decided to call my daughter, but the phone was dead. I put the needles away and thought quite pointlessly: at least I gained two and a half hours and one and a half socks, which makes four, only in this case it does not add up that way. The eerie, dreamlike sensation returned on the steps of the theater. "I feel the lumps of snow under my shoes," I kept repeating. "If I tried to walk away I wouldn't be able to move my leg. Like the black bird that couldn't soar in the air. I will have to paint all this."

That is when I noticed her standing in a large group of people. She was stomping her feet and writing down the names. I wanted to know whether she had already realized it was only a dream, but I understood I would be unable to approach her, because I couldn't lift my feet from the steps.

Just in case I tried the right foot first. I started cautiously to lift my heel, but I realized with amazement that my right foot moved easily on the snow. The same with the left one. I was standing a bit lower now and had a patch of smooth ice under my soles. So this is not a dream, I thought and felt a chill above my wrists.

I looked at the Subtenant again, I wanted to know whether she realized it was not a dream, but she kept on writing: there were more and more names.

Bernard R. was taken from his home in the morning. Someone knocked at the door. . . . They told him to get dressed and walk ahead. At the time we were standing on the steps Bernard was talking with a young man called Irek ("Irek, we've got Rajnicz," said one of the men who brought him in), who wanted to know why on earth Bernard R. got involved with all that stuff. Bernard tried to explain it, an infantile smile on his face, and looked with amazement at the wall behind Irek's back, but his interlocutor did not care to learn that Bernard R. was trying to rehabilitate the idea for which he had won over, many years ago, several bakers from the Lvov slums; he was more interested in names and addresses.

A portrait of Janek Krasicki was hanging on the wall behind Irek's back (perhaps all the interrogation rooms were occupied and they had to use the conference room of their youth organization?) which distracted Bernard R. quite a bit because he remembered how he recommended Janek for the Comsomol in Lvov, and how they were later glad to meet again during the war, and how they quarreled and parted in anger.* Bernard found somebody's abandoned jacket with pockets full of money, and he threw a lavish party with pork chops, mandarin oranges, and champagne for his colleagues in Dniepropietrovsk, and Janek scolded him like mad because a Communist should never feast during a war, so now Bernard felt terribly sorry. Janek left the restaurant without even tasting a pork chop and without saying goodbye, and they never saw each other again, except for this meeting on the wall behind Irek's back.

The conversation in the conference room is the last scene with Bernard R., so I should present it in more detail.

One could ponder, for example, what Bernard R. felt as he was entering the room.

Well, he felt sorrow. Quite recently he had finished his work on a mathematical model, or a formula, which explained a lot, but first of all it explained why the idea presented to the hunchbacked seamstress never triumphed in the world. Having finished his work Bernard R. wished to inform the world about his findings and he kept saying: Now I know why the idea did not win and I am going to explain everything to you. But the people, very busy with what was happening just then, kept saying: "Mr. Bernard, this is not

*Janek Krasicki, leader of Communist youth in Nazi-occupied Poland, murdered by the Germans.

the time for such things." "But this is very important," insisted Bernard R. "At last I know everything, and I have obtained a mathematical proof." But the people were trying to catch up on what was happening around them and said: "This is incredibly interesting, but perhaps some other time?" And now Bernard was entering a room in the headquarters of Internal Security with the full awareness that he will never manage to get the world interested in learning why the said idea never triumphed, and that the "some other time" promised to him will never come.

The place in which Bernard R. found himself on that day was also important. It was the same building where the major and his colleagues were brought for interrogation thirty-two years before. Their trial, however, was held somewhere else, in Military Information Headquarters.

Upon seeing the court and the major on the bench, Bernard R.—as we have already mentioned—remembered the porch, the officers waiting for their commander on a hot summer day, and himself passing a cigarette to a young lieutenant who was leaning against a warm pine tree. On the next day the major and the lieutenant were nowhere to be found. Bernard was standing on the porch alone, and he promised himself in the basement of Military Information Headquarters that this time he would not surrender his men. It would be in order, I presume, if the empty porch appeared one more time during the conversation with Irek and was accompanied by the familiar urge to go somewhere immediately, to save the people.

As a matter of fact Bernard should notice with some relief that this time he has no place to go. This time he himself is being interrogated and there is no place for him to go. Nobody stands between him and the young lieutenant leaning against the pine tree.

He is one of them,

at last one of them. . . .

Irek turned the knob, the anthem seeped in, and the room (it was probably a conference room of their youth organization) started to fill with Irek's colleagues, eager to hear the latest news.

A vigorous, masculine voice was giving information about the imposition of martial law. Bernard started to choke, rushed out of the room, yanked at the door, and leaned over a toilet bowl.

"You are a nervous wreck, Mr. Bernard," said Irek, peeking into the corridor because the rush of water in the toilet was drowning out the voice on the radio.

At the time when the Subtenant and I were standing on the steps, and Bernard R. was explaining why he had got involved, My Favorite Film Director of Semidocumentary Films, who wanted nothing more than to finish his movie, was putting a reel on the editing table. He pressed a button and Werner appeared on the screen. He was old and gray although he never had time to grow old and gray, and he began explaining to My Favorite Director that each generation needs its own light in the labyrinth of history. The scene pleased the director, so he rewound the film and Werner ran backward from the podium, which was as funny as any film running backward. When he finally sat down it turned out that he was speaking about the ugly pale hands with the ring from a spy. "If they have locked him up, he must be a spy, I kept telling her that for a whole year until she believed me," explains Werner to a young boy who is listening to his words with visible compassion. The presence of the boy on the screen never ceased to astonish me because I knew very well to whom, and where, Werner told the story about the spy's wife.

If the director rewound his film further back, he would probably see the embankment near the Old Town and

118

Werner grabbing the Subtenant's hand: "You were shouting 'at last' with the rest of them?"

and if he rewound it still further, Werner would have confessed (in the Security building, the same one where Bernard and the major . . . ) that he had killed Nowotko

and if he rewound it even further, Werner would be sitting on the windowsill with Jarek at the table and Anna pouring hot apricot preserves into her jars, and they all would be young, younger than Irek, and perhaps even younger than the boy in the final scene of the film, the boy whom the director told to act compassion mixed with contempt.


Around ten A.M. somebody said we couldn't keep on standing like that because there was a ban on all public gatherings. Our Subtenant put the list in her purse and left the steps. I asked her where she was going, and she said she was going to St. Anne's. I asked her why. "I don't know," she answered. "That's where one has to go." She was much calmer than before the general strike, when everybody was asking whether they would survive. She told the poet Ryszard K. how glad she was to have bought his book at the congress, and she told me to put on shoes with flat heels.

The sun was shining. We were walking through the blinding snow. We were passing tanks, patrols, and a few silent passersby.

"That's terrible," I said.

"Right," she agreed, looking curiously at the park. From Saxon Garden we turned into Victory Square and the sun was even more intense. The Subtenant stopped for a moment. "Everybody is terrified, right?" she said lifting her head as if, for some important though obscure reason, she wanted to have a good look at the sun, but she kept walking through the square and toward the church.

This book is coming to an end. Who knows, perhaps it has already ended and I haven't had the chance to say anything about the personal life of our heroine. This is absolutely necessary: her daughter, her home, her piece of land on the high embankment over the Narew River, and her husband? what about her husband? and her growing old?

I met my future husband long ago, during one of my visits to the Home. It was Jakubek, who thrilled the humanists because, just like Achilles, he didn't know he was a boy. Learning to be a boy at the age of ten can have a serious impact on one's personality. Just imagine the following scene: a Soviet officer—it all happens after the war—brings a homeless girl to the Home. What is your name, they ask, Zosia, do you have a mother? I don't know, never mind, you will be fine here . . . several simple, reassuring sentences spoken to a frightened girl in dirty rags, a girl who has to be, needless to say, solidly scrubbed, so they go to the bathroom, the tutor fills the tub with hot water, she turns toward Zosia with a foamy sponge, and she cannot believe her eyes. Zosia is a boy. "But you are a boy," shouts the tutor rather unceremoniously, but who would remember formalities under such circumstances. Zosia begins to cry, they explain to her why she had to be a girl, but she understands rather little, and how good it is that she is a boy, they tell her, she *should* be glad, they say, still using the feminine form because in fact sometimes Polish grammar can be quite confusing. Now they cut Zosia's shoulder-length hair, bring a pair of trousers, and introduce a new boy to the children. What is your name, asks somebody, and it turns out that in all the hair-clipping commotion Zosia has lost her old name, but hasn't acquired a new one. Never mind, says the tutor, we'll think of something later. Zosia spends a couple of hours without a name, but at dinner she is already Jakub— "This is a beautiful biblical name, you'll be glad to have it, you'll see."

120

This is Jakub's story.

Jakubek—Jakub—Kubuś—Kuba . . .

What can remain of the scene in the tub for the rest of your life?

Perhaps the memory of details: a fogged mirror against white tiles—hot steam—the smell of soap—a fat tutor looking at your body with amazement—her prying—your anger, as if somebody had treacherously stolen your secret—even if you didn't know it yourself—"what is your name?"—his shame.

It is interesting to see whether this scene will come back to him whenever he smells warm lather and steam. It could happen in a strangest possible place, like Ulan-Ude, where a hotel guest encounters a large cardboard object in the shape of a hoof, ponders its function, and since it reminds him of the collars worn by Mary Stuart he puts it around his neck, but the floor supervisor explains patiently that it is his personal, hygienic toilet seat which he should take with him to the common bathroom. Amused and still wearing his collar Jakub turns the tap, sees the mirror fog with steam, and he is engulfed—right there, in the capital of the Buryat Soviet Socialist Republic—by that warm soapy smell. . . .

It can also happen in an elegant place, like Tokyo for example, where he finds a kimono and a toothbrush in a beautiful case waiting for him in the bathroom. He puts on the kimono, turns the hot water tap . . .

But this will come much later. As for the childhood memories, there are gentlemen from the American charity institutions and humanists patting him affectionately on the head, the priest with chocolate, and a rich elderly couple who take him for a summer vacation. They are happy and cheerful people. One evening they go out for a dance. Jakub is left alone and he starts vomiting: he always starts vomiting when he is left alone, he sneaks out of the house and stops at the restaurant window. He sees a brightly lit room and men dressed in black suits scurrying around with dishes, the food is not important because Jakubek has no appetite, what enchants him is the bright, cheerful world and the men dressed in black. As he stands at the window—still a bit pale after vomiting, with drops of mucus on his chin, he promises himself that when he grows up a man dressed in a black suit will come to serve him and nobody else, he, Jakubek, will sit at the table and the man dressed in black will bustle around and bend toward him, only toward him, in a polite gesture. . . . ("My God . . . " I said to the Subtenant not long ago, when she was telling me about the dinner in Jakub's spacious office during which he was patiently explaining why the film by My Favorite Director will never be distributed. "So the man dressed in black served him dinner. . . . My God . . . ")

In high school Jakub has problems with his upper respiratory tract and talks through his nose as if suffering from a chronic cold, but his compositions are read aloud in front of the whole class, and one of them, about Pavka Korchagin, is submitted by the principal to a competition at a local newspaper.*

Jakub studies law. While in his senior year he publishes an article in *The Week* magazine and is discovered by an adviser to a certain influential politician. He lands a job even before graduating and by that time we should have already met because Jakub should start a family. Where have we met? In the office of *The Week*, where he brought his article, and I brought my drawings (if we stick to my painting). No, that doesn't make much sense. At the Subtenant's? Out of the question, a young, ambitious protégé of an influential politi-

*Pavka Korczagin, hero of the Soviet novel *Tempering of Steel*, by Nicolai Ostrowski.

cian's adviser does not cultivate such contacts, on the contrary, neither do I remember him from my visits to the Home, nor does he remember me; we shall probably discover this connection only much later, by pure accident, both taken by surprise. A friend from the university? If I am writing a dissertation on victimology, I could have studied law. That's it, a marriage of two students, and a rather successful one, compared with the others, because based on fairness. I contributed my bright, straightforward looks, slightly round but reassuring hips, my Christmas tree with white and red ribbons, my father the major, and Jan Kalasanty—the founder of the clan. Jakub donated his outrageous disrespect for all symbols and his rather charming inclination for paradoxes, with which he punctured my patriotic balloons—even the Christmas tree and the major—although he spared Jan Kalasanty because, despite everything else, he was always impressed by genealogies.

What remains of my marriage are several rather important things: my daughter, whom I systematically train in the art of survival, a piece of land on the high banks over the Narew, a certain amount of antidepressants, which I have not been using since the thirteenth of December, and an ironic disposition which has lately been irritating some of my friends. Especially the Subtenant—she detests my jokes about great and sacred things. "What else," she says, "can one expect of a person who was riding a bicycle when France was falling." I am dumbfounded and the Subtenant repeats with emphasis: "Yes, what were you doing in June, 1944, when France was falling? YOU WERE RIDING A BICYCLE. And we had to admonish you severly for that."

"My dear Martusia," I say when I cool down. "First of all you could not have admonished me, because you still weren't Our Subtenant. In fact you did not yet exist. Besides, what else could I do when France was falling but ride a bicycle?"

"I am not sure which one of us did not exist," she answers. "But this is not important. It is important, however, what you were doing when France fell. Carefree you were riding a bicycle. Perhaps that is why today you have such problems with understanding that there are certain things one should never ridicule. We live in slavery, and there are certain things . . . " "Maria," I interrupt her because she should be able to pronounce such formulas correctly by now, "You shouldn't laugh. The fatherland is in slavery. That's the correct form of the sentence."

My survival instructions for my daughter have recently become a bit more timely. Again, people have started telling one another that they are feeling something, that something is in the air, and that it will be terrible. We haven't seen anything yet, they say, everything may still happen, and it will surely be terrible. It would be a good idea to build a stove in our summer house, because if THAT happens in the winter it will be much easier to survive in the countryside. If you are thinking about the Narew—I am not so sure. During World War II the front line went right along the high embankment. There are still ditches, empty shells, and bones scattered around. Sometimes we wonder whether the people whose bones we find managed to notice the strange, spacious panorama of poplar trees, meadows, and the river with sand banks on the other side.

Listen, I say. First of all you should know that one never survives by accident. Look how few have survived, thirty thousand out of three million—exactly 1 percent. And if your mother managed to squeeze herself into that 1 percent, she must have known something about survival.

Therefore:

you have to concentrate on survival. Survival requires extraordinary concentration, and concentration requires strength. Survival requires a lot of strength, which may be why there is so little of it left for other things—like love, or writing.

Next:

you have to separate yourself from the world. Merging with the world and other people would relieve you of your responsibility for your own survival and ruin your concentration.

You should be wary of unnecessary sadness. Sadness can make you weak. Some say that only bad, insensitive people survive, but that is not true. Those who survived simply resolved to keep sadness, compassion, and suffering at a distance. If, for example, I ever come to you dressed in black, sit down on the edge of a chair and try to cry very quietly, you have to slip your hand from mine and say: "That's too bad, but I am still alive," after which you must quickly leave the room not to allow my sadness to catch up with you. It is awfully difficult to disentangle oneself from sadness, therefore it is better to be on guard all the time. "That's too bad," you have to say calmly, slip your hand out of my hand, and leave me sitting on the edge of the chair. . . .

And there is still something else.

Never allow your survival to be too important to you. They say one should not be too busy surviving, those who are not overly concerned seem to stand a much better chance. Therefore do not busy yourself but concentrate quietly, as though haphazardly, isolate yourself from the world, and don't let sadness get to you.

THIS could happen on the terrace over the Narew River. It would probably be aesthetic and radiant—maybe not as much as Krahelska's, but certainly more than Rywka Urman's. Until recently I thought that nothing reveals blackness and nothing confirms brightness like THIS, but lately I realized there are much simpler tests. Like the way of looking at the embankment. The bright ones walk up to it quickly and resolutely, they raise their eyes and look at everything simultaneously: at the dark green trees below, and the pale green meadow behind the trees, at the bushes growing in the meadow, at the light seeping through water, at the bend of the river, and the sand, and forests behind the sand, they look simultaneously at all the curtains of the forest—even the last one with a bright gap in the middle, which makes one wonder what stretches beyond. Some of them, like the owner of the stove with the rocaille, say: "Look, that's where I am, right there," and they point at the gap in the last, the darkest, curtain. They are thinking of course about their home, which is standing right there on some plot of land.

The dark ones would never look like that. The dark ones would make their eyes slide gently, gradually, down the slope, then they would lift them carefully to the level of the river, and finally they would dare to look at the bend and at the forest. Just imagine, a dark one would think, there they are—the bend and the forest. I've made it again.

In my opinion the banks of the Narew can be compared only with that fragment of the Sistine Chapel fresco in which God, having created Adam, tells him: Here you are. Now I am leaving you . . . and He starts to depart slowly, and Adam is still trying to touch Him with his finger—one more time, as a farewell.

The dark ones, if they look at anything directly, look at the woman with tied-up hair, whom God holds by the neck—already oblivious to her presence, already absorbed with Adam. "Don't look at Him like that," says a dark one to the woman, "do something about your eyes, don't look like that. . . ."

The bright ones, on the other hand, stretch out on their

backs, clasp their hands behind their heads, and look at the fingers of God and Adam.

The bright ones believe that they deserve everything, even our embankment, even the vault in the Sistine Chapel.

As a matter of fact looking should become part of my therapy for the dark ones. At first they could practice that resolute walk from the road and among junipers, and then looking directly at the forest on the other side of the river.

"You deserve this bank," I would tell the object of my therapy." "This is a terrible sin," the person would insist, convinced she deserves nothing apart from the barrack on the right side. "But we, the bright ones, take the sin upon ourselves," I would assure her. "Together with punishment, of course. It is true that punishment for the sin of our pride touches everybody, including you. Nevertheless, you get a lot in exchange."

"You can be with us.

"Only then in our fear and degradation, when they are shooting at everyone.

"Only then.

"Well, you get a lot.

YOU CAN BE WITH US, AT LAST.

The book is coming to an end, who knows, perhaps it has already ended, and I haven't even had a chance to write about

# TO OUTWIT GOD

*Translated by*
*Joanna Stasinska Weschler*
*and Lawrence Weschler*

That day you were wearing a sweater made of red, fluffy wool. "It was a beautiful sweater, made of angora. From a very rich Jew . . ." Two leather belts crisscrossed the sweater, and in the middle, atop your chest, a flashlight. "Hanna, I wish you could have seen me then!" you told me when I asked about that day, April 19th . . .

—Is that what I said? It was cold. In April, the nights are cold, especially for those who haven't been eating much. So I put the sweater on. It's true, I found it among some things that belonged to this Jew: one day they pulled his whole family out of their basement, and I took an angora sweater. It was top quality. That guy had loads of money: before the war he'd donated a plane or tank or something like that to the Fund for National Defense.

I know you like that sort of thing. That's probably why I mentioned it.

—Oh, no. You mentioned it because you wanted to show me something. The matter-of-factness and the calm. That's what you were trying to demonstrate.

—I simply talk about it the way we all spoke about it at the time.

—Well, the sweater, the crossing belts . . .

—Write also two guns. The guns completed the outfit, very

131

*de rigueur.* You figured in those days that if you had two guns, you had everything.

—April 19th: you were awakened by shooting, you got dressed . . .

—No, not yet. The shooting woke me up, true, but it was cold, and besides, the shooting was far away, and there was no reason to get up.

I got dressed around noon.

There was one guy with us who had smuggled in arms from the Aryan side. He was supposed to have headed back immediately, but it was already too late. When they started shooting, he told me that he had a daughter in Zamosc in a convent and that he knew he would not survive, but that I would, so that after the war I was supposed to take care of this daughter. I said: "All right, all right, stop talking nonsense."

—Well?

—Well what?

—Did you manage to find this daughter?

—Yes, I did. . . .

—Listen, we agreed that you would talk, right? It is April 19th. They have started shooting. You've gotten dressed. This guy from the Aryan side is talking about his daughter. What next?

—We went out to look around. We crossed the courtyard—there were a few Germans there. Actually, we should have killed them, but we hadn't had practice in killing yet, and besides, we were still a little afraid, so we didn't kill them.

After about three hours the shooting died down.

It got silent.

Our area was the so-called Brush Factory Ghetto—Franciszkanska, Swietojerska, Bonifraterska streets.

We had mined the factory gate.

The next day, when the Germans approached, we plunged the plug in, and about a hundred of them got wiped out. I don't remember exactly, you'd have to look it up somewhere. Actually, I remember less and less. About any of my patients, I could tell you ten times more.

After the mine's explosion, they started charging at us in an extended line. We loved it. Forty of us, a hundred of them, a whole column, in full battle array, crawling along. It was obvious that now they were taking us seriously.

Before the day had ended, they sent over three men with their guns held down, carrying white sashes. They called out that if we'd agree to a ceasefire, they would send us to a special camp. We shot at them. I later found that scene in Stroop's reports: them, parliamentarians with a white banner—us, bandits, opening fire. By the way, we missed, but it doesn't matter.

—How come it doesn't matter?

—The important thing was just that we were shooting. We had to show it. Not to the Germans. They knew better than us how to shoot. We had to show it to this other, the non-German world. People have always thought that shooting is the highest form of heroism. So we were shooting.

—Why did you choose that very day, April 19th?

—We didn't choose it. The Germans chose it. That was the day the liquidation of the Ghetto was scheduled to begin. There were phone calls from the Aryan side—that they were getting everything ready, that the walls were being surrounded on the outside. On the night of the 18th we met at Anielewicz's, all five of us, the whole command staff. I was probably the oldest one there, twenty-two years old; Anielewicz was a year younger. Together, all five of us, we were a hundred and ten years old.

There wasn't much to talk about by that time anymore. "Well?" "Have they called from the city?" Anielewicz takes the central Ghetto, his deputies—Geller and myself—we divvy up Toebbens' Sheds and the Brush Factory. "See you tomorrow." We did say good-bye to each other, the only thing we had never done before.

—Why was it Anielewicz who became your commander?

—He very much wanted to be a commander, so we chose him. He was a little childlike in this ambition, but he was a talented guy, well read, full of energy. Before the war he'd lived on Solec Street. His mother sold fish. When she had any left over, she would have him buy red paint and paint the gills so the fish would look fresh. He was constantly hungry. When he first came back to the Ghetto from Silesia and we gave him something to eat, he would shield the plate with his hand, so that nobody could take anything away from him.

He had a lot of youthful verve and enthusiasm, only he had never before seen an "action." He hadn't seen the people being loaded into trains at the Umschlagplatz. And such a thing—when you see four hundred thousand people being sent off to gas chambers—can break a person.

We did not meet on April 19th. I saw him the day after. He was already a different man. Celina told me: "You know, it happened to him yesterday. He was just sitting and muttering: 'We're all going to die. . . .' " He managed to get roused up again only once after that. We got a message from the Home Army* to wait in the northern part of the Ghetto. We didn't know exactly what it was all about, and in the end, it didn't work out anyway: the guy who went there to check it out got burned alive in Mila Street, we could hear him screaming all day. . . . Do you think that can impress anybody any-

*The Home Army, the principal and largest clandestine anti-Nazi armed organization in Poland.

more—one burning guy after four hundred thousand burned people?

—I think that one burned guy makes a bigger impression than four hundred thousand, and four hundred thousand a bigger impression than six million. So, you didn't know exactly what this message was about . . .

—He must have thought that some reinforcements were being sent. We kept trying to dissuade him: "Let it go, the area there is completely dead, we won't get through."

You know what?

I think that all along he had actually convinced himself of the possibility of some sort of victory.

Obviously, he never spoke about it before. On the contrary. "We are going to die," he would yell, "there is no way out, we'll die for our honor, for history. . . ." All the sorts of things one says in such cases. But today I think that all the time he maintained some kind of a childlike hope.

He had a girlfriend. Pretty, blond, warm. Her name was Mira. On May 7th he came with her to our place in Franciszkanska Street.

On May 8th he shot her first and then himself. Jurek Wilner had apparently declared: "Let's all die together." Lutek Rotblat shot his mother and sister, then everybody started shooting. By the time we managed to get back there, there were only a few people left alive; eighty people had committed suicide. "This is how it should have been," we were told later. "The nation has died, its soldiers have died. A symbolic death." You, too, probably like such symbols?

There was a young woman with them, Ruth. She shot herself seven times before she finally made it. She was such a pretty, tall girl with a peachy complexion, but she wasted six bullets.

There is a park now at that place, with a landmark, a rock, an inscription. When the weather turns nice, mothers with kids go there, and in the evenings young guys go there with their girls. It is actually a collective grave; we never dug the bones out.

—You had forty soldiers. Did it ever occur to you to do the same thing?

—Never. They should never have done it. Even though it was a very good symbol. You don't sacrifice a life for a symbol. I did not have any doubts about that—at least not during those twenty days. I was capable of bashing somebody in the face myself if they started to get hysterical. In general, I was able to do a lot of things then. To lose five men in a battle and not feel guilty. To nod off to sleep while the Germans were drilling holes in order to blow us up (I simply knew that there was nothing more to be done at the moment); and only when they'd break for lunch at noon, we'd quickly do whatever was necessary to get out. (I wasn't nervous—perhaps because actually nothing could happen. Nothing greater than death. It was always death that was at stake, not life. You see, maybe there was no drama at all there. Drama is when you can make a decision, when something depends on you, whereas there, everything had been predetermined. Nowadays, in the hospital, there it's life that's at stake—and each time I have to make a decision now, I get much more nervous.)

And I was capable of one other thing there. I was capable of telling a guy who'd asked me to give him the address of a contact on the Aryan side: "Not yet, it's too early." His name was Stasiek . . . you see, I can't remember last names. "Marek," he said, "there must be some place *over there* I can get to. . . ." Was I supposed to tell him that there was no such place? So I told him: "It is too early yet."

—Was it possible to see anything beyond the wall on the Aryan side?

—Oh yes. The wall only reached the second floor. And

136

already from the third floor one could see the *other* street. We could see a merry-go-round, people, we could hear music, and we were terribly afraid that this music would drown us out and that those people would never notice a thing, that nobody in the world would notice a thing: us, the struggle, the dead. . . . That this wall was so huge, that nothing, no message about us, would ever make it out.

But we later heard from London that General Sikorski posthumously awarded the Virtuti Militari Cross to Michal Klepfisz. The guy in our attic who managed to cover over that machine gun with his body, so that we could get through.

An engineer, in his twenties. An exceptionally good guy.

Thanks to him we forced back one attack—and a bit after that those three men with their white rosettes arrived. The parliamentarians.

I would stand in this place. Exactly here. Only the gate was wooden then. This cement post is the same, that barrack, and probably even those poplars.

Wait, why actually did I always stand on this side?

Oh, I see, because the crowd would march on by the other side. I was probably afraid that they would rake me in, too.

By that time I was working as a messenger at the hospital, and this was my job: to stand by the gate at the Umschlagplatz and select out "sick" people. Our people would pick out those who should be saved, and I would select them out as "sick."

I was merciless. One woman begged me to pull out her fourteen-year-old daughter, but I was only able to take one more person and I took Zosia, who was our best courier. I selected her out four times and each time ended up having to take her out all over again.

At the beginning it was the people without life tickets who were being paraded past me. The Germans had issued these tickets, and those who got them were promised survival. In those days everybody in the Ghetto had only one goal: to get a ticket. But later, they were even taking out those with the tickets.

Still later it was announced that the right to live was being reserved for employees of factories. Sewing machines were necessary in these factories, so people began thinking that sewing machines might save their lives and they were ready to pay any price for a sewing machine. But afterward, they started taking away even those with the machines.

Finally, they announced that they would distribute bread. That everybody who volunteered for hard labor would get three kilograms of bread and jam.

Listen, my dear. Do you have any idea what bread meant at that time in the Ghetto? Because if you don't, you will never understand how thousands of people could voluntarily come for the bread and go on with this bread to the camp at Treblinka. Nobody has understood it thus far.

They were giving out that bread right here, in this very place. Oblong, browned loaves of rye bread.

And you know what?

Those people would go, in order, by fours, to get this bread, and then right onto the train car. There were so many such volunteers that they had to wait in line! It was required that they send two trains a day to Treblinka—and still, there was not enough space for all those who were willing to go.

Yes, we knew.

In 1942 we'd sent a friend, Zygmunt, to find out what was going on with those trains. He'd gone with the railway workers. In Sokolow they'd told him that at that point the railroad divided in two, and that one sidetrack went to Treblinka. Every day a freight train loaded with people would pass that way and return empty; but food supplies were never sent there.

Zygmunt came back to the Ghetto, we wrote about it in

our newspaper—and nobody believed it. "Have you gone insane?" people would say when we were trying to convince them that they were not being taken to work. "Would they be sending us to death with bread? So much bread would be wasted!"

The action lasted from July 22nd till September 8th, 1942—six weeks. During those six weeks I stood by the gate. Here, at this spot. I saw four hundred thousand people off from this square. I was looking at the same cement post you are looking at now.

In the building of that vocational school over there, that was our hospital. They liquidated it on September 8th, the last day of the action. On the upper floor there were a few rooms with children. As the Germans were entering the ground floor, a woman doctor managed to poison the kids.

You see, Hanna, you don't understand anything. She saved these children from the gas chamber. People thought she was a hero.

In this hospital, sick people were lying on the floor waiting to be loaded onto the train cars, and the nurses were searching out their parents in the crowd and injecting them with poison. They saved this poison for their closest relatives. And she, this doctor, had given *her own* cyanide to kids who were complete strangers!

There was only one man who could have declared the truth out loud: Czerniakow. They would have believed him. But he had committed suicide.

That wasn't right: one should die with a bang. At that time this bang was most needed—one should die only after having called other people into the struggle.

Actually, this is the only thing we reproach him for.

—"We"?

—Me and my friends. The dead ones. We reproach him for having made his death his own private business.

We were convinced that it was necessary to die publicly, under the world's eyes.

We had several ideas. Dawid said that we should jump the walls—everybody, all those still alive in the Ghetto—force our way over to the Aryan side, and dig in along the inclined dikes of the Citadel, in rows, one above the other, and wait there until the Gestapo surrounded us with machine guns and shot us all, row by row.

Estera wanted to set fire to the Ghetto so that we would all burn in it. "Let the wind spread our ashes," she would say. At that time, that did not sound grandiloquent, just objective.

The majority of us favored an uprising. After all, humanity had agreed that dying with arms was more beautiful than without arms. Therefore we followed this consensus. In the Jewish Combat Organization there were only two hundred twenty of us left. Can you even call that an uprising? All it was about, finally, was that we not just let them slaughter us when our turn came.

It was only a choice as to the manner of dying.


That interview was translated into several foreign languages and angered many people. Mr. S., a writer, wrote to Edelman from the United States that he had had to defend him; he'd written three long articles to calm everyone down and the title had been "The Confession of the Last Living Commander of the Warsaw Ghetto."

People had sent letters to the editors about the interview—in French, English, Yiddish, and in some other European languages—that he had stripped everything of its magnitude, but basically it was about the fish. The fish whose gills Anielewicz used to paint red so that his mother in Solec Street could sell yesterday's merchandise.

Anielewicz, a peddler's son, painting fish gills red—that beat all! So that this writer, Mr. S., did not have an easy job. But there was also a certain German from Stuttgart who wrote a nice letter.

"*Sehr geehrter Herr Doktor,*" wrote that German, who during the war had spent time in the Warsaw Ghetto as a Wehrmacht soldier. "I saw there bodies of dead people lying in the streets, many bodies, covered with paper. I remember, it was horrible. We are both victims of that terrible war. Could you please drop me a few words?"

Obviously, he wrote the guy back, that he was pleased to have heard from him and fully understood the feelings of a young German soldier who for the first time saw bodies covered with paper.

This story about the writer, Mr. S., reminded Edelman of his trip to America in 1963. He was flown there for a meeting with union leaders. He remembers there was a table with some twenty gentlemen sitting around it. Their faces expressed concentration and emotion: these were the presidents of the trade unions that during the war had given money for arms for the Ghetto.

The chairman greets him and the discussion starts. What is human memory and is it proper to build monuments or maybe buildings—that sort of literary dilemma. Edelman was being very careful not to just blab out something improper, such as, for instance, "And what importance does any of it have today?" He had no right to harm them in this way. "Be careful," he kept saying to himself, "careful, they have tears in their eyes. They gave money for arms. They went to President Roosevelt to ask him if they were true, all these stories about the Ghetto. You have to be good to them."

(They must have gone to Roosevelt after one of the first reports prepared by "Waclaw," shortly after Tosia Goliborska ransomed him from the Gestapo with her Persian carpet. The report was smuggled out by a messenger in his tooth, inside a filling, on microfilm, and reached the United States via London. But they'd had a hard time crediting those thousands of people allegedly processed into soap and those thousands driven through the Umschlagplatz, so they'd gone to their president to ask if these things could be taken seriously.)

So he *was* good to them. He let them be moved and talk about human memory. But then, unintentionally, he hurt them so terribly: "Do you really think that it can be called an uprising?"

Coming back to the fish. In the French translation of the interview published in the weekly magazine *L'Express*, they were not fish but *du poisson*, and Anielewicz's mother, that Jewish peddler from Solec Street, would buy *un petit pot de peinture rouge*. Well—can one still take him seriously, this Anielewicz who puts *peinture rouge* on gills (*les ouïes*); is he still Anielewicz?

It is like attempting to tell one's cousins in England the story of their grandmother who was dying of hunger during the Ghetto uprising. Just before she died, the religious old lady had asked for something to eat. "Doesn't matter," she'd said, "it doesn't have to be kosher, it can even be a *kotlet wieprzowy*."

But one has to tell the story in English to one's English cousins, so in English, Grandma was asking not for a *kotlet wieprzowy* but for a *pork chop*, and at that moment she simply stops being that dying grandmother. It becomes possible to talk about her without hysteria, calmly, the way one might tell an interesting story at a civilized English dinner.

They insist that this couldn't be the real Anielewicz, this one with *peinture rouge*. And there must be some truth to that, since so many people insist on it. They write that one mustn't say such things about the Commander.

—Listen, Hanna, Edelman says, from now on we'll have to be careful. We'll choose our words carefully.

Of course, we shall.

We'll choose our words very thoughtfully. And we'll try not to hurt anybody.

One morning the American writer, Mr. S., calls. He is in Warsaw. He has seen Antek and Celina, and he wants to talk about it in person.

Well—this is serious business. Because one can neglect what everybody in the world says about these things, but there are two people whose opinions can't be ignored and those people are precisely Celina and Antek. Antek, Anielewicz's deputy and the representative of the ZOB (the Jewish Combat Organization) on the Aryan side, who had left the Ghetto shortly before the beginning of the uprising, and Celina, who was with them in the Ghetto all the time, from the first day till the evacuation through the sewers.

Antek has kept silent all this time. And here, Mr. S. arrives and says he's just seen Antek a week earlier.

I have a feeling that Edelman is a little nervous. For no reason, as it turns out. Mr. S. says that Antek reassures Edelman about his friendship and respect for him, and approves, except for a few details, of the entire interview.

"What details?" I ask Mr. S.

Antek has said, for instance, that there were not two hundred of them in the uprising, there were more: five hundred, maybe even six hundred of them.

(—Antek says there were six hundred of you. Shall we change this figure?

—No, Edelman says, there were two hundred and twenty of us.

—But Antek wants, Mr. S. wants, everybody wants you to be at least a little more . . . Shouldn't we just change it?

—After all, it doesn't matter, he says angrily. Can't all of you understand that none of it matters anymore?!)

Oh, and one more thing. Obviously: the fish problem.

It wasn't Anielewicz who painted them, it was his mother. "Write it down, Ms. Krall," says Mr. S., the writer. "That is *very* important."

I return to the problem of choosing words carefully.

Three days after Edelman's departure from the Ghetto, Celemenski arrived and took him to a clandestine meeting with representatives from the underground political parties who wanted to hear a report about the Ghetto uprising. He was the only surviving member of the uprising command and the commander's deputy, so he delivered a report: during those twenty days, he said, it might have been possible to have killed more Germans and to have saved more of our people. But, he said, they had not been properly trained and weren't able to conduct a proper battle. Besides, he said, the Germans also knew how to fight.

Those people looked on at him in total silence, until finally one of them said: "We must try to understand him. He is not a normal man. He is a human wreck."

Because, as it turned out, he was not talking the way he was supposed to talk.

"And how is one supposed to talk?" he asked.

One is supposed to talk with hatred, grandiloquence—one is supposed to scream. There's no other way to express all this except by screaming.

So, from the very beginning, he was no good at talking

about it because he was unable to scream. He was no good as a hero because he lacked grandiloquence.

What bad luck.

The one, the only one, who'd survived was no good as a hero.

Having understood that, he tactfully lapsed into silence. He was silent for quite a long time, for thirty years in fact, and when he finally spoke, it immediately became clear that it would have been better for everybody if he had simply never broken his silence.

He had taken a streetcar to that meeting with the representatives of the various parties. For the first time since leaving the Ghetto he was riding a streetcar, and a horrible thing suddenly happened to him. He was seized by the wish not to have a face. Not because he was afraid that someone would notice him and denounce him; no, he suddenly felt that he had a repugnant, sinister face. The face from the poster "JEWS— LICE—TYPHUS." Whereas everybody else around him had fair faces. They were handsome, relaxed. They could be relaxed because they were aware of their fairness and beauty.

He got off in the Zoliborz district, in an area of little houses. The street was empty and only one elderly woman was watering flowers in her garden. She looked at him from behind her garden's wire netting, and he tried almost not to exist, to take up as little room as possible in that sunny space.

Today, they showed Krystyna Krahelska on TV. Her hair was also fair. She was once Nitschowa's model for the statue of the mermaid which has become a symbol of Warsaw, she used to write poetry, she sang *dumky* (those Ukrainian folk songs), and she was killed during the 1944 Warsaw uprising among the sunflowers.

Some lady was telling Krahelska's story: how she'd been running through some gardens, but that she was so tall that even when bending she'd been unable to hide among those sunflowers.

So, it is a warm August day. She has tied this long, blond hair behind her. She has already written the underground anthem, "Hey, Boys, Affix Your Bayonets!", she's dressed somebody's wound, and now she is running in the sun.

What a beautiful life and a beautiful death! This is the only way a person should die. But this is the way beautiful and fair people live and die. The dark and ugly ones die in an unattractive way: in fear and darkness.

(One could perhaps have hidden at the place of this lady who's telling Krahelska's story. She's not wearing makeup, she certainly hasn't been to the hairdresser and, although you cannot see this on TV, she is probably too wide in the hips, and she hikes in the mountains with a sweater tied round her waist. Her husband wouldn't even have to know that she was hiding somebody, one would only have to be careful not to use the bathroom in the afternoon, between 3:30 and 4 P.M. He has a very regular stomach and uses the bathroom the moment he comes home, even before supper.)

The dark and ugly ones, sapped by hunger, between humid sheets, wait for someone to bring them oats cooked with water or perhaps something from the garbage can. Everything there is gray: faces, hair, sheets. The acetylene lamp is only used sparingly. In the streets, their children tear packages right out of pedestrians' hands in the hope that they might find bread within; they devour everything immediately. In the hospital, children swollen with hunger receive half a powdered egg and one vitamin C tablet each day—this has to be distributed by the physicians because the ward attendant, who is also swollen, cannot handle the torture of the distribution. (Only the doctors and the nurses get food rations: 500 grams of soup and 60 grams of bread. At a special meeting it is decided to sacrifice 200 grams of soup and 20 grams of bread

146

and divide it among the stokers and the ward attendants. Thus, everybody is getting the same: 300 grams of soup and 40 grams of bread per person.) At 18 Krochmalna Street a thirty-year-old woman, Rywka Urman, chewed off a piece of her child, Berek Urman, twelve years old, who had died of starvation the day before. People surrounded her in the court-yard in complete silence, without saying a word. She had gray, tousled hair, a gray face, and crazy eyes. Later, the police came and wrote it all down for the record. At 14 Krochmalna Street a child's body was found in decay. It had been abandoned by its mother, Chudesa Borensztajn, apartment #67. The child's name was Moszek. (The car from the Eternity Mortuary took the corpse away, and Borensztajn explained that she had abandoned it in the street because the community council didn't bury without payment, and besides, she would soon die herself.) People are being taken to the public baths for delousing. On Spokojna Street, they have already been waiting for a day and a night in front of the bath building, and when only enough soup is brought to feed the children, police have to be called to drive the crowd away because people are trying to take food away from the children.

Death by starvation is as unaesthetical as is the hungry life. "Some people fell asleep with a bite of bread in their mouth or during any sort of physical strain, for instance, while running, trying to get some bread."

This comes from a scientific paper.

Doctors in the Ghetto conducted research on hunger because the exact mechanism of death by inanition was at that time unclear from the medical point of view and it seemed wise to take advantage of the occasion. It was an extraordinary occasion. "Never before," the doctors wrote, "has medicine had such rich research material."

147

Still today, it continues to be an interesting problem for physicians.

"For instance," says Dr. Edelman, "the problem of upsetting the balance between water and albumin in a human body. Did they write there anything about electrolytes?" he asks. "Together with water, potassium and salt seep into the connective tissue. See whether they found out anything about the role of albumin."

No, they don't say anything about electrolytes. They note their disappointment that they had been unable to explain anything about this problem that is so interesting from a doctor's point of view—the mechanism of edema in hunger.

Perhaps they would have discovered the role of albumin if they hadn't suddenly had to stop their work, but, unfortunately, they had had to stop it, for which they excuse themselves in the introduction. They were unable to continue the research because "the scientific stock—the human material— was presently annihilated." The liquidation of the Ghetto had begun.

Shortly after the scientific material was annihilated, the researchers were also killed.

Only one of them is still alive: Dr. Teodozja Goliborska. She was investigating basal metabolism in hungry people.

She writes me from Australia that she had known from her readings that the basal metabolism in starving people was slower, but she hadn't suspected that it would prove so much slower, and that this was related to the lower number of breaths and their reduced depth, and in turn the smaller amount of oxygen used by a body in the state of inanition.

(I ask Dr. Goliborska whether later, as a physician, she ever had occasion to make any use of that research. She writes that no, all the people she has treated in Australia have been well fed, indeed some of them overfed.)

Here are some of the results of the research, presented in the paper "Starvation Sickness. Clinical Research Conducted in the Warsaw Ghetto in 1942."

There are three stages of emaciation: Stage I occurs as the excess of fat tissue is being used up. People look younger than usual at this stage. "In the pre-war period we would often find these symptoms in patients who had returned from the spas at Karlsbad, Vichy, etc." Almost all cases studied by the group belonged to Stage II. The exceptions were the cases of Stage III, that is, starvation decrepitude, which in most cases constituted the premortal phase.

Let's proceed to a description of changes in particular organs and systems.

Weight was usually between 30 and 40 kilograms, and it was about 20 to 25 percent lower than pre-war weight. The lowest weight registered was 24 kilograms in a thirty-year-old woman.

Skin is pale, sometimes pale purple.

Nails, especially fingernails, are clawlike . . .

(Perhaps we are discussing all of this at too great length and in too great detail, but this is because it is vital to understand the difference between a beautiful life and an unaesthetical life, and between a beautiful death and an unaesthetical one. It is important. Everything that happened later—everything that happened on April 19th, 1943—was a yearning for a beautiful dying.)

At the beginning, edemas are observed on the face in the eyelid area, on feet, and in some people even edemas of the whole cutaneous integument. If punctured, liquid comes out of subcutaneous tissue. In early fall, a tendency toward frostbite of the fingers and toes can be observed.

Faces are expressionless, masklike.

Thick hair growth can be observed all over the body, especially in women, on faces, in the form of mustaches and whiskers, and sometimes hairiness of the eyelids. In addition, long eyelashes are observed . . .

The mental state is characterized by a paucity of thoughts.

Active and energetic people become apathetic and lethargic. They are sleepy almost all the time. They seem to forget about their hunger, are unaware of its existence, although upon seeing bread, sweets, or meat, they suddenly become aggressive; they will try to devour it even at the risk of exposing themselves to beatings, which they are unable to avoid by running away.

The transition from life to death is slow, almost imperceptible. Death is similar, physiologically, to death in old age.

Autopsy material (3282 complete autopsies were included in the study):

Pigmentation in people who died of starvation: pale or cadaverous pale in 82.5 percent of cases, dark or russet in 17 percent.

There were edemas in one-third of all the bodies submitted to autopsy, in most cases on the lower limbs. The torso and upper limbs were swollen in fewer cases. In most cases edemas were observed in individuals with pale pigmentation. It can be concluded that pale pigmentation appears together with edemas, and russet pigmentation accompanies dry prostration.

Excerpts from an autopsy record (L. rec. aut. 8613):

"Woman, 16 years old. Diagnosis: *Inanitio permagna*. Nutrition very squalid. Brain 1300 grams, very soft, swollen. About 2 liters of clear, yellowish liquid in the abdominal cavity. Heart—smaller than the fist of the corpse."

Frequency of atrophy of particular organs:

In general, the heart, liver, kidneys, and pancreas deteriorate.

Heart atrophy was observed in 82 percent of cases, liver

atrophy in 83 percent, atrophy of pancreas and kidneys in 87 percent. In addition, bones deteriorate—they soften and become spongy.

Livers shrink the most—from about 2 kilograms in a healthy person to 54 grams.

The lowest heart weight was 110 grams.

Only the brain seems virtually not to diminish; it still weighs about 1300 grams.

During the same period the Professor had been working as a surgeon in Radom, in the Saint Casimir Hospital. (The Professor is a tall, grayish, refined man. He has beautiful hands. He likes music, used to play the violin himself. He speaks several foreign languages. His great-grandfather was a Napoleonic officer, his grandfather participated in an anti-Russian rebellion.)

Every day some newly injured partisans would be brought to this hospital.

The partisans usually had belly wounds. It was difficult to get the ones with head injuries to the hospital on time. So he tended to operate on stomachs, spleens, bladders, and large intestines; he was capable of operating on thirty, forty bellies a day.

In summer 1944 they started bringing in thorax cases, because the Warka bridgehead had been created. Many thoraxes were being brought, some mangled by shrapnel or by grenade fragments, or with a bullet-shattered window frame thrust into the chest. Hearts and lungs were sticking out of chest cavities, so it was necessary to repair them somehow and then shove them back into their place.

Once the January offensive started, heads were added: the

Red Army had better transportation than the partisans and now the wounded arrived on time.

"A surgeon has to exercise his fingers all the time," says the Professor. "Like a pianist. I had early and extensive practice."

War is an excellent school for a young surgeon: so the Professor achieved amazing skill in operating on bellies (thanks to the partisans), in operating on heads (thanks to the advancing front), but the Warka bridgehead turned out to provide the most important experience. For during the time of the Warka bridgehead, the Professor for the first time saw an open, beating heart.

Before the war, nobody had ever seen a heart beat. Maybe in an animal, but even this not too often, because there would have been no sense in maltreating an animal so badly, especially since it would have been of no use to medicine anyway. It wasn't until 1947 that for the first time in Poland a thorax was surgically opened. This was done by a Professor Crafoord, who'd come from Stockholm especially for the occasion, but even he hadn't opened up the pericardium. Everybody stood looking as if bewitched at the pericardium as it rhythmically moved, as if there were some small living animal hidden inside. And the Professor was the only one— for not even Professor Crafoord knew—the only one who knew exactly what this thing moving restlessly inside would look like. Because only he—and not the world-famous Swedish guest—had pulled out from the hearts of peasants pieces of rug, splinters, and window frames. It was thanks to this that just five years later, on June 20, 1952, he was able to open the heart of a certain Kwapisz Genowefa and operate on her mitral stenosis.

There is a close and logical relation between those hearts from the Warka area and all the others on which he would later operate, including, of course, also the heart of Mr. Rudny, the haberdashery machine specialist, and that of Mrs. Bubner (whose late husband was very active in the Jewish community, thanks to which she was quite relaxed before the operation, had even been calming the doctors down: "Please, don't worry," she'd told them; "my husband has a very good relationship with God, he will certainly arrange things here so that everything turns out quite all right."), and that of Mr. Rzewuski, president of the Automobile Club—those and many, many other hearts.

Rudny had to have a vein transplanted from his leg into his heart so as to create a wider passage for his blood at a moment just before a heart attack was otherwise about to start. Rzewuski required such a transplant when his heart attack had already started. Mrs. Bubner had to have her blood circulation changed. . . .

Is the Professor scared before such operations?

Oh, yes. He is very scared. He feels fear right here, here, in the belly.

Each time he hopes that at the last moment something will happen that will render it all impossible: the internists will forbid it, the patient will change his mind, maybe even he himself will run out from his office. . . .

What is the Professor so afraid of? God?

Oh, yes, certainly he is very scared of God, but that's not the worst.

Is he scared that the patient may die?

That too, but he knows—everybody knows—that without the operation the patient would die anyway, this is for sure.

So what is he afraid of?

He is afraid that his colleagues will say: *he is making experiments on human beings*. This is the most horrible of all the accusations that can be made.

Doctors have their own board of control regarding professional conduct, and the Professor relates how one day a certain surgeon hit a child with his car. He carried the child into his car, brought him to his hospital ward, cared for him, and cured him. The kid ended up fine, the mother didn't claim anything; only the professional board ruled that caring for this kid in his own hospital ward like that was against medical ethics and rebuked the doctor. He was thereafter unable to exercise his profession, and he soon died of heart disease.

The Professor tells this story just like that, for no particular reason. Because I asked him what a doctor is afraid of.

With these ethics, it becomes much more complicated than one would have thought.

For example: If he had not operated on President Rzewuski's heart, Rzewuski would certainly have died. Nothing special would have happened: dozens of people die during a heart attack. . . . Everybody would have understood, no explanations would have been needed.

However, if they performed the operation and *then* Rzewuski died—oh, that would be quite a different story. Someone might point out that, after all, nobody else in the world was even attempting such interventions. Somebody else might have asked if the Professor was not being too reckless sometimes, and that could already begin to sound like a general accusation . . .

So that now we might begin to imagine what the Professor is thinking of as he sits in his office before an intervention— before this particular intervention—and there, in the operating room, the anesthesiologist is beginning to bustle about, preparing Rzewuski.

Because the Professor has been sitting in his office for quite a while now, even though, if truth be told, it is not at all clear if this is because of Rzewuski. In the operating room they might just as well be bustling about Rudny or Mrs. Bubner. But it has to be admitted that the Professor was the most nervous before Rzewuski.

Because the Professor very much dislikes operating on the hearts of intellectuals. Intellectuals think too much before an operation, their imaginations are too vivid, they're constantly asking themselves and everybody else too many questions, and all this later reflects undesirably in the pulse rate, in the blood pressure, and in the entire process of the operation. A man like Rudny, by contrast, consigns himself into his surgeon's hands with much greater confidence, he does not ask the unnecessary questions, and therefore it is much easier to operate on him.

Thus, let it be Rzewuski, and let the Professor be sitting in his office before the operation that he is going to perform on this intellectual, whose heart is in a state of acute heart attack and who just a few hours before was rushed here from a Warsaw hospital in an emergency ambulance.

The Professor is absolutely alone.

Nearby, just beyond the door, Dr. Edelman is sitting, smoking cigarettes.

What is the problem?

The problem is that it's precisely Edelman who has insisted that Mr. Rzewuski can be operated on during his heart attack; if it were not for this, the whole issue would not have even come up.

For that matter, Mr. Rudny would not have existed either. The Professor had operated on him as the heart attack was just about to begin, and all the manuals of heart surgery declare that this is precisely the state in which a patient mustn't be operated on.

For that matter, there would not have been any idea of reversing Mrs. Bubner's blood flow (and perhaps there wouldn't be Mrs. Bubner herself anymore; this thought, however, doesn't strictly belong with these considerations).

Since the scene in the Professor's office for us, after all, is a mere pretext, we can leave him for a moment at that desk and explain what is actually at stake here with the blood-flow system.

Namely, during one such operation, earlier, an assistant doctor had questioned whether the Professor had taken up an artery or rather a vein—it happens sometimes that blood vessels look similar. Everybody had insisted that it was okay, that it was an artery, but the assistant had persisted: "It is definitely a vein." After coming home, Edelman, who had been at this operation, began to think what actually would have happened had it really been a vein. He began to draw out a sketch on a piece of paper: the oxygenated blood, which, as we know from school, in the pulmonary circulation flows in arteries, could be directed from the main artery directly to the veins—these are still pliable because they haven't been attacked by sclerosis, therefore they would not provoke a heart attack. This blood would flow away through . . .

Edelman is still not quite sure where this blood would flow away, but the next day he shows his sketch to the Professor. The Professor gives it a glance. "It is possible, Professor, right here, and the muscle would be supplied with blood . . . ," Edelman says, and the Professor nods politely. "Oh yes," he says, "that's very interesting," because what, except polite-ness, can you show someone who suggests that blood can arrive at the heart not through veins but rather through arteries?

Edelman goes back to his hospital and the Professor, back at his house, at night, places the sketch on a little night table next to his bed. The Professor always sleeps with the light on, so as to be able to pull himself together quickly in case he awakens during the night. So this time he also leaves his lamp on, and when, after four hours, he wakes up, he immediately reaches for the piece of paper with Edelman's drawing.

It is difficult to state at which moment the Professor stops staring at the drawing and begins to sketch something himself on another piece of paper (he is drawing a bridge linking the main artery with veins), but the fact is that one day he suddenly asks Edelman: "Well, and what is gonna happen with this used blood, if the vein assumes the role of the artery?"

Edelman and Dr. Elzbieta Chetkowska reply that a certain lady, Ratajczak-Pakalska, is working on her Ph.D. on the anatomy of heart veins, and her research shows that blood would be able to flow away through other confluences, through the valve of Vieussens and the thebesian veins.

Edelman and Elzbieta subsequently try it out on corpses' hearts—they inject methylene blue into veins in order to see if it flows away. It does.

But the Professor says, "So what? After all, there was no pressure on those veins."

They inject the blue liquid under pressure and it again finds an outlet.

But the Professor says, "So what? After all, this is just a model. How would a live heart react?"

Well, this is a question nobody can answer because nobody has made such a test on a live heart before. In order to know how a live heart would react, it would be necessary to operate on a live heart.

And on whose live heart is the Professor supposed to operate?

Just a second, we have forgotten about Aga, and Aga has just gone to the library.

Aga Zuchowska goes to the library whenever a new idea comes up. Before she goes there, she says: "Fat chance." For instance, Edelman says: "Who knows, maybe it is possible to operate on bypasses in an acute state." And Aga says, "Fat chance," goes to do some reading, comes back with *The*

*American Heart Journal*, and triumphantly announces: "Here they say that you are just spewing nonsense." And then a bypass in an acute state is attempted, and everything works out perfectly.

Nowadays, Aga says that when one has pronounced "Fat chance" enough times and then has gone on to see that the man, despite all the experts, turns out to be right, one eventually stops shrugging one's shoulders. Furthermore, one begins to try to forget what all these experts have been writing and instead, upon hearing about some new idea, one quickly tries to adjust to this new way of thinking.

But in those days, Dr. Zuchowska still used to say "Fat chance." So she went to the library and brought back an article from *The Encyclopedia of Thoracic Surgery*. Over thirty years earlier, it turns out, an American surgeon, Claude Beck, used to do something similar but the rate of mortality had proven so high that he'd given up on it. . . .

So, whose live heart? . . .

Now, we have to detour from our subject for a moment to talk about the anterior myocardial infarction with left anterior hemiblock.

This is very important because, up till now, it has never been possible to rescue anybody from this sort of heart attack.

People die in these circumstances in a somewhat peculiar way: they lie quiet, silent, more silent still, yet more quiet, with every passing hour, and gradually everything inside them slowly dies. Legs—liver—kidneys—brain . . . Until one day the heart simply stops and the person is dead. It happens so very quietly, so inadvertently, that a patient on the next bed may not even notice.

When a person with an anterior myocardial infarction with left anterior hemiblock is brought to the hospital, one can be sure that this patient is going to die.

So one day a woman with such a heart attack is brought in. Edelman calls the Professor at his clinic. "This woman is going to die within a few days. The only thing that can save her is a reversal of her blood circulation." Now, this woman doesn't look at all as if she is going to die.

Still, after a few days the woman dies.

Some time later, a man with the same kind of heart attack is brought in. They call the Professor: "If you don't operate on this man . . ."

Within a few days, the man dies. Later, there is another man. Later some young guy, then two women . . .

The Professor comes in every time. He no longer suggests that these people may survive without an operation. He simply looks on in silence, or he asks Edelman: "What do you actually want from me? Do you want me to perform an operation nobody has ever succeeded with before?" To which Edelman answers: "Professor, I am only saying that we won't otherwise have any chance of curing this patient, and nobody but you is capable of performing that operation."

A year passes.

Twelve or thirteen people die.

By the fourteenth case the Professor says: "All right. We'll try."

So let's get back to the Professor's office.

As we recall, he is alone. On the desk in front of him lie Mr. Rzewuski's coronograms, and Mr. Rzewuski is lying in the operating ward.

On the other side of the door, on a chair, Dr. Edelman is sitting and smoking his cigarettes.

The biggest problem at this moment is precisely the fact that Dr. Edelman is sitting in that chair and certainly will not be moving from there.

Why is this such a big problem?

It's simple.

There is only one exit from the office, and it's blocked by Dr. Edelman.

Couldn't the Professor, for instance, say, "Excuse me, just for a moment," and quickly bypass Edelman, and walk away?

Yes, he could. He has even done so once. Before Mr. Rudny. And what? He came back himself, before the day was over, and Mr. Rudny was still waiting for him in the surgery ward, and Edelman with Chetkowska and Zuchowska were still sitting on the chairs of his waiting room.

Anyway, where could he possibly have gone?

Home? They would have found him in no time.

To one of his kids? They would have found him at the latest by the next day.

Out of town? Maybe. . . . But eventually he would always have to come back—and then he would find all of them: Mr. Rzewuski, Edelman, Zuchowska. . . . But perhaps he would not find Mr. Rzewuski anymore.

Mr. Rudny, the one whom he'd come back for before the end of the day, is still alive.

And Mrs. Bubner, the one with blood circulation, is also still alive.

That's right, we have been talking about blood circulation.

"All right, we'll try." This is the point we stopped at before, at that point, and now the Professor is beginning the operation. The other one—on Mrs. Bubner's heart. Let's not mix these two cases. It even makes sense that the Professor is thinking now about this other operation. He is trying to brace himself.

(That time also everybody was saying to him: "But it's crazy, her heart will choke with blood. . . .")

The operating room is silent.

The Professor takes up the main vein, in order to stop the blood leak and see what happens.

*160*

(Claude Beck had not taken up the leak, which later caused right heart asthenia and death. So the Professor improves on that method—no, he doesn't allow the use of that word *improve*—he only *alters* Claude Beck's method.)

He is waiting . . .

The heart is working normally. He now joins the main artery to the vein with a special bridge. Arterial blood is beginning to flow into the veins.

He waits again.

The heart moves. Another spasm. Then a few more fast spasms and the heart begins to work slowly, regularly. The blue veins become red from arterial blood and begin to throb. The blood is flowing away—nobody knows exactly where, but it is finding some outlet through some of the smaller runoffs.

Several more minutes pass in silence. The heart is still beating, without any interference.

The Professor mentally finishes off that operation and once again happily realizes that Mrs. Bubner is still alive.

The successful operation on Mr. Rudny had been all over the papers. This story of the reversed blood circulation of Mrs. Bubner he'd reported to a convention of heart surgeons in Bad Nauheim, West Germany, and everybody had risen from their chairs and applauded. Professors Borst and Hoffmeister of West Germany even suggested that this method would now solve the problem of coronary sclerosis, and surgeons in Pittsburgh, for the first time in the United States, started performing this sort of operation based on the Professor's method. However, if the operation on Mr. Rzewuski proved unsuccessful, was anyone going to say, "But at least Mr. Rudny and Mrs. Bubner are still alive"?

No, nobody was going to say that.

Everybody would instead say, "He operated during a heart attack, so he is guilty of Mr. Rzewuski's death."

At this point someone may begin to feel that the Professor has been sitting in his office far too long already, and that it wouldn't hurt to add some dynamics to our story.

Unfortunately, an attempt at escape, which certainly would have animated the whole story, failed. What more was left?

Oh, right, God was left.

But not the one with whom the religious Jew, Mr. Bubner, arranged the successful outcome of his wife's operation.

Rather, the God the Professor prays to every Sunday at eleven accompanied by his wife, three children, children-in-law, and a handful of grandchildren.

So the Professor could pray, even in his office. But what for?

Indeed, what for?

That at the last moment, already on the operating table, Rzewuski would change his mind and revoke his consent to the operation? Or maybe that his wife, who is even now crying just outside in the hall, might all of a sudden say no?

Yes, this is what the Professor might now like to pray for.

But—just a second—in refusing to undergo an operation, this man (as the Professor knows very well) would be signing his own death sentence. So is he supposed to be praying for the guy's certain death?

It is true that such operations have not been performed before, or at least, when performed, they were performed differently. But, then, nobody transplanted a heart before Christiaan Barnard either. There always has to be someone who risks, if medicine is going to make any progress at all. (As we can see, the Professor is now including social motivation.) And when is one allowed to risk? When one has deep confidence in the value of such an operation. The Professor has such confidence. He has thoroughly thought through every detail of the proposed intervention, and all his knowledge, his expertise, and his intuition—everything confirms the logic and necessity of what he is planning to do. Besides, there is nothing to be lost here. He knows that without the operation this man is going to die anyway. (Is it certain that Mr. Rzewuski would die without the operation?)

He calls in the general-medicine doctor.

"Are you sure that Mr. Rzewuski would die without this operation?"

"Professor, it is his second heart attack. His second, *extensive* heart attack."

"In that case, he will not survive the operation. . . . Why should we torture him further?"

"Professor, they brought him here all the way from Warsaw not so that he die here, but so that we save him."

This was Dr. Edelman talking now. Oh, it's easy for Dr. Edelman to say such things. If anything happens, nobody will reproach him.

Edelman is absolutely certain that he's right. The Professor is also certain. But it is the Professor, and only the Professor, who will have to confirm it with his own hands.

—Why, I ask Edelman, were you convinced that it was right to operate?

—Because. Because I saw the sense of it and knew that it would work out all right.

—Listen, Marek, I say, perhaps you go for such things so easily because you are so familiar with death . . . ? You were much more familiar with death than, for example, the Professor?

—No, he says. I hope it's not because of that. It's just that when one knows death so well, one has more responsibility for life. Any, even the smallest chance for life becomes extremely important.

(A chance for death was there all the while. The important thing was to make a chance for life.)

163

Careful now. The Professor is about to introduce a new character. Dr. Wroblowna.

"Bring in Doctor Wroblowna," he says.

Everything is clear.

Dr. Wroblowna is an elderly, shy, careful lady, a cardiologist from the Professor's clinic. She would never advise him to do anything improper, to take any kind of untoward risk.

The Professor will ask, "Well, Miss Zofia? What is your advice?" And Miss Zofia will answer, "The best thing is to wait, Professor. After all, we don't know how such a heart will react. . . ." And then the Professor will be able to turn triumphantly to Edelman: "You see, Doctor, my cardiologists won't let me!" (He will stress the word *my*, because Dr. Wroblowna is from his clinic and Dr. Edelman is from the city hospital. Or maybe that's just my mistaken impression, and the word *my* simply implies that the Professor, the head of the clinic, has to take into account the opinions of his doctors.)

So Dr. Wroblowna comes in. Shy, she blushes, looks down. Then she says in a very low voice:

"It is necessary to operate, Professor."

No! That beats all!

"Wroblowna," the Professor cries, "even you're against me, too?"

He pretends that he is joking, but he begins to have an odd feeling, a feeling that will not leave him till the end of the day.

When he gets up from behind his desk—gathering up the coronograms and heading toward the operating room where Mr. Rzewuski, asleep, already awaits him, along with the surgeons in their blue masks and the nurses—he will be unable to shake the feeling that he is absolutely alone, despite the presence of all these people.

Alone with the heart, which is moving in its sack like a tiny, frightened animal.

For it is still moving.

Everything I've written so far I've shown to various people—and they don't understand a thing. Why haven't I talked about how he managed to survive? It isn't even clear how he managed to survive, and already we have him sitting behind the door of the Professor's office. And, after all, he *has* to be sitting there; otherwise, if he weren't, the Professor would have gotten home a long time ago, he'd be in the middle of watching the TV news, all relaxed and quiet.

Therefore he has to be behind that door, along with Aga and Elzbieta Chetkowska. Although there is no Elzbieta anymore. I mean—she is there while they are sitting there waiting, but she no longer exists as I write about that waiting. All that's left of her is the Dr. Elzbieta Chetkowska Prize awarded for outstanding achievements in the field of cardiology.

They founded that prize based on royalties from their book *Infarction*. During that research on starvation Edelman hadn't been able to participate because at the Ghetto hospital he'd only been a messenger, but now, with this one, he'd been able to describe everything he knew about people with heart diseases. Tosia Goliborska told me that in the Ghetto hospital they had had an inkling of his other activities—and that they should not ask him questions about them—so that therefore they did not demand much from him, only that each day he deliver the blood from the typhoid victims to the epidemiology station. The rest of the day he could spend at his place

*165*

in the Umschlagplatz, standing there every day for six weeks until four hundred thousand people had passed by him on their way into the train cars.

The movie *Requiem for 500,000* shows them filing in. One can even see the bread loaves in their hands. A German cameraman stood at the train car's entrance and photographed the surging crowd, the stumbling old women, the mothers dragging their children by the hands. They are running with this bread toward us and toward the Swedish journalists who have come here to Warsaw to gather material about the Ghetto; they are running toward Inger, a Swedish journalist who is looking at the screen with dumbfounded blue eyes, trying to comprehend why so many people are running toward the train car—and then, suddenly, the shots are heard. What a relief it is when they start shooting! What a relief it is when puffs of dust veil the running crowd and their loaves of bread and the narrator informs us about the outbreak of the uprising, so that it now becomes possible to explain it all to Inger in a matter-of-fact way (*The uprising's broken out, this is April forty-three*). . . .

I tell Marek about this scene and I say how it's really a well-thought-out sequence. It's great how the explosions veil the people—and at that point he begins to scream. He screams that I probably consider the people who were surging into the train cars to have been worse than the ones who were shooting. Of course, I do, absolutely, everybody does, even that American, the professor who recently visited Marek and told him, "You were going like sheep to your deaths." That American professor landed once on some French beach, scrambled for four or five hundred meters under withering fire without swerving or even crouching down, got wounded, and now he believes that if one has run across such a beach, he later has the right to say "Men should run," or "Men should shoot," or "You were going like sheep." The professor's wife added that those shots were needed by future generations: the death of people dying in silence means nothing because it leaves nothing behind, whereas those who shoot leave a legend behind—for her and her American children.

He'd very well understood why the professor—who still had the scars from his wounds, had medals and academic tenure—why he wanted to include those shots in his history. But he nevertheless tried to explain to him several things— how to die in a gas chamber is by no means worse than to die in battle, and that the only undignified death is when one attempts to survive at the expense of somebody else. But he'd been unable to explain anything, and instead he'd started yelling all over again. Some woman who was in the room tried to offer apologies on his behalf: "Excuse him, please," she'd pleaded in embarrassment. "One has to excuse him . . ."

—My dear, Edelman says, you have to understand this once and for all. Those people went quietly and with dignity. It is a horrendous thing, when one is going so quietly to one's death. It is infinitely more difficult than to go out shooting. After all, it is much easier to die firing—for us it was much easier to die than it was for someone who first boarded a train car, then rode the train, then dug a hole, then undressed naked. . . . Do you understand now? he asks.

—Yes, I say. I see. Because it is indeed easier, even for us, to look at their death when they are shooting than when they are digging a hole for themselves. . . .

I once saw a crowd on Zelazna Street. People on the street were swarming around this barrel—a simple wooden barrel with a Jew on top of it. He was old and short, and he had a long beard.

Next to him there were two German officers. (Two beautiful, tall men next to this small, bowed Jew.) And those Germans, tuft by tuft, were chopping off this Jew's long beard with huge tailor's shears, splitting their sides with laughter all the while.

The surrounding crowd was also laughing. Because, objectively, it really was funny: a little man on a wooden barrel with his beard growing shorter by the moment as it disappeared under the tailor's shears. Just like a movie gag.

At that time the Ghetto did not exist yet, and one might not have sensed the grim premonition in that scene. After all, nothing really horrible was happening to that Jew: only that it was now possible to put him on a barrel with impunity, that people were beginning to realize that such activity wouldn't be punished and that it provoked laughter.

But you know what?

At that moment I realized that the most important thing on earth was going to be never letting myself be pushed onto the top of that barrel. Never, by anybody. Do you understand?

Everything I was to do later, I was doing in order not to let myself get pushed up there.

—It was the beginning of the war and you could still have left the country. Your friends were still fleeing to places without barrels . . .

—Those were different kinds of people. They were wonderful boys from civilized families. They had excellent grades at school, telephones in their houses, and beautiful paintings on their walls. Originals, not some reproductions. I was nothing compared to them. I wasn't any member of the high life. I had poorer grades, I couldn't sing as well, I couldn't ride a bicycle, and I didn't even have a house because my mother died when I was fourteen. (*Colitis ulceroza*. It's odd: later, the first patient I had in my life suffered from the same thing. Only, by that time there existed prednisone and penicillin, so we cured him in a couple of weeks.)

What were we talking about?

—That some friends did leave.

—You see, Hanna, before the war I was telling my fellow Jews that their place was here, in Poland. That we would build socialism here, and that they should stay here. So when they stayed, and the war then began, and everything that was to happen in this war to the Jews was beginning to happen—how was I supposed to leave?

After the war, some of those friends turned out to be managers of Japanese corporations, or physicists in American nuclear agencies, or professors at colleges. As I told you, they were talented people.

—But by that time you had already pulled yourself up to their level. You had hero status. They could accept you in their glorious class.

—They would ask me to come. But I had seen four hundred thousand people off at the Umschlagplatz. I myself, me, in person. They'd all passed by me while I stood there at the gate . . .

Listen, Hanna, do me a favor, stop asking me those nonsense questions. "Why did you stay?" "Why did you stay?"

—But I am not asking you about it at all.

— . . .

—Well?

—Well what?

—Tell me about the flowers. Or whatever. It doesn't matter what. But it can be about the flowers. How you get them every year on the anniversary of the uprising, without knowing who they are from. Thirty-two bunches so far.

—Thirty-one. In 1968, I didn't get any flowers.* I felt bad about that, but already the next year I was getting them again, and I am still getting them up to this day. Once they were marsh marigolds, last year they were roses—always yellow flowers of some sort. They are delivered by a florist without so much as a word.

—I am not sure, Marek, whether we should write about this. I mean, anonymous yellow flowers? It smacks of cheap literature. I must say that kitschy stories somehow seem to stick to you. Those prostitutes, for instance, who would give you a bagel every day. By the way, do you think it would be proper to write that there were prostitutes in the Ghetto?

—I don't know. Probably it wouldn't be. In the Ghetto there should only have been martyrs and Joans of Arc, right? But if you want to know, in the bunker on Mila Street, together with Anielewicz's group, there were some prostitutes and even a pimp. A big, tattooed guy, with huge biceps, who was their boss. They were good, clever, resourceful girls. Our group got to that bunker after our area began to burn. They were all there—Anielewicz, Celina, Lutek, Jurek Wilner—and we were so happy that we were together again. These girls gave us some food, and Guta had Juno cigarettes. That was one of the best days in the Ghetto.

When we came back later on and everything had already happened to them—there wasn't any Anielewicz anymore, nor Lutek, nor Jurek Wilner—we found those girls in the basement next door.

The next day we headed down into the sewers.

Everybody got in, I was the last one, and one of the girls

---

*During 1968, a power struggle in the Polish Communist Party included an astonishingly virulent anti-Semitic campaign. Thousands of Jewish professionals were sacked from their jobs and many left the country.

asked whether she could join us in escaping to the Aryan side. And I said no.

So you see.

I only ask you one thing: don't make me explain today why I said no then.

—Earlier did you ever have a chance of getting from the Ghetto to the Aryan side?

—Actually, I used to go to the Aryan side, legally, every day. As the hospital messenger, every day I carried blood samples from the typhoid victims for tests at a lab over on Nowogrodzka Street.

I had a pass. There were just a few passes in the Ghetto at that time: at the hospital in Czyste, at the community council, and at our hospital, where I was the only one who had one. Those people from the council, they were dignitaries, they would go to offices and travel in carriages. But I would just walk, wearing my armband on the street, among people, and all those people would gaze at me and at that armband. With curiosity, with sympathy, sometimes with a sneer . . .

I would walk like that every day around 8 A.M. for a couple of years, and in the end nothing bad ever happened to me. Nobody ever stopped me, nobody called a policeman, no one even laughed. People only looked at me. Only looked at me. . . .

—What I meant, Marek, is why didn't you simply stay on the Aryan side?

—I don't know. Today one no longer knows things like why.

—You were a nobody before the war. So, how did it happen that three years later you became a member of the command group of the Jewish Combat Organization? You were one of five people chosen from among the three hundred thousand people who were still there.

—I wasn't the one who was supposed to be there. It should

have been . . . Well, it doesn't matter. Let's call him "Adam." He graduated before the war from military college and took part in the September 1939 campaign and in the defense of Modlin. He was famous for his courage. For many years he was a real idol of mine.

One day the two of us were walking together along Leszno Street, there were crowds of people, and all of a sudden some SS men started shooting.

The crowd scrambled away desperately. And so did he.

You know, I had never before suspected that he could be afraid of anything. And there he was, my idol, running away.

Because he was used to always having a weapon by his side: in the military college, later in the defense of Warsaw in September, and in Modlin. The others had weapons, but he had a weapon, too, so therefore he could be brave. But when it happened that the others were firing their arms and he couldn't shoot, he became another man.

It all actually happened without a single word, from one day to the next: he simply quit all activity. And when the first meeting of the command group was about to be held, he was useless for participating in it. So I went instead.

He had a girlfriend, Ania. One day, they took her to Pawiak Prison—she managed to get out later on—but the day they took her, he broke down completely. He came to see us, leaned his hands on the table, and started telling us that we were all lost, that they would slaughter us all, and that since we were young we should escape to the forest and join the partisans instead of attempting to form an underground here in the city.

Nobody interrupted him.

After he'd left, somebody said: "It's because they have taken her away. He has no reason to live anymore. Now he will get killed." Everybody had to have somebody to act for, somebody to be the center of his life. Activity was the only chance for survival. One had to do something, to have somewhere to go.

All this bustle might not have had any importance, because everybody was getting killed anyway, but at least one wasn't just waiting his turn idly.

I was busy at the Umschlagplatz. With the aid of our people in the Ghetto police, I was supposed to select out those whom we needed the most at the time. One day I pulled out a guy and a young woman—he had worked in the printing shop, and she had been an excellent liaison officer. They both died soon afterward—he in the uprising, and she by way of a later trip to the Umschlagplatz—but before that he managed to print an underground paper and she managed to distribute this paper.

I know. You want to ask, what sense did it have?

No sense at all. Thanks to that, one wasn't standing on a barrel. That's all.

There was an emergency room at the Umschlagplatz. Students from the nurses' college worked there—this was, by the way, the only school in the Ghetto. Luba Blum was the headmistress and she made sure that everything there was run like in a real, first-rate school: snow-white robes, starched caps, perfect discipline. In order to pull somebody out from the lines at the Umschlagplatz, it was necessary to prove to the Germans that the person was seriously ill. They would send those sick people home in ambulances: till the last moment, the Germans tried to maintain the illusion in people that they were leaving in those trains to work, and only a healthy person could work, right? So these girls from the emergency room, those nurses, would break the legs of those people who had to be saved. They would wedge a leg up against a wooden block and then smash it with another block. All this in their shiny white robes of model students.

People who were waiting to be loaded onto the trains were herded together in a school building. They would take them out floor by floor, so that from the first floor the people would tend to flee up to the second floor, and from the second to the third, but there were only four floors and on the fourth floor their activity and energy would simply give out, because it was impossible to go any higher. There was a big gym on this fourth floor, and several hundred people would be lying there on the floor. Nobody would stand or walk, nobody would even move. People would just be lying there, apathetic and silent.

There was a niche in this gym. And in this niche one day several Ukrainian guards—six, maybe eight—were raping a young girl. They waited in line and then raped her. After the line was finished, this girl left the niche and she walked across the whole gym, stumbling against the reclining people. She was very pale, naked, and bleeding, and she slouched down into a corner. The crowd saw everything, and nobody said a word. Nobody so much as moved, and the silence continued.

—Did you see that yourself, or somebody told you?

—I saw it. I was standing at the end of the gym and saw everything.

—You were standing in that gym?

—Yes. One day I told Elzbieta about this incident. She asked me, "And you? What did you do then?" "I didn't do anything," I told her. "Anyway, I can see that it's no use talking to you about it. You don't understand a thing!"

—I don't understand why you got so mad. Elzbieta's response was the reaction of any normal person.

—I know. I also know what a normal person is supposed to do in such circumstances. When a woman is being raped, every normal person rushes to her rescue, right?

—If you'd rushed by yourself, they would have killed you.

But if you had all gotten up from the floor, all of you could have easily overpowered those Ukrainians.

—Well, nobody got up. Nobody was any longer capable of getting up from that floor. Those people were capable of only one thing: waiting for the trains. But, why are we talking about it?

—I don't know. You were saying before how it was necessary to keep busy.

—I was busy at the Umschlagplatz. . . . And that girl is still alive, you know?

My word of honor. She is married, has two kids, and is very happy.

—You were busy at the Umschlagplatz . . .

—And one day I selected out Pola Lifszyc. The next day she went to her house and she saw that her mother wasn't there—her mother was already in a column marching toward the Umschlagplatz. Pola ran after this column alone, she ran after this column from Leszno Street to Stawki—her fiancé gave her a lift in his riksa so that she could catch up—and she made it. At the last minute she managed to merge into the crowd so as to be able to get on the train with her mother.

Everybody knows about Korczak, right?* Korczak was a hero because he went to death with his children of his own free will.

But Pola Lifszyc, who went with her mother—who knows about Pola Lifszyc?

And Pola could have easily crossed to the Aryan side because she was young, pretty, she didn't look Jewish, and she'd have had a hundred times better chance.

---

*Janusz Korczak (né Henryk Goldszmit) was a famous writer of children's books and director of a Warsaw orphanage who, though exempted from deportation, chose to accompany his young wards to Treblinka.

—Marek, you once mentioned the life tickets. Who distributed them?

—There were forty thousand tickets—little white chits of paper with a stamp. The Germans gave them to the community council and said: "Distribute them among yourselves. Those who have the tickets will stay in the Ghetto. All the others must go to the Umschlagplatz."

It was two days before the conclusion of the liquidation action, in September. The head doctor of our hospital, Mrs. Heller, got some fifteen tickets, and said: "I'm not going to pass these out."

Any of the doctors could have distributed these tickets but everybody thought that she would give them to those who deserved them most.

Listen to me: "Who deserved them most." Is there any standard that can be used to decide who has the right to live? There is no such standard. But delegations of people went to Mrs. Heller begging her to distribute the tickets, so finally she agreed to.

She gave Frania a ticket. And Frania had a mother and a sister. All those who had tickets were being gathered together near Zamenhofa Street, and all about them a crowd of people who didn't have tickets was scrambling. Among those people, Frania's mother was standing. She didn't want to leave Frania, even though Frania had already joined the ranks of the reprieved. Frania kept saying: "Mother, go already." She was pushing her away with her hand. "Mother, go away."

Yes, Frania did survive.

She later saved the lives of a dozen or so people. She carried one guy out of the Warsaw uprising. In general, she behaved extraordinarily.

One such ticket went to Mrs. Tenenbaum, the head nurse. She was a friend of Berenson, the famous attorney, the defense lawyer in the Brzesc trial. She had a daughter who hadn't gotten a ticket. So Mrs. Tenenbaum gave her ticket to her daughter and said, "Hold this for a second, I'll be right back," and she went upstairs and swallowed a flaskful of Luminal.

We found her the next day, she was still alive.

Do you think we should have tried to save her?

—What happened to the daughter who now had the ticket?

—First, answer: Should we have tried to save her?

—You know, Tosia Goliborska told me that her mother also swallowed poison. "And that moron, my brother-in-law," she told me, "he saved her. Can you imagine such a moron? To save her just so that a few days later she could be dragged to the Umschlagplatz. . . ."

—When the liquidation action started and they were gathering up people from the first floor of our hospital, one woman upstairs was in labor. A doctor and a nurse were with her. And when the baby was born, the doctor handed it to the nurse, and the nurse laid it on one pillow, and smothered it with another one. The baby whimpered for a while and then grew silent.

This woman was nineteen years old. The doctor didn't say a thing to her. Not a word. And this woman knew herself what she was supposed to do.

I'm glad that you haven't asked me today, "And did this woman survive?" the way you asked about the doctor who gave cyanide to the children.

Yes, she did survive. She is a very famous pediatrician.

—So what happened to Mrs. Tenenbaum's daughter?

—Nothing; she also died. But before that she had a few really good months: she was in love with a guy, and in his presence she was always serene, smiling. She had some really good months.

177

That French guy from *L'Express* asked me whether people in the Ghetto fell in love. Well . . .

—Excuse me. Did you also get a ticket?

—Yes. I was standing in the fifteenth row of five, in the same column in which Frania and Mrs. Tenenbaum's daughter were already standing, and I noticed a friend of mine and her brother. So I quickly pulled them into the column. Only, other people had been doing the same thing, so that in our crowd there were already not forty thousand but forty-four thousand people.

Therefore the Germans simply counted out the people and sent the last four thousand to the Umschlagplatz. Somehow I managed to squeeze in with the first forty thousand.

—So this French guy was asking you . . .

—. . . whether people fell in love. Well, to be with someone was the only way to survive in the Ghetto. One would secret oneself somewhere with the other person—in a bed, in a basement, anywhere—and until the next action one was not alone anymore.

One person had had his mother taken away, somebody else's father had been shot and killed, or a sister taken away in a shipment. So if someone, somehow, by some miracle escaped and was still alive, he had to stick to some other living human being.

People were drawn to one another as never before, as never in normal life. During the last liquidation action they would run to the Jewish Council in search of a rabbi or anybody who could marry them, and then they would go to the Umschlagplatz as a married couple.

Tosia's niece went with her boyfriend to Pawia Street—at 1 Pawia Street lived some rabbi who married them—and immediately after that wedding, some Ukrainians arrived and wanted to take her away. One of them put the barrel of his rifle up against her belly. So he, her husband, pushed that barrel away, covering her belly with his hand. She, by the way, ended up going to the Umschlagplatz anyway, and he, with a blown hand, managed to run away to the Aryan side and later died in the 1944 Warsaw uprising.

But this was precisely what mattered: that there be someone ready to cover your belly with his hand should that prove necessary.

—When the whole operation started, the Umschlagplatz and all that, did you—you and your friends—immediately understand what it meant?

—Oh, yes. On July 22, 1942, an ordinance about "relocation of the population to the East" was posted all over the Ghetto, and that very night we were pasting pieces of paper over the ordinance: "Relocation means Death."

The next day, prisoners from jail and old people were taken to the Umschlagplatz. It took the whole day because there were six thousand prisoners to be transported. People were standing along sidewalks, looking—and you know, it was completely silent. It all happened in such an eerie silence . . .

Later, there were no more prisoners and no more old people, and no more beggars, and it was still necessary to deliver ten thousand people a day to the Umschlagplatz. The Jewish police were supposed to accomplish this under German supervision. The Germans would say: things will be quiet and nobody will be shot so long as every day, by 4 P.M., you deliver ten thousand people to the trains. (Because at four the transport was scheduled to leave.) So people were told: "We have to deliver ten thousand, the rest will survive." And the Jewish police would gather up the people themselves: first in the street, then they would circle a house, pull people from apartments . . .

179

We later executed some of those policemen. The police commander, Szerynski, Lejkin, a few more.

The second day of the action, on July 23rd, representatives of all the political parties gathered and for the first time they discussed armed resistance. Everybody was already determined and the question was only how to get arms, but after a few hours someone came in and announced that the action had been interrupted and that there would be no more relocations. Not everyone believed this, but the news immediately calmed the atmosphere down and no decisions were made.

And actually, the majority of people still didn't believe that it meant death. "Is it conceivable that they would kill a *whole* nation?" they would ask themselves, and this would reassure them. It is necessary to deliver those ten thousand to the square, in order to save the rest . . .

In the evening of the first day of the action, Czerniakow, the community council chairman, committed suicide. It was the only rainy day. Except for this one day, during the entire action, it was sunny every day. The day Czerniakow died, the setting sun was red and we were sure that it would rain the next day, but it turned out sunny.

—What did you need rain for?

—For nothing. I am just telling you how it was.

As far as Czerniakow goes, we were resentful. We thought that he shouldn't have . . .

—I know, we have spoken about that already.

—Oh, yes?

You know, Hanna, after the war was over someone told me that Lejkin, this policeman we killed in the Ghetto, at that time, after seventeen years of marriage, had had his first child, and he'd thought that he might save that child's life with that cleverness of his.

—Do you want to tell me anything more about the action?

—No. The action was over.
I was alive.

It so happened that all of them—Mr. Rudny, Mrs. Bubner, and Mr. Wilczkowski, the well-known Alpinist—had their heart attacks on Friday during the day or at night, and Saturday was for each of them a day when they suddenly had no more errands to run. Saturday found each of them lying immobile, under a Xylocaine drip, thinking.

Engineer Wilczkowski, for example, was thinking about the mountains, more precisely, about a specific mountain peak goldened by sunshine (this is how he expressed it, poetically), atop which he was sitting and unfurling rope—not any of the mountaintops in the Alps or in Ethiopia, not even one in the Himalayas, but rather a peak in the Polish Tatra mountains, Mieguszowiecki, or perhaps Zabi Mnich, where one September he had accomplished a very pretty climb up the west face. Mr. Rudny (first vein transplant in acute state) for his part was envisioning machinery, all modern, of course, imported, British or Swiss, and all of it in working order because no parts were missing. Mrs. Bubner, on the other hand (reversed blood circulation), had before her eyes an injection molding machine. Her employee was using it to manufacture plastic parts, but later it was she herself who would put them into boiling paint because this was the most responsible part of the work. Later still, she would assemble the whole ballpoint pen (obviously, she had a certificate from Customs for the Swiss end pieces she had managed to get through private channels), slap on a label, and put the whole pen into a box.

This was what Dr. Edelman's patients were thinking about, lying under the Xylocaine drip.

Under the drip, one usually ends up thinking about the most important things.

For the head doctor, Mrs. Heller, the most important thing had been who deserved the life ticket. And for Mr. Rudny, the most important thing was the spare parts for the machines. If Mrs. Heller gave the ticket to Mr. Rudny, it would have been a ticket for machines, because they are Mr. Rudny's life, as Mrs. Bubner's life is ballpoint pens, and Mr. Wilczkowski's mountain peaks.

As far as Mr. Rzewuski is concerned, he wasn't thinking at all.

If Mr. Rzewuski, like Mrs. Bubner or Mr. Rudny, had been thinking about the best thing in his life, he would doubtlessly have been thinking of a factory that was turned over to him when he was twenty-eight years old and taken away from him when he was forty-three. He would have been sensing a metallic smell and hearing someone coming in with a blueprint and he would know that something was just being created, something was going to be possible to look at, possible to check on, to measure, and he would be feeling impatient, watching as the metal was being shaped, because he so much wanted already to be able to touch the prototype he had seen moments earlier in the drawing. . . .

("The factory," Mr. Rzewuski once said, "was for me the same as the Ghetto was for Doctor Edelman: the most important thing that happened in my life. Activity. A chance to test oneself. *A truly macho adventure.*")

Mr. Rzewuski would have certainly been thinking about all that as he lay under the i.v. drip, if he thought about anything at all. But, as I have said, he was not thinking about anything while the Professor was still sitting in his office, sunk in thought, and the anesthesiologist was already busying himself around his body, nor a few hours later, when the Professor and Edelman and Dr. Chetkowska looked on gladly as the blinking light traversed the screen of the monitor. All that time he'd been experiencing only one sensation—pain—and nothing could have been more important than easing that pain, if only for a moment.

It was the first attempt through the middle of western approaches and probably it was not September after all; in any case, it was very sunny there during the climb. Later, looking down from above, they saw the Morskie Oko lake, and in the background, the jagged world and the Babia Gora mountain. The Englishman Mallory, when asked why he was trying to climb Mount Everest, replied: *because it is there.* Because it is there. That golden peak remained far away throughout the day all Saturday (prednisone was added to the Xylocaine), he was scaling it, he could see it very clearly but was unable to approach it even by a single millimeter, and he suddenly realized that he would never make it to that sunny place.

He started thinking about his chances. He hadn't had an accident so far in the mountains, but this did not calm him down, because someone could always cross the line of his destiny. After all, there are hobgoblins who bring bad luck to mountain people. Before his group's expedition to Ethiopia, their hobgoblin (it only turned out later that he was a hobgoblin) had been assigned luggage container number eight, which he did not want to carry; somebody else took it. There were eight men, they departed on the eighth, and the man who took container number eight slipped off the moving truck's canvas, something no one was ever able to understand since they had all been sleeping on that canvas tied down with ropes. On Deyrenfurth's expedition to Mount Everest a Hindu died of exhaustion and the hobgoblin was the last person who saw him, and that Hindu, by the way, had been wearing the hobgoblin's parka. The whole night from Saturday to Sunday, Wilczkowski was thinking about his own place, and even though he was doing his best to think absolutely objectively, he arrived at a conclusion that his co-ordinate did not cross anything suspicious, which reassured him a lot.

The four reels in the British machine should be adjusted in such a way that they all are synchronized, so that there isn't any stress and the material doesn't snap. One adjusts them through a sort of box that includes a lock ring around a conical disk, and when the material on the reels—be it ribbon, or elastic, or some other sort of strap—has achieved the requisite humidity and speed, and all the reels are perfectly synchronized one to the next, *that* is a wonderful moment, because one knows one has achieved total mastery over the entire machine.

The machines were then oiled, the cylinders he'd managed to adjust perfectly were swinging rhythmically, and Mr. Rudny could spend a few moments daydreaming about his little lot, how it was going to be necessary to dig it up, and how actually it might not be bad to build some sort of bower there.

His wife said that who knows, maybe they should build a little house there, you know, a summer cabin—everybody is having such cabins built nowadays.

His wife used to tell him that, so far, anyway, they had always managed to achieve everything they'd most wanted in their lives: he had filled their apartment with that highly fashionable, light-colored furniture—only the cabinet's doors were lacquered black—they had gotten the coupon for a washing machine without having to wait at all, they were managing a family vacation every year, and it had never ever happened that they'd sold out the boneless veal before they reached her turn at the store. So certainly, if they only busied themselves a bit, they were going to be able to have this cabin—his wife used to talk like that. Until she saw him that day from a distance through the half-open door of the intensive care unit, she'd imagined that they'd managed to put together everything that really matters in a person's life.

Ballpoint pens could be sold only through bookstores. Newsstands and stationery shops were not allowed to take merchandise from small private factories like hers, so she was totally dependent on the bookstores. A bookstore's manager could take a thousand or two at a pop, and Mrs. Bubner had to do everything to avoid having her merchandise remain unsold.

She had her heart attack just after she came home from the trial (she received a one-year sentence, suspended to three years' probation). During the trial it turned out that the rate had been standardized: all the makers of ballpoint pens bribed the bookstore managers exactly 6 percent, that is, between ten and twenty thousand zlotys for each consignment.

In the court it also turned out that it wasn't just the ones who gave the bribes who had heart problems. Those who served as intermediaries were in even worse shape: one of the intermediaries had to take nitroglycerin every once in a while, and the woman judge would order a short recess each time: "Just a second," she would say. "Let's wait for the nitroglycerin to dissolve; and please, don't be so anxious."

In the worst shape of all, however, were those who *accepted* the bribes: the bookstore managers themselves. One had already had a heart attack, and the court doctor authorized him to testify for only one hour, so that the woman judge had to look at her watch all the while, and after exactly one hour she would order a recess. In fairness, it should be stressed that this judge had a really good and understanding attitude toward all those suffering from heart disorders: manufacturers, intermediaries, and bookstore managers.

As far as she, Mrs. Bubner, was concerned, during the trial she had not yet required medical care. She had her heart attack only after the trial, at her home, and she'd even managed to rise from her stretcher and ask her neighbor to put her dachshund to sleep with the best shot available.

"Doctor Edelman approached me later and said, 'You have to have the operation, Mrs. Bubner.' So I started crying, and at first I said, 'No.' He said, 'Believe me, Mrs. Bubner, you really should agree to it.' "

(Because Mrs. Bubner's case was precisely an anterior myocardial infarction with left anterior hemiblock—the kind with which people grow more and more silent and quiescent because everything inside them is slowly, gradually dying. And Mrs. Bubner was the fourteenth person, when the Professor no longer asked, "What actually do you want from me?" and only said, "All right, we'll try." And so Dr. Edelman was saying, "You really should agree, Mrs. Bubner, believe me. . . .")

". . . and it occurred to me at that moment how my late husband had been such a good, religious man. He used to say, 'Well, Mania, but God *does* exist.' He was very active in the Jewish community. After meetings in the Guild he would never go to Malinowa Restaurant with the others; instead he'd come directly home. And if I sometimes wanted to have a drink with some of the other people, he would say, 'All right, Mania, only give me your purse, so that you don't lose it.' So if a man like this requests something of his God, surely this God would not refuse him. Even while I was in Mostowski Jail for a month, before the trial, I remained calm, for I knew that the door would eventually open up because it was impossible that my late husband wouldn't arrange it for me. And guess what, Mrs. Krall? He did, didn't he? A bookkeeper from the Guild came and paid my bail and I was allowed conditional freedom until the trial.

"So that time I also ended up saying, 'Don't worry, Doctor, you'll see, he is going to arrange everything just right.' "

(Soon after she'd spoken those words, the Professor was taking up the main vein in Mrs. Bubner's heart in order to block the blood flow and redirect the arterial blood into the veins, and as it turned out, to everyone's happiness, that blood somehow was finding its confluence. . . .)

Before they brought in the new, imported machines, they had sent Mr. Rudny to England, to Newcastle, for training. Mr. Rudny noticed there that far fewer mistakes had to be ferreted out by the English quality-control people than by the ones in his factory and that in England it simply never happened that a machine had to be stopped for lack of a spare part.

When he returned to Lodz he would dream of attaining the same efficiency as the machines in Newcastle. Unfortunately, one could fret oneself to one's very limits and still not be able to find the various required parts, there was still all sorts of waste, and on top of everything, he couldn't find a common language with the young workers.

The head of the factory says that in the old days the loyalty toward one's boss was different because it was difficult to find jobs. Today, workers' kids go to college; this is all to the good, it's only that later there are no people left to work in the factories and whenever a new person does come to work, especially those with vocational training, he immediately becomes all fresh and everything because he well understands his position.

So when Mr. Rudny came back from the hospital after the operation (it was that intervention in acute state when for a while the question had been who was going to get there first: the heart attack or the doctors, the doctors or God—it was that intervention before which the Professor had tried to leave the clinic and not come back; but he had come back, that very day, late in the afternoon; and, as a matter of fact, the Professor was not the only one who'd left. Edelman had also left, even though he had insisted so strongly that they perform that operation; he'd said: "I'm going to go and think," because he also knew of books where it was said that such interventions should not be performed; he'd come back after a couple of hours, and then it had been Elzbieta Chetkowska who was yelling, "Where did you go? Don't you know that every minute counts?!")—when Mr. Rudny came back to the factory after that operation that had been covered all over in the press, he was immediately transferred to a quieter department. In particular, they had looked for a place without imported machines with their impossible-to-find spare parts and young, highly trained workers, so they'd moved him over to the oil department. "Mr. Rudny's health, and nothing but his health, was the reason for this transfer," the manager points out, "and not, as Mr. Rudny falsely believes, the fact that he'd gone to the safety-control board and told them that Mr. Nowak, who had been on sick leave for ten days, wasn't just sick, but that he had had a work-related accident. It is very embarrassing for the factory when a work-related accident only gets reported after a ten-day delay like that, but, as I have said, that wasn't the case here and this was not the reason we gave Mr. Rudny the quieter job."

At his new workplace, Mr. Rudny was checking up on the greases. What kind of work was that! Look at a machine, write a report, that's all. Mr. Rudny understood very well that it was important, responsible work, because as long as a high-speed machine is well oiled it will work for many years, but there were no immediate rewards with such work.

The manager does not understand what I am getting at with all my interest in Mr. Rudny's health.

Perhaps I think that the factory was responsible for Mr. Rudny's illness? I don't think so at all. The manager adds that after each trip to a cooperating factory, where he has to beg for spare parts and a higher quality of thread, his own stomach ulcer acts up all over again. And the chief mechanic, Mr. Rudny's immediate boss (spare parts not for a few machines but for the whole factory!), has already twice been taken to a hospital on the very verge of a heart attack, and if I want, he'll measure his own blood pressure right then and there, it's the end of the trimester and he's certain it won't be less than 180/110.

All three of them, Mrs. Bubner, the engineer Wilczkowski, and Mr. Rudny, had all kinds of time to think those Saturdays. And what each of them was thinking was how they sure didn't want another heart attack.

One can resolve not to have another heart attack; in the same way, by choosing a certain life-style, one can accept the good possibility of a heart attack.

Therefore, upon returning home, Mrs. Bubner closed down her shop. It is obligatory to save all the documentation for five years and she still has her ballpoint pens, one from each model. From time to time, she takes them out, cleans them, and examines them—shiny, four colors each, with labels and invoice included. And then she puts them back into the box, stores them away, and slowly goes out for a walk.

Mr. Rudny, on the other hand, who recently has been transferred back to his old department because some imported machines have again arrived (this time from Switzerland), says to himself: "Calmly. Calmly. Even if there is a part missing, I do not have to try to revive an old one or to twist my neck in order to make a new one myself. If there is a part missing, all I'm supposed to do is to file a formal order, and everything'll be okay."

And indeed: he files a written order, and everything is okay.

And if sometimes he breaks his word to himself, it really is just for a moment. And if he feels pain coming on in his breastbone area, he goes to a doctor, hears the advice—"Mr. Rudny, you should enjoy your life and not worry so much about machines"—and returns to filing his orders once again.

He doesn't feel pain anymore and he comes to the hospital only for social reasons, as a guest. On June 5th, the anniversary of his operation, he brings three bunches of flowers. He hands one to the Professor, the other one to Dr. Edelman, and he takes the third one to Dr. Chetkowska and puts it on her grave in the Radogoszcz Cemetery.

Ihe action was over and you were alive . . .

—There were sixty thousand Jews left in the Ghetto. Those who'd managed to survive now understood everything: just what "relocation" meant and that it was impossible to wait any longer. We decided to create one military organization for the whole Ghetto, which was not simple because we didn't have confidence in each other, we in the Zionists or they in us, but at that point, of course, it didn't matter anymore. We created one organization: the Jewish Combat Organization.

There were five hundred of us. In January there was another action and there were only eighty people left. During that January action, for the first time, some people were refusing to go to their deaths voluntarily. We shot and killed a few Germans on Muranowska, Franciszkanska, Mila, and Zamenhofa streets. Those were the first shots in the Ghetto, and they made a big impression on the Aryan side: this was before the big armed operations of the Polish resistance movement. Wladyslaw Szlengel, a poet who continued to compose poetry in the Ghetto in which he expressed his revulsion at the prospect of submissive acquiescence in one's own death, managed to write a poem about those shots. It was called "Counterattack":

... *Do you hear, oh German God,*
*the Jews praying in their wild houses,*
*grasping crowbars and wrenched-out stakes in their hands?*
*We beseech you, God, for bloody struggle,*
*we beg you for a sudden death.*
*Let our eyes before their dimming*
*not be forced to gaze upon slowly moving rails,*
*but Lord, give our hands precision. ...*
*Like the scarlet, blood-red flowers*
*on Niska and Mila streets, in Muranow*
*the fire blossoms from our barrels.*
*This is our spring, this, our counterattack,*
*this, the wine of battle gone to our heads,*
*this is* our *partisan forest—*
*the back alleys of Dzika and Ostrowska. ...*

For the sake of exactitude I'll tell you that those "our barrels" from which the fire blossomed—at that time there were ten of them in the Ghetto. We'd gotten those guns from the Popular Army.*

Anielewicz's group, which was taken to the Umschlagplatz and did not have arms, started hitting the Germans with bare fists. The group of Pelc, the eighteen-year-old printer, when taken to the square, refused to board the train, and van

---

*Popular Army (AL), one of the independent clandestine armed organizations operating in Poland during the war; this one was affiliated with the Moscow-oriented Communist party.

Oeppen, the commander of the Treblinka camp, shot all of them, sixty men, on the spot. I remember, the Kosciuszko radio station then started broadcasting appeals encouraging people to struggle. Some woman kept shouting "To arms, to arms" with a sound-effects background imitating the jangle of weapons. We were wondering what they were using to make that sound, because as far as we were concerned, we had sixty guns at that point, from the Polish Workers' Party and from the Home Army, and that was all the guns there were.

—And you know who it was that was shouting? Rysia Hanin.

At the radio station in Kuybishev at that time she read the communiqués, poems, and appeals. She told me that it couldn't be ruled out that it was she who was encouraging you to struggle. . . . But they did not use weapons to jangle. Rysia Hanin says that over the radio nothing sounds as false as authentic sounds. . . .

—One day Anielewicz wanted to get one more gun. He killed a *werkschutz*, a German paramilitary guard, on Mila Street, and the same day in the afternoon the Germans came and as revenge pulled out every single person from the block of Zamenhofa between Mila Street and Muranowski Square, several hundred of them. We were furious at him. We even wanted to . . . Well, it doesn't matter.

In the house where they started taking people away, at the corner of Mila and Zamenhofa streets, lived my friend Hennoch Rus. (He was the one who'd prevailed in the decision about creating one armed organization in the Ghetto: the discussion had been going on for many hours and there had been several votes, but it was impossible to decide anything because each time there were the same number of votes in favor as against. In the end, it was finally Hennoch who changed his mind and raised his hand, the decision about creating the Jewish Combat Organization thereby being made.)

Hennoch Rus had had a little son. At the beginning of the war the boy got sick and a transfusion proved necessary, so I gave him some of my blood, but immediately after the transfusion, the kid died. It was probably because of the shock caused by the transfusion; it happens sometimes. Hennoch didn't say anything, but from that moment on he tended to steer clear of me: after all, it had been my blood that killed his child. Only, once the action started, he said to me: "Thanks to you my son died at home, like a human being. I am grateful to you."

We were accumulating weapons then.

We would smuggle them from the Aryan side (we were forcefully taking money from various institutions and private people); we also published newspapers, and our liaison girls took them all over Poland . . .

—How much did you have to pay for a revolver?

—Between three and fifteen thousand. The closer to April, the greater the cost: market demand was growing ever larger.

—And how much did you have to pay for hiding a Jew on the Aryan side?

—Two, five thousand. Different prices. It depended on whether the person looked Jewish, whether they had an accent, whether it was a man or a woman.

—That means that for the price of a single gun it would have been possible to hide one person for a month. Or perhaps two people, maybe even three.

—It was also possible with a gun to ransom a Jew from a *szmalcownik*.*

*Szmalcownik*—a dark new "profession" that came into being during the war in Poland in which people would blackmail hiding Jews or the Poles who were helping to hide them—agreeing not to turn them in to the Gestapo for a fee.

—If you were then faced with a choice—one revolver or a single person's life for a month . . .

—We weren't ever faced with that kind of choice. Perhaps it's better that we weren't.

—Your courier girls took the newspapers all over Poland . . .

—One of them would smuggle them over to the Piotrkow Ghetto. In the Piotrkow Ghetto our people were in the community council, so there was an unusual degree of order there: there were no swindles, and the food and work were divided fairly. But we were very young and rigid in those days, and we believed that one shouldn't work in any of the community councils because that constituted collaboration with the enemy. So we ordered them to abandon that place, and a few of the people turned up in Warsaw, where it proved necessary to hide them because the Germans were out searching for all those council members from Piotrkow. I was supposed to take care of the Kellerman family. Two days before the conclusion of the liquidation action, as they were leading us from the Umschlagplatz to get the tickets, I saw Mr. Kellerman. He was standing behind the hospital door—it used to be a glass door, but the glass had been broken and the door had been covered over with wooden planks—and through a slit between these planks I saw his face. I signaled with my hand that I'd noticed him and would come back to get him—and then they took us away. I came back a couple of hours later, but nobody was behind that door any longer.

You know, I saw so many people dragged through the Umschlagplatz, both before that incident and after, but it's only toward those two that I would like to be able to explain myself—because I was supposed to take care of them, I told them I'd come back, right up till the last moment they must have been waiting for me, and I came too late.

—What about the liaison girl who used to travel to Piotr-kow?

—Oh, nothing. Once, on her way back, some Ukrainians caught her and were about to kill her, but our people some-how managed to pass them some money; the Ukrainians put her at the edge of a grave and shot her with blanks, she pretended to fall, and later she resumed carrying those news-papers.

We printed those newspapers on a duplicator. The machine was on Walowa Street, and one day we had to move it. On our way we met up with some Jewish policemen. We were carrying the machine, and they surrounded us and were about to cart us off to the Umschlagplatz. Their boss was a certain attorney who previously had been behaving impeccably, hadn't beaten anybody, and would feign that he didn't notice when people were escaping. Well, in this case we somehow managed to wrench ourselves free, and afterward I said to my friends, "Look, what a pig, after all." They excused it, explaining to me that he had probably been broken, that anyway this was probably the end both for us and for him. Later on, Maslanko said the same thing when the three of us were heading to West Germany to testify as witnesses. After the war I hadn't said a word to that attorney, but Maslanko said (we were having some drinks in that train): "What sense does it make to remember all that today?"

In fact. What sense—to remember?

A few days after the killing of the *werkschutz* and the massacre, in April, we were walking down the street—Antek, Anielewicz, and myself—and all of a sudden we came upon some of our own people in Muranowski Square. It was warm, a sunny day, and these folks had crawled out of their base-ments to be in the sun. "God," I said, "how can they possibly have come up? What are they doing that for?" And Antek, referring to me, muttered, "How much he must hate them, he would rather they stayed down there in the darkness. . . ." Because, as far as I was concerned, people were only supposed to come out during the night. If they came out in daylight, when they could be seen, it meant that they could die at any moment.

Antek, I remember, was the first one to predict during a meeting of the Command Group that the Germans would set the Ghetto on fire. When we were still pondering what to do, what kind of death to choose—whether to hurl ourselves at the walls, or to let ourselves be killed on the Citadel, or to set the Ghetto on fire and all of us burn together—Antek said, "What if they set the fire themselves?" We all said, "Don't talk nonsense. They wouldn't want to burn the whole town down." But on the second day of the uprising, they did indeed set a fire. We were in a shelter at that moment, and suddenly somebody burst in, desperately shouting that the place was on fire. Panic broke out. "That's it, the end, we're lost!" And that was the point where I had to slap this guy's face to calm him down.

We went out to the backyard, and they had indeed set fires all over, but luckily the central Ghetto wasn't burning yet, only our area, the Brush Factory, so I announced that we would have to break through the fire. Ania, that friend of Adam's who had managed to escape from Pawiak Prison, said she wasn't going to come because she had to stay with her mother. So we left her and scrambled across the backyard. Somehow we managed to reach the wall along Franciszkanska Street, where there was a breach in the wall, but it was lit up by a searchlight. People began to get hysterical all over again, how they couldn't possibly continue through there, how in that light we'd just get picked off one by one. And I said: "Suit yourselves, but then you're on your own." And they did stay behind, some six of them. Zygmunt provided cover, shooting at the searchlight with the only rifle we had, and we managed somehow to tear through. (Zygmunt was the guy who'd said that I would survive and he wouldn't and that I was supposed to find his daughter in Zamosc.)

You like this number with the searchlight, don't you? Better style than dying in a basement. One has more dignity leaping over a wall than suffocating to death in the dark, right?

—Sure.

—Then I can offer you something else in that style. Before the uprising, when the action in the little ghetto had just started, someone told me that they had taken Abrasza Blum away. He was an exceptionally thoughtful and wise man, our leader from before the war, so I went to see if I could find out what had happened with him.

I saw people arranged in ranks of four along Ciepla Street, and along both sides, every five, ten lines, there were Ukrainians. The street was cordoned off. I had to get in deeper, to see if I could spot Blum, but it was dangerous to walk behind the back of the Ukrainians or through the area where the crowd was standing because they might have raked me in as well. So I decided to walk between the Ukrainians and the crowd, so that everybody would see me. I walked real fast, very purposefully, as if I were simply entitled to be walking there. And you know what? Nobody even stopped me.

—I get the feeling that you yourself like stories of this kind—about fast, purposeful walks or shooting at searchlights—that you like them better than talking about basements.

—No.

—I think you do.

—Actually, I told you the story about the Ukrainians for quite a different reason. Because when I came back home that evening, there was Stasia, this girl with the long, thick braids, crying. "What are you crying about?" I asked her. "Because I thought they had taken you away."

That's all.

Everybody'd been busy with all their various important businesses, and Stasia had spent the whole day waiting for me to come back.

—We seemed to have dropped a stitch with that story about the searchlight. Although, to be honest, I am not at all sure that there is any particular thread to these conversations.

—Is that so bad?

—Of course not. We are not writing history, after all. We are writing about remembering. But let's get back to this searchlight: Zygmunt shot it out, you guys ran quickly. . . . Wait, what happened with Zygmunt's child in the convent at Zamosc?

—With Elzunia? I found her as soon as the war was over.

—Where is she now?

—She isn't anymore. She went to America. Some rich people adopted her and loved her a lot. She was beautiful and wise. And later she committed suicide.

—Why?

—I don't know. When I was in America, I went to see these parents. They showed me her bedroom. They hadn't changed a thing there since her death. But I still don't know why she did it.

—All the stories you tell, almost all of them, end with death.

—Really? That's because we're talking about *those* stories; that's the kind of story they are. The ones I tell about my patients end with life, after all.

—Zygmunt, Elzunia's father, shot the searchlight . . .

—. . . we jumped over the wall and ran into the central ghetto, Franciszkanska Street. And there, in the courtyard, were Blum (who, as it turned out, had not been taken away in that action after all) and Gepner.* The guy from whose suitcase I'd looted the red sweater. The one with the real, fluffy wool, that beautiful sweater . . .

—I know. Tosia recently sent you another one from Australia just exactly like it. And I have read a poem about Gepner: "Canto About an Iron Merchant, Abram Gepner." It says, among other things, that his friends on the Aryan side had implored him to get out, but he refused and stayed in the Ghetto till the end. Have you noticed how often in these stories that theme recurs: a chance to get out and the decision to stay? Korczak, Gepner, you guys . . . Maybe it's because making this decision between life and death afforded the last chance at preserving one's dignity. . . .

—Blum told us (in this courtyard in Franciszkanska Street) that there had been an assault by a group from the Home Army against the wall along Franciszkanska Street but that they'd failed and that Anielewicz was now a broken man, that there were no more arms, and that we couldn't count on getting any more. . . . I said, "All right, all right, let's not stand around here like this." And they asked, "Well, where shall we go, then?" There were more than thirty of us, and Gepner and Blum, and everybody was waiting for some kind of orders, and I didn't have a clue myself where to go.

For the time being, we went back down into the basements. And in the evening Adam said that he wanted to go back and get Ania. He asked me to give him a group of people; I asked if anyone wanted to go, and two or three people volunteered. They went there and later came back to say that that shelter with Ania and her mother had already been buried and that

*Gepner, the rich Jew of the first anecdote in this narrative, had somehow escaped after he and his family had been hauled out of their basement, so that he resurfaces here.

those six guys who hadn't wanted to come along with us at the searchlight were also dead.

Perhaps you want to ask me whether I have a guilty conscience over how I left them behind?

—I don't want to.

—No, I don't feel guilty, no. But I do feel sorry about it all the time.

And the next day we joined up with everybody: Anielewicz, Celina, Jurek Wilner. We got to their bunker. Those girls, these two prostitutes, prepared something for us to eat and Guta handed out cigarettes. It was a good, quiet day.

What do you think, can one tell the people about things like that?

—What do you mean?

—About those guys I left in the backyard?

Should a doctor tell people about such things? After all, in medicine, every life, every chance, even the smallest chance at saving life, counts.

—Maybe instead we should talk about the searchlight, about leaping over the wall, that sort of thing?

—But everything alternates, you see. You run somewhere, then someone gets killed, then you run again, then Adam sticks his head out of the basement and a grenade begins to roll along the molding, and I yell "Adam, a grenade!" and the grenade explodes right on top of his head. Then I jump out of the basement, there are some Germans in the backyard but I have these two guns, you know, the ones with the two crisscrossing belts, I shoot . . .

—And you manage to hit with both of them?

—Of course not, I don't hit with either of them, but I do manage to get to the building, and the soldiers come running after me, so I run onto the roof—is this the right kind of story?

—Excellent. First rate.

—Do you think it is prettier to run along a roof than to sit in a basement?

—I prefer it when you're running along the roofs.

—I didn't see any difference then. But I saw it later, in the general Warsaw uprising, in 1944, when everything was already happening during the day, in sunlight, in open spaces without walls. We were able to attack, to withdraw, to run. The Germans were shooting, but I was shooting, too, I had my own rifle, a white-and-red armband, there were other people around with white-and-red armbands—lots of people—listen, what a terrific, congenial fight that was!

—Shall we get back to the roof?

—I ran on the roof over to another building. All that in this red sweater, and a red sweater like that on a roof makes an excellent target. But it was difficult to shoot into the sun, so that I was hard to hit. In this other building there turned out to be a young guy lying on a big sack of biscuits.

I stopped and hid alongside this guy. He gave me one biscuit, then another one, but then he didn't want to give me anymore. It was noon. By about 6 P.M. the guy had died, and I had the sackful of biscuits all to myself. Unfortunately, it is difficult to jump with a sack, and I later had to jump again. When I eventually got out to the backyard, there were five of our boys lying there killed. One of them was named Stasiek. That very morning he had asked me for an address on the other side, and I'd told him, "Not yet, it's too early." And he'd been saying: "But this *is* the end, give me that address, please." And I didn't have any address. A moment later he'd jumped out into the backyard, and now I'd found him again.

It was necessary to bury these guys.

We dug the grave in the courtyard at 30 Franciszkanska Street. It is a tremendous job to dig a grave for five people. We buried them and, since it was May 1st, we sang over their grave in very low voices the first verse of "The Internationale." Can you believe that? One had to be totally out of one's mind to sing in a courtyard on Franciszkanska Street.

Later, we managed to get some sugar and we were drinking sweet water. At that point I happened to have a small rebellion in my group. These rebels thought that I was being unfair with them, not giving them enough weapons, so they organized a hunger strike against me: they refused to drink this water.

You know what the worst part of it was?

How more and more people were waiting for me to order them what to do next.

—How did the strike end? (A hunger strike in the Ghetto, good God!)

—As usual with such things: they were forced to drink that water. Don't you know how you force people to do things during a war?

So more and more people, older than me and more experienced, were asking me what to do and I didn't have a clue myself. I felt absolutely alone.

That entire day as I'd lain there next to that guy who was dying on his biscuits, this had been the only thing on my mind.

On May 6th, Anielewicz and Mira came to us. We were supposed to have some kind of meeting, but actually there was nothing to talk about anymore, so he went to sleep. And so did I. The next morning I said, "Stay with us. What are you going back for?" But he wanted to go. We saw them off and the day after that, the eighth, we went to their bunker at 18 Mila Street (it was night already), and we shouted—but nobody answered. Finally some guy said: "They don't exist anymore. They all committed suicide." A few people were still left and those two girls, the prostitutes. We took them with us, and the moment we got back to our place it turned out that Kazik from the Aryan side was already there with the sewermen and that we were going to be heading out. (The two girls asked whether they could join us. I said no.) Our guides through the sewers had been sent by Jozwiak— "Witold" from the Polish Workers' Party. They led us through the sewers to a manhole under Prosta Street, where we waited a night, and a day, and then another night, and finally, on May 10th at ten in the morning, the hatch was lifted, a car was waiting with our people and "Krzaczek" who'd been sent by "Witold." A crowd of people was standing around, looking at us with horror. We were dark and dirty, with weapons—there was total silence as we clambered out into the blinding light of May.

Andrzej Wajda would like to make a movie about the Ghetto. He says he would use some footage from the archives and have Edelman tell the whole story in front of the camera.

He would be speaking at the places where the events he was describing had actually taken place.

For instance, next to the bunker at 18 Mila Street (today snow lay there and little boys were sledding).

Or at the entrance to the Umschlagplatz, next to the gate.

The gate, by the way, does not exist anymore. The old wall collapsed while the Inflancka housing project was under construction. Now several tall gray buildings rise there—exactly along what used to be the loading platform. My friend Anna Stronska lives in one of those buildings. I tell her how just outside her kitchen window the last cars of the train once stood, because the engine car was just over there by the poplars. Stronska, who has a heart problem, grows pale.

"Listen," she says. "I was always good to them. The ghosts wouldn't harm me, would they?"

"Of course not," I say. "They'll only protect you, you'll see."

"You think so?" asks Stronska, and she relaxes a bit.

So when they were tidying up after the construction, the old wall collapsed, but a new one, made of healthy white bricks, was quickly erected in the very same place. Commemorative plaques and candle holders were slotted in, and little green flower boxes were hung, and grass was planted all around, and very soon everything was tidy, neat, and new.

Or, for instance, Wajda might use the monument.

On April 19th, the day of the anniversary, the Orbis state tourist buses would arrive as usual with their foreign guests, and ladies in spring suits and men with cameras would get off these buses. All over the park, old women sitting with baby carriages would stare at the buses and the delegations from factories ready to lay wreaths. "In our basement," one of the women would say, "one of them was hiding under the coal and it was necessary to pass her food through a little window from the street." (It might also happen that the one to whom they had been passing the food would be standing now in a spring suit, brought by a tour bus.) Later, there would be the sound of drums, and the delegations with wreaths would move on; after the delegations some private people would start to approach, with little bunches of flowers in their hands or with one yellow jonquil, and after everything, after the snare drums and the flowers, an old man with a white beard would emerge suddenly from the crowd and would start reciting the Kaddish. He would stand at the foot of the monument, below the burning torches, and with a breaking voice he would start to chant his plaintive prayer. For six million dead. Such a lonely old man, in a long black coat.

The crowd would mingle. "Marek," someone would shout, "how are you?!" "Marysia, you always look so young," he would declare happily, because it would be Marysia Sawicka, the same girl who before the war used to run the eight hundred meters at the Skra sports club along with Michal Klepfisz's sister, and who later hid this sister-runner at her place, along with Michal's wife, and his daughter. . . .

The daughter and the wife survived, and Michal, who stayed behind at Bonifraterska Street, in that attic where he covered a machine gun with his body so that the others could pass—he has a symbolic grave in the Jewish cemetery with an inscription that reads:

ENGINEER MICHAL KLEPFISZ
4/17/1913–4/20/1943

That would probably be the next place for Wajda to train his cameras.

Nearby there is Jurek Blones's grave, his twenty-year-old sister Guta's, and their twelve-year-old brother Lusiek's, and then Fajgele Goldsztajn's (which one was she, Marek does not even remember her face), and Zygmunt Frydrych's, Elzunia's father who'd told him that first day, "You will survive, but remember: in Zamosc, in a convent . . ."

In this case, it's not a symbolic grave:

After that group had escaped through the sewers, they'd been driven to Zielonka, where a hideaway had been prepared for them, but ten minutes later, the Germans had arrived. They were buried in Zielonka, next to a fence, so that it was easy to find their bodies after the war.

Another group lies a few hundred feet farther on, deeper along the path, having been brought there after the war from near the Bug River. After they'd clambered out of the sewers, they were supposed to have headed east to cross the river and join the partisans, but they'd been fired on while still in the middle of the river. (They'd climbed out of the sewers at Prosta Street. The manhole cover suddenly opened, and "Krzaczek" was already yelling "Out! Out!" but eight people were missing. Edelman had ordered those eight to head over to a wider sewer, because having waited throughout a night and day and into another night underneath that closed-off manhole cover, they'd been beginning to asphyxiate and die owing to the water reeking of feces and methane. Now, with the cover up, Edelman ordered someone to call them and bring them back, but nobody moved. Nobody wanted to move away from the outlet, the cover having now been lifted open, all that fresh air and light pouring in; they could already hear the voices of the people who had come to rescue them. Edelman then told Szlamek Szuster to run and fetch the others, and he did. But up there it was "Krzaczek" and Kazik who were in charge of everything, and they were yelling that they had to drive off immediately, that there would be another truck, and despite the fact that Celina pulled out her revolver and shouted "Stop or I'll shoot!" the truck drove off. This emergence from the sewers had been organized by Kazik. He was nineteen years old at the time, and what he accomplished was truly extraordinary, only that now he calls Marek sometimes from a city three thousand kilometers away and says that it was all his fault, because he didn't force "Krzaczek" to wait. To which Edelman answers that that's not true, that Kazik performed marvelously, and that the only one responsible was he himself, since it was he who told the others to move away from the outlet in the first place. At which point Kazik, still from his city three thousand kilometers away, says, "Stop it. After all, it's the Germans who were responsible." And he adds: "Why is it that ever since that time nobody asks me about those who survived? They always ask only about the dead." The manhole cover, which is in Prosta Street, in what is now the Za Zelazna Brama housing project, would also do as a location for Wajda's film.)

At the very end of the cemetery path, where the graves end and some sort of a field begins—a flat field with high grass, spreading out toward Powazkowska Street, right up to the wall—there aren't any plaques at all anymore. Here lie all those who died before the final liquidation of the Ghetto—the ones who starved to death, who died of typhoid or of exhaustion, in the streets, in deserted apartments. Every morning the laborers from the Eternity Company would go out with their pushcarts and collect the bodies, placing them one on top of the next in piles on the carts, and finally they'd cross Okopowa Street, enter the cemetery (which was on the Aryan side), and trudge right this way, along this path, toward that wall.

At first, they buried the corpses alongside the wall, but then, as the influx of the bodies swelled, they gradually overflowed into the interior of the cemetery, until the entire field was filled.

Over the graves of Michal Klepfisz, Abrasza Blum, and the others killed in Zielonka, there stands a monument: an upright man with a rifle in one hand, a grenade upraised in the other one, he has a cartridge pouch sashed about his waist, a bag with maps at his side, and a belt across his chest. None of them had ever looked like this: they didn't have rifles, cartridge pouches, or maps; besides, they were dark and dirty. But in the monument they look the way they were ideally supposed to. On the monument, everything is bright and beautiful.

Next to Abrasza Blum lies his wife, Luba, the one who was the head of the nurses' college in the Ghetto. She got five life tickets for her school, and there were sixty students; so she said: "These should go to the ones with the best grades in nursing"—and she had them answer a single question:

"Describe the appropriate nursing care for a patient during the first days following a heart attack." The five students who answered best got the tickets.

After the war Luba Blum ran an orphanage. Children found in closets, convents, coal trunks, and cemetery vaults were brought to her orphanage. These kids were subsequently shaved bald, dressed in clothes from the United Nations Relief and Rehabilitation Administration, taught to play piano and how they shouldn't smack while eating. One of the girls had been born after her mother was raped by Germans and kids kept calling her "Kraut." Another one was completely bald, because all her hair had fallen out due to lack of vitamins. A third one, who had been hiding out in the countryside, had to be asked several times by her teacher not to keep telling everyone what the peasants would do with her in the attic, since proper little ladies were not supposed to tell such stories in society.

Luba Blum, who in the Ghetto used to make sure that all her students wore the cleanest possible starched bonnets, and in the orphanage used to instruct all her wards that they should politely answer, and in full sentences, all the questions put to them by the visiting gentlemen, questions about how and in what manner their daddies had been killed, because these gentlemen would presently return to America and later on send packages, lots of packages with dresses and halvah— Luba Blum today lies on the main, orderly path. If one diverges slightly into the interior of the cemetery, there is an increasingly dense thicket of twigs, broken columns, overgrown graves, plaques—eighteen hundred . . . nineteen hundred thirty . . . citizen of Praga . . . doctor at law . . . the bereaved—traces of a world that must actually have existed once upon a time.

Along a side path, "Engineer Adam Czerniakow, Chairman of the Warsaw Ghetto, died on July 23, 1942," and a fragment of Norwid's poem on Mickiewicz's death: "So that it little matters in what urn you rest, / Because they will open your grave again someday, /And assess your merits differently." ("This is the only thing we reproach him for: that he made his death his own private business.")

A funeral. It proceeds along an ordered, busy path, several people, wreaths, sashes (from the pensioners' club, from the local union cell . . .). An elderly man approaches everyone and, discreetly whispering, asks, "Excuse me, are you perhaps Jewish?"—and continuing on—"Excuse me, are you . . . ?" He needs to have ten Jews in order to recite the Kaddish over the coffin, and he's managed to gather only seven.

"In this crowd?"

"You can see for yourself, madam, I am asking everybody, and it always ends up being seven."

He counts them out on his meticulously extended fingers: seven, in the entire cemetery, the *Jewish* cemetery. It is impossible even to recite the Kaddish.

The Jews are at the Umschlagplatz, in Stronska's apartment, at the loading platform.

Bearded, in gaberdines, yarmulkes, some of them in hats bordered with red fox fur, two of them even in *maciejowkas*\* . . . Crowds, throngs of Jews: on shelves, tables, above the couch, along the walls . . .

My friend Anna Stronska collects folk art, and the folk artists like to recreate their neighbors from before the war.

Stronska collects her Jews from everywhere, from all over Poland—from Przemysl, where they sell her the most beautiful pieces and give her the best price because her father was a foreman there before the war; from the Kielce area; but the most valuable are those from Krakow. On the second day of

---

\**Maciejowkas*, the visored caps emblematic of Marshal Jozef Pilsudski's legions.

Easter, in front of Norbetanki Church in Salwator, there is an annual church fair, and only there can one still get the Jews in their black robes and white satin tallithim, the tefillin on their heads, everything arrayed just so, according to the rules, exactly as it should be.

They cluster in groups. Figurines.

Some of them gesticulate animatedly in the midst of lively conversations; nearby, one fellow reads a paper, but the other group has been talking so loudly that he's raised his eyes from the page and is now listening in. A few are praying. Two men in reddish robes are splitting their sides with laughter for some reason; an elderly man with a stick and a little suitcase passes by: perhaps a doctor?

Everybody is busy and involved with something, because they are *those* Jews, from before everything. So I bring Edelman to Stronska's, to let him see those Jews from the normal time, and as we are about to leave, Stronska reports that a neighbor who lives a few blocks away, on Mila Street, keeps telling her about an eerie dream.

This neighbor has been dreaming this same dream, every night, ever since the day she moved into that apartment. Actually, she is not entirely sure that it's a dream, because she dreams that she's awake and just lying there in her room, only it seems not quite to be her room. There is old furniture in it, a huge stove, a window in a blind wall. And because she returns here every night, she has gotten used to all the pieces of furniture and is already able to recognize trinkets left on the armchairs and the dresser. Sometimes she is visited by a feeling that behind the door there is somebody. This sensation of somebody's presence becomes so strong that sometimes she gets up and checks whether it isn't a thief—but no, nobody is there.

One night she sees herself once again in this room of hers—no, not her room. Everything is in its usual place: the stoves, the trinkets on the dresser. And then, all of a sudden, the door opens and a young woman, a Jew, enters the room.

She approaches the bed.

She stops.

They look at each other intently. Neither of them says a word, but it is obvious what they would like to say. The young woman stares: "Oh, so it's you here . . ." And the other one, the dreamer, starts explaining—that the building is new, that she was, after all, assigned this apartment. . . . The young woman makes a calming gesture: everything is all right, she just wanted to see who was here now, simple curiosity . . . and she drifts over to the window and casts herself out to the street below from the fifth floor.

From the night of this variation, the dream has never again recurred, and that sensation of somebody else's presence has likewise disappeared.

So that it's precisely in places like this, and in many others, that Wajda might shoot his movie. Only Edelman says that he would not utter a single word before Wajda's cameras, because he could tell it all only once.

And he has told it.

Why did you become a doctor?

—Because I had to continue doing what I was doing before, in the Ghetto. In the Ghetto we made the decision for forty thousand people—there were forty thousand of them left in April 1943. We decided that they would not voluntarily collaborate in their own deaths. As a doctor I could continue to be responsible for the life of at least one person—so I became a doctor.

You would have liked me to answer like this, right? It would have sounded good? But it didn't quite happen like that. What happened was that the war ended. The war—a victory for everybody. Only for me it was a lost war, and all the time I was haunted by a feeling that I still had something to do, somewhere to go, that somebody was still counting on me and I had to go rescue him. Something seemed to propel me from one town to another and from country to country, but when I'd arrive, it would turn out that nobody was waiting, that there wasn't anybody counting on me for help anymore, and that, in general, there was nothing more to do. So I came back (people kept asking me, "Do you want to look at those walls again, those empty streets?" and I knew that yes, indeed, I had to come back here and look at them). So I came back and I lay in bed and simply stayed like that. I slept. I slept for days and weeks. From time to time friends would wake me up and tell me that, after all, seriously, I had to do something about myself. For a while, it seemed to me I might study economics. I don't remember why anymore. But finally Ala registered me in medical school.

Ala was already my wife. I'd met her when she came with a patrol organized by Dr. Swital from the Home Army to lead us out of a bunker in the Zoliborz district. We'd been left there, on Promyka Street, after the general Warsaw uprising in 1944—Antek, Celina, Tosia Goliborska, and I, among others—and in November they sent this patrol around to fetch us. (Promyka Street runs along the Vistula River, so it was still the front line, and everything was mined. I remember Ala's taking her shoes off and crossing the mine field barefoot, because she imagined that if she happened to step on a mine barefoot, for some reason it wouldn't go off.)

As I was saying, Ala registered me in medical school, so I

started going there. But I wasn't the least bit interested, and when we'd get back home, I would throw myself back onto the bed. Everybody else was studying assiduously, and because I was lying there with my face to the wall all the time, some of my friends began drawing things for me on this wall, so that at least I would be memorizing something. One day, for instance, they would draw a stomach, another day a heart—always with great precision, by the way, you know, the ventricles, the auricles, the aorta. . . .

Things continued more or less like this for about two years. Occasionally people would call and invite me to participate in a panel discussion about the Ghetto . . .

—You'd already acquired hero status?

—Sort of. Or they would come by and say: "Mr. Edelman, please tell us, tell us how it was." But I was rather subdued, and I tended to prove rather pale and ineffectual on those panels.

Do you know what I remember best from this period?

Mikolaj's death. The one who was a member of the Zegota (the Council to Aid the Jews) as a representative of our underground.

Mikolaj got sick and died.

He died—Hanna, do you understand?—normally, in a hospital, *in bed*! He was the first of the people I knew who simply died and was not killed. The day before, I'd visited him in the hospital and he said: "Mr. Marek, should anything happen to me, here, under the pillow is the notebook and everything is accounted for there, to the last penny. Folks may ask about it one day, so please, remember that it's all balanced and there is even a slight surplus."

Can you imagine, Hanna, what he had there? It was a thick notebook with a black cover in which throughout the whole war he'd been recording how he was spending all the dollars. The dollars we'd received in the drops to buy arms. Almost a hundred was left, and the bank notes were all there in the back of the notebook.

—Did you give the cash and the notebook to those union leaders in America, those hosts who seemed so profoundly moved in 1963?

—You know, I didn't even take this notebook from the hospital. I told Antek and Celina about it and—I remember—we laughed a lot about the whole thing, about the notebook and how Mikolaj was dying in such a bizarre way, you know, lying between clean sheets, in bed. We almost split our sides laughing, and Celina finally had to remind us that, after all, such behavior was slightly improper.

—Did your friends eventually stop having to draw those hearts on the wall?

—Yes.

One day I happened to pop in during some lecture—probably only to get some forms signed—but I heard a professor say: "When a doctor knows what his patient's eyes look like, and his skin, and his tongue, he should be able to tell what's wrong with him." I liked that. I realized that a patient's illness is like a puzzle and if one put the pieces together correctly, one should know what's going on inside that patient.

From that moment I took up medicine, and from then on the stuff you were wanting me to say at the outset applies. But I only understood it much, much later: how by being a doctor I could continue to be responsible for human life.

—Why actually do you feel you have to be responsible for human life?

—Probably because everything else seems to me less important.

—Perhaps it was a question of your having been twenty then? If one has lived the most important moments of one's life by the age of twenty, afterward it can get rather difficult finding an equally significant job . . .

—You know, Hanna, in the clinic where I later worked, there was a big, tall palm tree there in the hall. I would stand underneath that palm tree sometimes—and I'd look out over the rooms where my patients were lying. This was a long time ago, when we didn't yet have today's medications or operations or devices available, and the majority of the people in those rooms were in effect simply condemned to death. My assignment was to save as many as possible—and I realized, that day under the palm, that actually it was the same assignment as I'd had there, at the Umschlagplatz. There, too, I would stand at the gate and pull out individuals from the throngs of those condemned to die.

—And all your life you have been standing at this gate, right?

—Actually, yes. And when I can't accomplish anything else, there is always one thing left: to assure them the most comfortable death possible. So that they might not know, not suffer, not be afraid. So that they need not humiliate themselves.

You have to provide them with a way of dying such that they don't become like *those*—the ones from the fourth floor at the Umschlagplatz.

—People have told me, Marek, that when you're taking care of simple and not terribly serious cases, you do it in a way out of a sense of duty, that you only really light up when the game begins, when the race with death begins.

—This is, after all, my role.

God is trying to blow out the candle and I'm quickly trying to shield the flame, taking advantage of His brief inattention. To keep the flame flickering, even if only for a little while longer than He would wish.

It is important: He is not terribly just. It can also be very satisfying, because whenever something does work out, it means you have, after all, fooled Him . . .

—A race with God? How delicious!

—You know, when you've had to see all those people off on the trains, later on you can have some things to settle with Him. And they all passed by me because I stood there by that gate from the first day till the last. All of them. Four hundred thousand people passed right by me.

Of course, every life ends in the same way, but what counts is postponing the sentence for eight, ten, or fifteen years. That's not nothing. When, thanks to that ticket, Mrs. Tenenbaum's daughter lived those extra three months—that was a lot because she managed to get to know love during those three months. And the girls we cure of stenosis or of narrowed valves, they have time to grow up and make love and have babies—then how much more do they manage to live than Mrs. Tenenbaum's daughter?

I had such a nine-year-old girl once, Urszula, with contraction of the dual lung valve; she was spitting pink, foamy sputum, and suffocating—but at that time we weren't yet operating on children. For that matter, they were only then just beginning to operate on heart defects in Poland at all. But she was already dying, so I called the Professor and told him that this little one was going to suffocate at any moment. He flew up within a few hours and he operated on her that very day. She quickly got better, left the hospital, graduated. . . . Over the years she's come to visit us from time to time, once with a husband, later divorced, pretty, tall, with dark hair. Before she used to be slightly disfigured by a squint, but we got her an operation with a very good ophthalmologist and her eyes are all right now.

Then we had Teresa with a heart defect, swollen like a barrel, dying. After we'd operated and the swelling had subsided, she immediately demanded, "Send me home." It was strange because during all that time, nobody from her home had ever come to see her. I went there. It was a back room with a concrete floor. She lived with a sick mother and two younger sisters. She said she had to go home because someone had to take care of those sisters—she was ten at that time—and she went. She later had a baby. After the labor we had to pull her out of lung swelling, but as soon as she could breathe, she said she had to leave to take care of her baby. Sometimes she comes to us and says she has everything she's ever wanted to have—a home, a baby, a husband, and what's most important, she says, she's escaped that tiny room at the back of a store.

Later we had Grazyna from the orphanage, whose alcoholic father died in a mental hospital and whose mother died of TB. I used to tell her she should never have a baby, but she's gone ahead and had one and she's coming back to us with circulatory system asthenia. She's getting weaker and weaker, she can't work anymore, she can't hold this baby anymore, but she puts him in a stroller, proud that she has had a baby like any normal woman. Her husband loves her a lot and won't consent to an operation. We don't have the courage to insist, so Grazyna is slowly fading.

Maybe I am getting some of this wrong, but I don't remember all of them clearly anymore. It's strange. When they are here—when you're having to help them—they become your closest people in the world, and you know everything about them. You know that this one has a concrete floor at home; that this other one's father drinks and her mother is mentally ill; that this third one has problems with mathematics at school; and that this fourth one's husband is not good for her at all; or that there are exams at college right now so that it's necessary to get a cab to take this new one together with a nurse and medication to that exam. And you also know all about their hearts: that the withdrawal from their various valves is either too narrow or too wide (if it is too narrow there is ischemia—if it's too wide, there is blood stasis and the blood doesn't make it through the circuit). You look at a patient, and when she is so pretty, skinny, with pink complexion, it means that she developed peripheral blood stasis and it resulted in dilatation of capillary blood vessels; or if she is pale and her blood vessels in her neck throb, her aorta outlet is too wide. . . . You know all about them, and they are your closest people during those few days of mortal danger. And then they get better. They leave for their homes, you forget their faces, somebody new arrives, and already this new person alone is the most important.

A few days ago they brought in a seventy-year-old lady with asthenia. The Professor operated on her. It was a really risky operation—an acute circulation asthenia. As she was falling asleep, she was praying. "God," she said, "bless the hands of the Professor and the thoughts of the doctors from Pirogow."

The doctors from Pirogow—that's us, me and Aga Zuchowska.

Well, tell me, to whom else but my patient—a little old lady—would it occur to pray *for my thoughts?*


Isn't it high time already we put a little bit of order here? After all, people are expecting numbers from us, dates, data about soldiers and their weapons. People are very strongly attached to the importance of historical facts and chronology.

For instance: there were 220 insurgents, 2090 Germans.

The Germans have their air force, artillery, armored vehicles, flamethrowers, 82 machine guns, 135 submachine guns, 1358 rifles. Each insurgent, according to the report of the uprising commander's deputy, has one pistol, five grenades, and five incendiary bottles. There are three rifles in each area. For the entire Ghetto, there are only two mines and one submachine gun.

The Germans enter on April 19th at 4 A.M. The first battles occur on Muranowski Square, Zamenhofa and Gesia streets. At 2 P.M. the Germans withdraw without having taken a single person to the Umschlagplatz. ("At that point we believed it was very important that they hadn't been able to take anybody away that day. We even considered it a victory.")

April 20th: there are no Germans at all till past noon (for a full twenty-four hours there has not been a single German in the Ghetto!); they return at 2 P.M. They approach the Brush Factory area. They're trying to open the gate. A mine explodes, they withdraw. (This is one of the two mines in the Ghetto. The other one, on Nowolipie Street, never goes off.) They force their way into the attic. Michal Klepfisz smothers a German machine gun with his body, the group manages to get through—the radio station Dawn will presently broadcast the news that Michal had fallen on the field of glory and read General Sikorski's order awarding him the Virtuti Military Cross, fifth class.

Now comes the scene with the three SS officers. Wearing white rosettes and with their machine guns pointed down, they propose a truce and a removal of the wounded. The insurgents shoot at the officers, but they fail to hit any of them.

In the American author John Hersey's book *The Wall*, this scene is described in great detail.

Felix, one of the imaginary characters, reports it with ambivalence and embarrassment. There is still in him, the author points out, a longing, so typical in the Western tradition, for rules of warfare, a need to honor a basic sense of "fair play," even in a deadly struggle. . . .

*219*

It was Zygmunt who shot at the SS men. They had only one rifle and Zygmunt was the best shot because he'd managed to put in some actual military service before the war. Seeing the approaching officers with their white rosettes, Edelman had said, "Fire," and Zygmunt had fired.

Edelman is the only survivor from among all the people who participated in that scene—at any rate, on the insurgents' side. I ask him whether he felt embarrassed violating the rules of war, that basic sense of "fair play" so typical of the Western tradition.

He says he felt no embarrassment whatsoever, because those three Germans were exactly the same fellows who had already transported four hundred thousand people to the Treblinka camp, only now they happened to be wearing the white rosettes . . .

(In his report, Stroop mentioned those "parliamentarians" and the "bandits" who fired on them.

Soon after the war Edelman encountered Stroop.

The prosecutor's office and the Commission to Investigate Nazi Crimes asked him to help determine some particulars in a confrontation with Stroop: whether there was a wall in a particular place, whether there was a gate, a few topographical details.

They were sitting at a table—the prosecutor, the Commission's representative, and he—and a tall, cleanly shaven man in shiny boots was escorted into the room. He came to attention before them. "I also rose. The prosecutor told Stroop who I was. Stroop drew himself up, clicked his heels, and turned his head toward me. In the military, they call this 'rendering military honors' or something like that. I was asked whether I'd seen him kill people. I answered that I had never seen this man before, that I was seeing him for the first time. Later, they asked me whether it was possible that there was a gate at such-and-such a place and that the tanks had approached from that direction, because this was what Stroop was declaring and it didn't seem to fit in. I said: 'It's possible that there was a gate there and that the tanks came from there.' I felt sorry. This man was standing before me at attention, without his belt; he had already received one death sentence. What difference did it make where the wall was and where the gate? I just wanted to leave that room as quickly as possible.")

The parliamentarians leave (Zygmunt, unfortunately, missed), and in the evening everybody goes down to the basements.

During the night a boy runs in shouting that there is fire. Panic breaks out. . . .

Excuse me. "A boy runs in shouting . . ." We don't need that density of detail for a serious historical report. Nor do we need the fact that, after the boy's shout, a few thousand people started to panic, which extinguished the candles so that it became necessary quickly to reprimand the boy. All of this is too thorough for History. . . . Well, at any rate, after a moment people begin to calm down: they can see that someone is taking charge. ("People should always have this sense that someone is in charge here.")

So the Germans are beginning to set the Ghetto on fire. The Brush Factory area is already in flames. It is necessary to break through these flames into the central ghetto.

When a building is burning, at first the floors burn, and then burning posts begin to fall from above, but between the first falling post and the next one, a few minutes pass, and this is when one should run. It is terribly hot: broken glass and asphalt melt under one's feet. People are running through the flames between those falling posts. A wall. A hole in the wall with a searchlight trained on it. "We are not going."

221

"So, stay here." A shot into the searchlight, the people are running. A backyard, six guys, shooting, running. Five guys, a grave, Stasiek, Adam, "The Internationale." . . .

One more thing: that same day when they dug the grave and softly sang the first verse of "The Internationale," they had had to make their way through basements to another building. Four men went down to dig an opening while upstairs the Germans started throwing grenades into the basement. Smoke and poison gas began to penetrate through, and Edelman ordered them to seal up the opening. There was still one guy left on the other side, but people were beginning to suffocate and it was impossible to wait for him.

And here we have a strict chronology. We know already that the first one to die was Michal Klepfisz, then those six guys, then the five guys, then Stasiek, then Adam, and then the guy who'd had to be buried. And then several hundred people in the shelter. But this happened later, when the whole Ghetto was on fire and everybody had moved into the basements. "It was terribly hot there and some woman had let her child go out for a moment; the Germans gave him a candy, asking him, 'And where is your mom?' and the kid led them back so that the Germans then blew up the whole shelter, several hundred people. Some of us later felt that we should have shot this kid the moment he got out. But this wouldn't have helped any, because the Germans had sound-detection devices and were using them to track down the people in the basements."

So this is the chronology of the events.

Historical order turns out to be nothing more than the order of dying.

History is happening on the other side of the wall, where the reports are being written, radio announcements are being sent to the world, and help is being demanded from the world. Any expert today knows the texts of the cables and governmental communications. But who knows about the boy who had to be buried because poisonous gas was penetrating into the basement? Who today knows about that boy?

These reports are being written on the Aryan side by "Waclaw." For example: "Communiqué #3. Wac. A/9, April 21: Jewish Combat Organization directing the struggle of the Warsaw Ghetto rejected a German ultimatum to throw down their arms by 10 A.M. Tuesday. . . . The Germans deployed artillery, tanks, and armored brigades. The state of siege of the Ghetto and the struggle of the Jewish militants are virtually the sole subject of conversation in this city of a million people. . . ."

"Waclaw" had previously broadcast information about the Ghetto liquidation action, and it was precisely from him the world learned about the existence of the Umschlagplatz, about the transports, the gas chambers, and the Treblinka camp. "Waclaw"—Henryk Wolinski—who has been mentioned in every account of the Ghetto, was the head of the Jewish Department of the Chief Command of the Home Army. He was the liaison between the ZOB (the Jewish Combat Organization) and the Command of the AK (the Home Army). Among other things, he transmitted to the chief commander the first declaration of the creation of the ZOB, and to Jurek Wilner, Home Army Commander Grot-Rowecki's order subordinating the ZOB to the Home Army. He put the Jews in touch with Colonel Monter and the other officers who later supplied them with arms and taught them how to use them. In most cases, the teacher was Zbigniew Lewandowski— "Szyna"—the head of the Technical Research Office of the Home Army. Today Dr. Lewandowski says that only two people from the Ghetto attended those "classes," a man and a woman; at the beginning he was concerned about this, but it quickly became evident that the man was a chemist and he was catching on to everything very fast and passing the instructions on to his friends in the Ghetto. In addition to instructions, they also received potassium chlorate, to which they could themselves add sulfuric acid, gasoline, paper, sugar, and glue to make ignition bottles. "Molotov cocktails?" I ask to make sure, but Dr. Lewandowski huffs: "You can't even compare them. Our bottles were delicate, sophisticated, covered over with this chlorate and wrapped in paper, and the ignition points went around the whole surface. Really, a sophisticated, elegant item: the newest achievement of the Home Army's Technical Research Office. In general, everything we were giving to the ZOB—the bottles, the people, the arms—were the best available to us at the time."

Up till today Dr. Lewandowski hasn't known the name of that man who'd come to his place at 62 Marszalkowska Street (first floor, in the backyard to the left). "He was a tall man, with brown hair," he says. "Not one of those aggressive types, those 'pistols'; rather, silent and quiet. But," the doctor adds, "in particularly dangerous actions the 'pistols' were seldom the best, but rather the inconspicuous ones."

So I tell the doctor that the man he had been teaching was Michal Klepfisz.

Together with Stanislaw Herbst, "Waclaw" described the first big liquidation action in the Ghetto, and this report, in the form of a microfilm, was transmitted by a courier via Paris and Lisbon, such that just before Christmas Eve, 1942, General Sikorski confirmed having received it. Jurek Wilner, the ZOB's representative on the Aryan side, brought news from the Ghetto every day, thanks to which the reports were updated and current information could be broadcast to London all the time. For instance:

*An atmosphere of crazy panic: the action is supposed to start at 6:30 and everybody is prepared that he or she can be taken away at any moment, from any place . . .*

*The last phase of the liquidation started on Sunday. At 10 o'clock that morning, all Jews were required to be in front of the Jewish Council building. There they started to distribute life tickets. Everybody is required to wear them on their chests. They consist of yellowish chits of paper with a handwritten number, the Jewish Council seal, and a signature. The tickets don't have names . . .*

*Last week at the Umschlagplatz people were paying 1000 (1 thousand) zlotys for 1 kilogram of bread, 3 zlotys for a cigarette.*

*When the gendarmes came to take him, Seweryn Majde threw a heavy ashtray at one of them, hitting him on his head. Majde was obviously executed. This has been the only known case of intentional self-defense . . .*

*Travelers going through Treblinka have observed that the trains don't stop at this station.*

Every day like that: Wilner brings information from the Ghetto, "Waclaw" writes the reports, radio operators transmit them to London, and the London radio—contrary to its practice heretofore—does not include any information about the matter in its programming. The clandestine radio operators back in Poland, at the insistence of their bosses, ask the reason, but the BBC remains silent. Only after a month does it include in its information service the first news about the ten thousand people a day and about the Umschlagplatz. Because—as it turns out later—all along London has not been believing "Waclaw's" reports. "We thought that you were exaggerating a little with all that anti-German propaganda . . . ," they explain, once they get confirmation from their own sources. . . . So Jurek Wilner would smuggle out from the Ghetto, alongside the news, additional texts for telegrams, like the one to be sent to the Jewish Congress in the United States, which ended with the following lines: "Brothers! The remaining Jews in Poland live convinced that in the most horrible days in our history you did not lend us your help. Say something. This is our last appeal to you."

In April 1943 "Waclaw" delivers to the ZOB Command Group's Antek a dispatch from Colonel Monter "welcoming the armed action of the Warsaw Jews" and subsequently informs him that the Home Army will try to break through the Ghetto wall on the side of Bonifraterska Street and the Powazki Cemetery.

Up till today, "Waclaw" does not know whether this message made it to the Ghetto at all, but it seems it did because Anielewicz was saying something about an expected attack and they even sent a boy there who did not make it (they burned him alive on Mila Street, the whole day one could hear him screaming), the moment Anielewicz got the message having been the sole time he seemed to regain any hope, even though everyone was telling him that it was impossible, that nobody would be able to force their way through there.

The burning boy was screaming on Mila Street, and meanwhile, on the other side of the wall, two guys lay on the street—they were supposed to have placed 50 kilograms of explosives at the Ghetto wall. The AK partisan, Zbigniew Mlynarski, who used the pseudonym "Kret," says that precisely this was the most horrible—that these two were killed at the very outset and that therefore nobody was going to get the explosives to the wall.

"The street was empty. The Germans were shooting at us from all over. The machine gun on the hospital roof that had been shooting into the Ghetto before was now shooting at us. Behind us, in Krasinski Square, an SS company was stationed, so that when Pszenny exploded that mine that was supposed to collapse the wall—instead, it went off in the street and mangled the bodies of our two guys. So we began to withdraw.

"Today," continues Mlynarski, "I know what we should have done: we should have entered the Ghetto, fired the explosives *inside*, and our people should have been waiting on the other side to lead the insurgents out.

"Only, when one thinks about it, how many of them would have still been there to leave? Not more than fifteen. And would even all of *them* have agreed to go?

"For them," continues Mlynarski, "there was this prestige aspect. Late, but in the end, they did commit themselves to make this painful sacrifice. And it's good that they did so because at least they preserved Jewish honor."

Exactly the same sort of comment is offered by Henryk Grabowski, in whose apartment Jurek Wilner used to hide arms and who later managed to spring Jurek from the clutches of the Gestapo:

"Those people did not want to live anymore anyway and one should consider it to their credit that they had the common sense to want to die in a battle. Because they were going to die in any case, so it's better to die with a weapon in one's hand than in some indecent manner."

Mr. Grabowski tells me how he came to understand this himself—how it is better to die putting up a fight—when he was stopped near the Ghetto one day as he was leaving, carrying a package of letters from Mordka Anielewicz. "Excuse me," Grabowski corrects himself, "I mean, from *Mordechaj*; one must be respectful of rank and position." They made him stand up against the wall, with a rifle barrel right in front of him, like this, at the level of this vase on the cabinet, and then he'd thought, "To at least be able to bite that Hun, to gouge his eyes out . . ." (Luckily, there had been a Polish policeman, a Mr. Wislocki, among the Germans, to whom he'd said: "All right, Mr. Wislocki, do your duty, but you should understand that I am not alone, so watch out that you don't have serious problems later on because of this . . ." Mr.

Wislocki had understood immediately, and they let him go at once.)

Mr. Grabowski had known Mordka for many years, since before the war. "He was, after all, one of us from down there, from the Powisle slum. We were in the same gang, we would always band together for brawls, or we'd go fight the boys from other districts like Wola or Gorny Mokotow."

There was the same sort of poverty at Mrs. Grabowski's as at Mrs. Anielewicz's. The one sold fish, the other bread, and if she sold ten loaves, forty bagels, and a few vegetables each day, that was it.

Already then, in Powisle, it was obvious that Mordka knew how to fight, so Mr. Grabowski wasn't all that surprised when he met him in the Ghetto, transformed into Mordechaj. On the contrary, it seemed to him quite natural: who, after all, should be the commander if not their guy from Powisle? (At that first meeting, Mordechaj told him what to convey to the boys in Wilno: that they should gather money, arms, and strong, committed young people.)

Mr. Grabowski had been a Boy Scout before the war, and all his friends from the older Scout troops had been executed in Palmiry within weeks of the Nazi invasion in 1939, all fifty of them. He'd survived and gotten an order from the Scout leadership to go to Wilno and organize Jews for the struggle.

In Wilno Kolonia, Mr. Grabowski met Jurek Wilner. There was a Dominican nunnery in Kolonia, and the Mother Superior was hiding a few Jews at her place. ("I told my sisters, 'Remember, Christ used to say that there is no greater love for God than when you give your life for your friends.' And they'd understood. . . .")

Jurek Wilner was the favorite of the Mother Superior— blond hair, blue eyes, he reminded her of her own brother who'd been taken away as a prisoner. So they often conversed: she would tell him about God, he would tell her about Marx. And when he was leaving for Warsaw, for the Ghetto, from which he would never return, he left her the most valuable thing he had: a notebook filled with poems. He would record in it the things he valued most and considered most important, and this notebook, in its brown plastic cover, its yellowed pages covered with Jurek's handwriting (it was she who had given him this name: Jurek had been Arie before), the Mother Superior has kept up till this day. "This book has come through a lot: a Gestapo visit, concentration camp, prison. Before I die I'd like to place it in some deserving hands."

From Jurek Wilner's notebook:

*Don't look—don't—don't look—don't—*
                              *what's there ahead, before you*
*(Shoes—shoes—shoes—shoes—up, down, up, down)*
    *People—people—people—people—*
                              *Obsessed with this vista*
                         *Well, there is no respite in war*
*Try—think—think—think—about something prior,*
                              *something different*
    *Oh my God—God—God—spare this mind*
                              *from madness!*
*(Shoes—shoes—shoes—shoes—up, down, up, down)*
                         *There is no respite in war*
    *We—can—stand—hunger—cold—thirst—weariness*
    *But—not—not—not—not—not this continuous vista*
*(Shoes—shoes—shoes—shoes—up, down, up, down)*
*There is no respite in war.*

So Mr. Grabowski met Jurek in Wilno Kolonia, and when Jurek came to Warsaw, he moved in with Mr. Grabowski, on Podchorazych Street. All the Jews from Wilno arriving in Warsaw would first stay at Mr. Grabowski's, and he would immediately take them to the marketplace to buy them some adequate clothing. "Ski caps were very fashionable then, those caps with their little eye shades, but those boys didn't look good in them because in some odd way the eye shades accentuated their noses, so I would tell them, 'Bicycle caps, yes, hats, yes, but ski caps—absolutely under no condition!' " He also corrected their behavior, even the way they walked, so that they would move "without a Jewish accent."

Mr. Grabowski offered an interesting observation: the more afraid a person was, the uglier he became—his features would somehow become distorted. Those who were not afraid, on the other hand, fellows like Wilner and Anielewicz—they were really handsome guys and their faces really looked quite different.

As the ZOB's representative on the Aryan side (Mr. Grabowski would only learn later, after the war, the nature of his mission; in those days he preferred to know as little as possible, in order not to even be capable of spilling anything under interrogation), Jurek used to get in touch all the time with "Waclaw" and the officers, and when he was unable to take all the packets to the Ghetto, he would leave them at Mr. Grabowski's or with the barefoot Carmelite nuns on Wolska Street: sometimes guns, sometimes knives, or even explosives. At that time the barefoot Carmelite nuns did not have strictures as severe as those they observe today and they were allowed to show their faces to strangers, so Jurek, tired after carrying sacks, used to rest on a cot behind a screen in the locutory. I am sitting now in the same locutory on one side of a black iron bar, with the Mother Superior in a nook on the other side, at dusk, and we are talking about those arms transports for the Ghetto that went through the convent for almost a year. Didn't they have any misgivings? The Mother Superior does not understand . . .

"After all, arms in such a place?"

"You mean, perhaps, that arms serve to kill people?" asks the Mother Superior. No, for some reason she had never thought about it that way. Her only thought was for the fact that Jurek would eventually be making use of these arms and that when his last hour came, it would be good if he managed to make an act of contrition and make his peace with God. She even asked him to promise this to her, and now she asks me what I think; did he remember the promise when he shot himself in the bunker, at 18 Mila Street?

While Jurek and his friends were making use of those arms, the sky in this part of the town became quite red and this glow even reached into the convent's vestibule. That's why precisely there, and not in the chapel, the barefoot Carmelite nuns would gather each night and read psalms ("Yea, for Thy sake are we killed all the day long, we are counted as sheep for the slaughter. Awake! Why sleepest thou, oh Lord?"), and she prayed to God that Jurek Wilner might meet his death without fear.

So Jurek was gathering arms, and Mr. Grabowski, for his part, was busy helping him by complementing his purchases. Once, he managed to get a few hundred kilos of saltpeter and wood coal to make the explosives (he bought them from Stefan Oskroba, a drugstore owner at Narutowicz Square); another time, two hundred grams of cyanide the Jews wanted to have on themselves in case of arrest. The cyanide came in small blue-gray cubes, and Henryk first tested the stuff on a cat. He scratched off a little powder, sprinkled it over a piece of sausage, and the cat died at once—so that Henryk could give it to Wilner without any compunctions. Because Henryk, as the owner of a bacon and meat stand, had his peddler's honor and couldn't sell bad merchandise to a friend.

Henryk "Baconman"—because this was Mr. Grabowski's pseudonym—and Jurek Wilner were very close friends. When they slept on the same pallet (Henryk's wife and daughter slept on the bed, under which were stored the packs of knives and grenades), they would talk about everything. That it had turned cold, how they were hungry, that killings were going on all around, and how it would soon be necessary to risk their own heads. "As far as his intellect went," remembers Henryk, "Jurek had a philosophical mind, so we often spoke about what the point of it all was, and he had such a humanistic attitude toward life in general."

From Jurek Wilner's notebook:

*And in a day—*
*we'll not meet each other anymore*
*And in a week—*
*we'll not greet each other anymore*
*And in a month—*
*we'll have forgotten each other*
*And in a year*
*we won't even recognize each other*
*And today the night over this black river*
*is like a coffin lid*
*which I try to pry open with my scream:*
*Listen—save me!*
*Listen—I love you!*
*Can you hear me?—*
*It's already too far.*

During the first days of March 1943 Jurek Wilner was arrested by the Gestapo.

"The morning of that day," says attorney Wolinski, "I'd been at his place in Wspolna Street, and around two in the afternoon the Germans surrounded the building and took him with his documents and arms.

"We had an unwritten law that if someone got arrested, he had to keep silent for at least three days. After that, if he was broken, nobody would blame him for that. They tortured Jurek Wilner for a month, and he gave not a thing away—no contacts, no addresses, although he knew plenty of them, both on the Jewish side and on the Aryan side as well.

"He escaped by a miracle, at the end of March, but he went back to the Ghetto, and he was useless after that for any work: his feet were smashed and he couldn't walk."

The miraculous escape attorney Wolinski speaks about had been arranged for Jurek by his friend Henryk "Baconman." He found out that Jurek was being kept in a camp in the Grochow district, he sneaked in through the swamps, got him out, and took him home.

Jurek's nails, kidneys, and feet were all smashed, he had been tortured every day, and one day he'd joined a group destined for execution, hoping that this would end it all faster. It turned out that the group was being taken to a work camp in Grochow instead, and that was where Mr. Grabowski found him.

Everybody set to caring for him—Mr. Grabowski, his mother, his wife, they would rub his nails with something (these nails were just peeling off his fingers), they gave him pills after which he would pee blue. Finally Jurek got better and said he wanted to go back to the Ghetto. Mr. Grabowski told him: "Jurek, what do you need that for? I'll take you to the country. . . ." But Jurek said he had to go back. To which Mr. Grabowski replied: "You'll see, I can hide you real well, nobody will find you till the end of the war. . . ."

They didn't even say good-bye to each other. When his friends came to pick Jurek up, Henryk happened to be out. And after the Ghetto uprising broke out, Henryk understood immediately that this would be the end for Jurek—that from this adventure he was certainly not destined to escape. Not the adventure, of course, but the tragedy that was about to transpire.

And indeed, Jurek did not escape—and from one of the last ZOB reports, we learn that it was precisely he who called for suicide on May 8th in the bunker at 18 Mila Street.

"Because of the hopeless situation and to avoid falling into the Germans' hands alive, Arie Wilner called on the fighters to commit suicide. As the first one, Lutek Rotblat initially shot his mother and then himself. In the bunker most of the members of the Combat Organization found their deaths, including Commander Mordechaj Anielewicz."

After the war Henryk (he initially had a repair garage, then a taxi cab, and then he worked in transportation, as a clerk in the technical department) often pondered whether he'd done the right thing letting Jurek go. In the country he would certainly have been cured, become stronger . . . "But, on the other hand, had he survived, perhaps he would have been angry with me? He would certainly have been angry to be alive, and it would have been even worse. . . ."

From Jurek Wilner's notebook:

*So once again a little more*
*why does someone always have to spoil it for me,*
*to cut the halter?*
*Yesterday I could already feel death in my bones*
*Had eternity complete*
*inside.*
*They handed me a spoon,*
*a spoonful of life.*
*I didn't want it, I don't want this drink:*
*Let me throw it up.*
*I know life is a full pot*
*and that the world is good and healthy,*
*but life doesn't make it into my blood,*
*it only gives me cerebral congestion.*
*It feeds others, but it saps me . . .*

"I wrote a letter to him in the Ghetto," says "Waclaw" (attorney Wolinski). "I don't remember exactly what I wrote, but they were tender words, the kind it is so difficult to write.

"His death was very painful to me. The death of every single one of those men was painful to me.

"Such honorable men.

"So heroic.

"So Polish."

After Jurek Wilner's arrest in March, Antek became the ZOB's representative on the Aryan side.

"He was a very nice and brave man," says attorney Wolinski. "Only he had a horrible habit: he always carried a bag full of grenades around with him. It made me a bit nervous because I always thought they would explode."

One of the first telegrams "Waclaw" had sent to London concerned money. Those under his charge needed it for arms, and at first, $5000 arrived in the drops.

"I gave it to Mikolaj from the 'Bund,' and all of a sudden Borowski, a Zionist, came to me with a complaint. 'Mr. Waclaw,' he said, 'he took everything and doesn't want to give any of it to me, please tell him something.'"

But Mikolaj by that time had already given the money to Edelman, and Edelman had given it to Tosia, and Tosia had hidden it under a polishing broom, and, as they were soon to experience, this was a brilliant idea, because during a search the whole apartment was ransacked, but it hadn't occurred to anybody to look under the floor polisher. With this money they were later able to buy some arms on the Aryan side.

Tosia subsequently ransomed "Waclaw" from the Gestapo: someone sent her a message that he had been arrested, and she immediately thought, "Who knows, maybe something can be arranged with a Persian rug." And indeed, thanks to the rug, "Waclaw" got out. "Why, yes," says Tosia, "it was really a beautiful rug. One of those beige ones, with selvage around the border and a medallion in the center."

Tosia—Dr. Teodozja Goliborska—the last of the doctors who participated in the research on hunger in the Ghetto—has come from Australia to visit for a few days, so there are many people today at attorney Wolinski's house. There is a lot of social animation, a hum, and everybody is competing at telling funny stories. For example, all the problems "Waclaw" had with those people from the ZOB who were always liquidating the Nazi collaborators too quickly. The sentence was supposed to come first and then the execution, but they'd come up to him and say: "Mr. Waclaw, we've already taken care of him." "And what was I supposed to do? I had to write to the executions committee to arrange for a post-facto formal sentence."

Or, perhaps, the story of what happened with that big drop. One hundred and twenty thousand dollars arrived and. . . . "Just a second," says Edelman. "Was it one hundred and twenty thousand dollars? We got only half of that."

"Mr. Marek," says Waclaw, "you guys got it all and you bought guns with it."

"Those fifty guns?"

"Of course not. Those fifty guns you didn't buy, those you got from us, from the Home Army. Well, actually not quite all of them, because one of them was sent to Czestochowa and that Jew used it, you remember? And twenty of them were sent to Poniatow . . ."

So everybody is chatting like this, and Tosia also recalls the red sweater Marek was wearing as he ran along the rooftops. She says that it was a real *shmate* compared to the sweater she will immediately send him as soon as she gets back to Australia. And now, when we are already on our way home, Edelman suddenly turns to me and says: "It wasn't a month. It was a few days, a week at most."

He's talking about Jurek Wilner. That he withstood a week and not a month of torture at the hands of the Gestapo.

Now, just a second. "Waclaw" spoke about one month, Mr. Grabowski about two weeks . . .

"I remember precisely that he was there for one week."

This is beginning to get annoying.

If "Waclaw" said it was a month, he must have known what he was talking about.

But what does it come down to? That all of us want very much for Jurek Wilner to have withstood the Gestapo tortures for as long as possible. It is, after all, a big difference: to maintain that silence for a week as opposed to a month. Really, we very much want Jurek Wilner to have held his tongue for the whole month.

"All right," he says, "Antek wants us to have been five hundred, that writer Mr. S. wants the mother to have been the one who painted the fish, and you all want him to have been in prison for a month. So let it be a month. After all, it doesn't matter at this point."

It is the same with the banners.

They'd been hanging over the Ghetto from the first day of the uprising: white and red, and blue and white. They provoked an outpouring of affection on the Aryan side, and the Germans finally took them down, with the greatest difficulty and the greatest satisfaction, as war trophies.

He says that if there were any banners there, it could only have been his people who hung them, and his people had not hung any banners. They would have liked to hang them, if they had had some white and red fabric, but they hadn't.

"Perhaps somebody else hung them, it doesn't matter who."

"Oh, yes," he says. "Possibly." Only, he didn't see any banners at all. He only learned about them after the war.

"That's impossible. Everybody saw them!"

237

"Well, if everybody saw them, they must have been there, these banners. And besides," he says, "what does it matter? All that's important is that people saw them."

This is the worst part: that in the end he agrees to everything. And it doesn't even make any sense to try to convince him.

"What difference does it make today?" he asks, and then he agrees.

W e have to write about one more thing," he says.

Why he is alive.

When the first soldier of the liberating army came in, he stopped him and asked, "You're Jewish—so how come you're alive?" The question seemed laced with suspicion: perhaps he'd turned somebody in? Perhaps he'd taken somebody else's bread? So I should ask him now whether by chance he didn't survive on somebody else's account, and if not, then why he actually did survive.

And then he will try to explain himself. For instance, he will tell me about the day he went to Nowolipki Street, number seven, where their conspiracy had a local safehouse, to tell somebody that Irka, a woman doctor from the Leszno hospital, was lying unconscious in an apartment across the street. When the entire hospital was being taken to the Um-schlagplatz, Irka had swallowed a bottle of Luminal, put on a nightgown, and gone to bed. He'd found her in this pink gown and brought her to a house where everybody else had already been taken away, and now he wanted to tell the others that if she was to survive, it would be necessary to get her out of there.

There was a wall just across the street at Nowolipki Street—on the other side it was already the Aryan part. All of a sudden an SS man leaned out from behind that wall and started shooting. He shot more than fifteen times—each time, less than half a meter to his right. Perhaps the SS man was astigmatic—it is the sort of visual defect that can be corrected by glasses, but the German apparently had an uncorrected astigmatism, so he missed.

"Is that all?" I ask. "Simply that the German soldier didn't have the right glasses?"

But there comes another story, this one about Mietek Dab.

One day, the contingent of people in the Umschlagplatz was a little short of the required ten thousand, and some people, Edelman included, were simply gathered up from a nearby street, piled onto a platform cart, and transported down to Stawki Street toward the Umschlagplatz. The cart was being pulled by two horses; a Jewish policeman was sitting next to the driver and there was a German at the back.

They were already passing Nowolipki Street when Marek suddenly noticed Mietek Dab walking down the street. He was a member of the Socialist Party, he had been assigned to serve in the Ghetto police, he happened to live on Nowolipki Street, and he was heading home from work.

"Mietek, I got caught," Marek yelled, and Mietek came running up close, told the policeman that he was his brother, and they let him off the cart.

Then they went to Mietek's house.

Mietek's father was there—short, thin, hungry. He looked at them with distaste:

"Mietek managed to save somebody from the cart again, right? And as usual, he didn't take a penny for it?

"He could have made thousands already.

"He might at least have been able to buy some rationed bread with the money.

"But what does he do? He gets people off for free."

"Daddy," said Mietek, "don't worry. It will count to my credit as an act of kindness and I'll go to heaven."

"What heaven? What God!? Can't you see what's going on? Don't you see that there hasn't been any God for a long time? And even if there is," the little old man lowered his voice, *"He is on THEIR side."*

The next day they took Mietek's dad. Mietek didn't get back in time to get him off the cart, and soon thereafter, Mietek escaped into the forest, to join the partisans.

This is the second example: when he should have died for certain, and again some coincidence saved him. In the first case, he was saved by the SS man's astigmatism; in the second, by the fact that Mietek Dab happened to be walking down the street on his way home from work.

Those girls brought in with pink sputum foaming on their lips (the ones who'd still manage to grow up and make love and have babies, that is, still manage so much more than Mrs. Tenenbaum's daughter ever managed to do), they were often suffering from narrowed valves. Valves are somewhat like rhythmically moving petals that allow the blood to flow through. When they are narrowed, not enough blood flows and lung edema can occur—the heart begins to work faster in order to transmit more blood, but it can only beat so fast, because the ventricles need time to fill with blood. . . . The optimum workload is four thousand two hundred heartbeats per hour, more than a hundred thousand a day, during which time the heart pumps seven thousand liters of blood, which is to say, five tons! I know all this from Sejdak the engineer, who says that a heart is just a machine like any other machine and, like all machines, has certain specific properties: it has big reserves of efficiency, and the use of material is low because it is able to regenerate used parts, in other words, to renovate itself day by day.

When the heart is not able to conduct its self-renovation properly, it begins to fall sick. And most often it is precisely the heart's valves that begin to break down first, which is actually quite understandable, says Sejdak the engineer, because they are precisely valves, and in any machine it's the valves that break first—take, for instance, your car.

Understanding the essence of a heart's work was therefore not that difficult for Sejdak the engineer, thanks to which in a year and a half he managed to build a machine for the Professor that could temporarily replace the real heart during its repair, which is to say, its surgery.

The cost of this mechanical heart was four hundred thousand zlotys. It was a unique, world-class invention for which Sejdak the engineer procured a patent, but when the work was finally completed, an inspector came to the Merinotex plant and found out that these accounting costs had not been recorded in the column where they should have been, which meant that Sejdak the engineer had caused losses for the factory, which in turn meant that he had committed an economic crime.

Luckily, Sejdak the engineer managed to pull together the necessary official documentation forms, and he was acquitted of this charge of transgression; the inspector was even kind enough not to include mention of the case in his report.

Sejdak is currently working on a new machine. It will help the heart pump blood through narrowed valves, and it will make it possible for patients to survive the time between a heart attack and the subsequent surgery. Most people in this situation die almost immediately after the heart attack and don't even make it to the operation. If this machine really turns out to work, it should save the lives of many people, or at least (says Edelman) it may shield the flame for one more moment.

One obviously shouldn't exaggerate this hope. After all, He is looking on very carefully both at Sejdak and at the Professor and at all these efforts of theirs, and He is always capable of striking in the most unexpected ways. For instance, they all imagined that everything had gone well, that they were all home free, and Stefan, Marysia Sawicka's brother, was maybe the happiest of them all because he was just seventeen and he had been given his first gun. Marysia Sawicka was the one who before the war used to run the eight hundred meters with Michal Klepfisz's sister in the Skra club. So Stefan was seventeen and he had his first weapon and his happiness at having taken part in an action (he'd been in the group safeguarding their removal from the sewers) was almost making him burst. He was unable to stay put at home, and he'd run downstairs to the confectionery, and at precisely that moment a German soldier just happened to enter the shop and notice the gun in Stefan's pocket; he simply took him outside and killed him on the spot, in front of the building, right beneath Marysia's windows.

Sometimes it is a real race, and right up till the very end, He does not spare you His petty, small-minded nastinesses. Take the Rudny case, where He seemed to be busy scrambling up everything: the coronography doctor was missing, the light bulb in the X-ray unit went out, the operating room was locked up, the scrub nurses weren't around. . . . All the while, Rudny's pain was increasing, each stab of pain might have been his last, and they were all still looking for cars, doctors, bulbs, and nurses. But that time they made it. At 3 A.M. as they were thanking the Professor, and the Professor was thanking them, as blood was already flowing through the wider channels in Rudny's veins and his heart was once again working normally—they had to agree that this time they'd succeeded, they'd succeeded once more.

Before Rudny's surgery Edelman hadn't been quite sure if it was going to be possible to operate in an acute state such as this because he had read in all the books how one shouldn't, and he left the hospital to think it over one more time in calm. He'd run into Dr. Zadrozna, and he'd asked her: "Should we operate? What do you think?" and Dr. Zadrozna had been very surprised. "What?" she'd said, "in *your* situation?" Because at the time they had been having some minor problems at work, or actually he had been, because he'd gotten fired and Elzbieta Chetkowska and Aga Zuchowska had decided to resign in solidarity with him—some insignificant matter, but serious enough so that Dr. Zadrozna could be surprised, since an unsuccessful operation would not have made it any easier for them to find new jobs. But the minute he'd heard "What? . . . ." he'd immediately realized that there was nothing more to think about, the decision was made, and was even made in a way without him. So he went back to the hospital and announced, "We are operating," and Elzbieta trounced him for even having gone out at all when he knew so well how much every minute counted.

Or, for instance, a patient is brought in, and everybody says that she is suffering from catatonia, a version of schizophrenia where the afflicted patient doesn't eat or move, just sleeps, and it is impossible to wake her up. She has been treated for catatonia for fifteen years. While she is still asleep, they do a blood test, and it turns out that she registers at more than 30 milligrams of sugar, and it suddenly occurs to everyone that this isn't schizophrenia at all, but rather some dysfunction of the pancreas. They operate on the pancreas and then the biggest tension starts: immediately after the operation, she's up at 130 milligrams of sugar, a bit too much;

after two hours—60, a bit too little—everyone gets nervous that the count is decreasing too fast; but after another four hours, it's still 60, so perhaps things have stabilized after all.

The pancreas problem ends. Everyday life resumes, but then a patient suffering from kidney disease arrives with a mysterious upsurge in his calcium. So it becomes necessary to ask one's colleagues what the clinical symptoms of an overacute parathyroid are, and obviously nobody knows because this sort of thing only happens once every few years. They call Paris, to the calcium experts at Professor Royuxe's center, who tell them to send a hormone sample for testing in a container chilled to minus thirty-two degrees Celsius, but the patient's calcium count has already reached sixteen and one dies at twenty, so they rush him for surgery to Warsaw, perhaps the count will remain stable during the transit; only exactly at the moment he is being put on the operating table, his count reaches twenty, and the patient fades. . . .

The parathyroid problem ends. Everyday life resumes.

I mention all this to Zbigniew Mlynarski—pseudonym "Mole"—the one who was getting ready to blow up the wall on Bonifraterska Street. He'd been aiming his gun at exactly the same moment that, on the other side of the wall, at Edelman's, they'd exploded that single mine of theirs. (Mlynarski had been aiming at a German cop who was aiming at him: luckily Mlynarski was better by a fraction of a second.) So I ask Mlynarski whether he understands all this about Edelman, and he says he understands, he understands it very well. He himself, for example, after the war became chairman of a fur makers' cooperative. He remembers that period very well because he had to act quickly and make risky decisions. For instance, once he used the cooperative's floating capital to repair the roof. Rain was flooding the furs. But he got into trouble, was threatened with prosecution. He said, "All right, take me to court. So I spent two million without any formal clearance. I saved thirty." It ended up that nobody did anything to him, but that decision had really required courage: to use the floating capital in those years for a roof. And that's exactly what matters in life, Mlynarski concludes: the ability to make quick, manly decisions.

After the cooperative, Mlynarski had a private shop making furs for state-owned companies. He employed four workers and had no more problems with the finance department. One of the workers would stretch the skins, the second would cut them, the third one would measure them out, and the fourth one would finish up. He himself had the most responsible job: matching them together—because the most important thing in the fur maker's profession is to make one skin match another.

But actually it was only during the war that Mlynarski lived a full life: "I am insignificant as a man—60 kilos and 163 centimeters—and yet back in those days I was braver than all those guys over 180." Later he put together the material to make skins match. "Can one take it seriously?" he asks. "After all that—ending up matching astrakhan furs?" That's why he understands Dr. Edelman so well.

The only thing that matters is to shield the flame.

But, as we have said, He sits above, carefully observing all these efforts, and is capable of lashing out so suddenly that it is then too late to do a thing: they test her blood and it turns out that it is glutethimide, and nothing can be done anymore. Why did she take glutethimide? Or with this other one: it might have been a hematoma at the back of her skull. She was confusing words, couldn't remember the easiest symbols, she'd forget an address now and then or how to turn a light on, things like that. . . . She had everything—loving parents, a room with expensive toys, and later a wonderful degree and a handsome fiancé, but one day she swallowed sleeping pills and all that remains is that beautiful room, willow green and white, where her good American father doesn't let anyone move even a single thing and says it will remain like this forever. The American father asked Dr. Edelman why she'd done it, but he was unable to answer, even though it was Elzunia, the daughter of Zygmunt, the one who had said: "I will not survive but you will, so remember that in Zamosc, in a convent, there is a child. . . ." Later, Zygmunt shot into the searchlight, thanks to which they managed to jump the wall, and immediately after the war Edelman found Elzunia. He wasn't able to help either of them: Elzunia who died in New York, or the other woman who died here. . . .

So you never know who's outsmarted whom. Sometimes you are happy that you've succeeded, you have checked everything thoroughly and you know that nothing bad should happen anymore, and then Stefan, Marysia's brother, dies because he was overwhelmed with happiness, or Celina, the one who got out with them through the sewers on Prosta Street, lies dying and all he can promise her is that she will die in a dignified manner and without fear.

(Edelman later went to Celina's funeral and there were three of them there from that sewer on Prosta Street: he, Masza, and Pnina. And Masza, the moment she noticed him, whispered: "You know, I heard him again today." "Whom?" he asked. "Don't try to pretend that you don't know," she got angry. He was later told that Masza kept hearing the scream of that boy who'd gone to find out what the message "Wait in the northern part of the Ghetto" meant. They burned him on Mila Street and he screamed the whole day; and Masza, who spent that day in a nearby bunker, today, in Jerusalem, a town three thousand kilometers away from Mila Street and from that bunker, lurks and waits for Pnina to go shopping and then whispers: "Listen, I heard him again today. Very clearly.")

Or, the super knocks at the door of Abrasza Blum's landlady, hisses, "There is a Jew in your apartment," locks the door, and goes to the telephone (the Home Army later sentenced this super to death, Abrasza jumped out the window to a roof, he broke his legs and lay crumpled like that until the Gestapo came); or a patient dies on the operating table because it was a circumferential infarction, which gave no picture on either the coronography or the EKG. So you well remember all these tricks and even when the operation seems to end, well—you wait.

There will be long days of waiting, because only gradually will it be revealed whether the heart will adapt to the patched-up veins, to the new aortas, and to the medication. Later, gradually, you get calmer, you become more confident. . . . And as this tension and later this happiness gradually leave you, only then do you finally realize the proportion: one to four hundred thousand.

1:400,000.

It is simply ludicrous.

But every life is a full one hundred percent for each individual, so that perhaps it makes some sense after all.